THE JOKER

LARS SAAYBE CHRISTENSEN

Translated by Steven Michael Nordby

WHITE PINE PRESS

© 1991 Lars Saaybe Christensen

Translation © 1991 Steven Nordby

Originally published in Norway as Jokeren by J.W. Cappelens Forlag, Oslo
© 1981 J.W. Cappelens Forlag

Book design by Watershed Design

Printed in the United States of America

The publication of this book was made possible, in part, by grants from
Norwegian Literature Abroad (NORLA), the National Endowment for the
Arts, and the New York State Council on the Arts.

ISBN 1-877727-11-3

WHITE PINE PRESS
76 Center Street
Fredonia, N.Y. 14063

THE JOKER

1

But I wasn't dead.

But that's what it said in the newspaper.

I got up slowly from the chair, went over to the television and let a sleepy index finger with a black rim at the edge of a bluish nail fall down on the switch. The picture puckered up and was gone. The man reading bleak weather reports disappeared from my room. He probably went to the neighbor's and served up more unpleasant temperatures there. I listened absent-mindedly for awhile to the streetcar clattering down Thereses Street, some voices that spoke too loudly to be friendly, and a record player that had fallen in love with Jens Book-Jenssen. It took some time before my mind was on top of the situation, or to be more precise, I needed a few minutes to get used to the hereafter. Then I nodded to the angels and went back to the chair.

It was no spectacular announcement. No "our dear departed" or "indispensable" or columns with fine names that would remember me with melancholy. Just my name. Hans Georg Windelband. He didn't leave anyone. He just went away. From Oslo. February 15, 1978. It was February 18th, Saturday. Hans Georg Windelband would be interred Tuesday, February 21st at West Crematorium.

From a cupboard that didn't need an incantation to open by it-self, I got out a bottle with a coating of calvados in the bottom. I poured it into a green glass, sat down nice and straight in the chair and waited for the congratulations.

But no congratulations came. The telephone sat there like a cold iron. *Aftenposten* lay in front of me with the death announcements' simple crossword making faces at me. And in the middle of all the meaningless names was mine. Hans Georg Windelband.

I thought: it's the first time I've had my name in the paper.

That thought made no small impression on me. But on the other hand, can you believe everything you read in *Aftenposten?*

At ten o'clock I called The Butcher. He was standing telephone watch. He answered before the first ring ended.

"Yes," he just said.

"It's Hans Georg."

"Oh yeah. So this is Hans Georg. Windelband. And where are you calling from?"

"From Limbo. I'm standing here with Dante and Raymond Chandler."

"Hold the baloney."

"I'm at home," I said wearily.

The Butcher breathed heavily into the receiver.

"What kind of hole have you gotten yourself into now?" he said with a mixture of resignation and rage.

"No idea," I answered honestly. "I really have no idea."

I leaned forward over the table and fished out a Hobby cigarette.

"Are you there!" yelled The Butcher.

"Yeah. Just getting a smoke."

"Listen here." Now his voice was serious. "It's nice that you're doing fine and got into the newspaper, but I hope you realize that your debut doesn't bode well."

"I realize that," I said.

Actually, it wasn't the first time that there was something about me in the paper. But I had never had my *name* in print, except in the church newsletter when I was baptized.

"And what do you intend to do about it?"

"Maybe we could talk about it a little. That's why I called. How about Tørteberg?"

"We!"

The horn was silent. A new Book-Jenssen record played on the floor above: "When the Chestnuts Bloom on Bygdøy Avenue." Outside, snow tumbled down.

"Not Tørteberg," said The Butcher finally. "Rosenborg. In fifteen minutes."

I heard a click in my ear.

"It's Our Spring This Spring."

The snow was thick and nasty in the air when I came out the front door and crossed Thereses Street toward Matkroken supermarket. The clock at the watchmaker's next door said eight minutes past ten. A streetcar rattled behind me. I hopped onto the sidewalk and saw a row of white faces disappear down toward Bislett Stadium and the city.

The streets were deserted. The ugly houses were closed and locked. Here and there a glow shined out of the windows, and the urinals by Fagerborg Church stunk worse than ever. The only living thing I saw was a blind man with a white cane shaking a heavy, sad head. At a quarter past ten I went up the steep steps to Rosenborg Restaurant.

I put a coin in the slot machine by the entrance and lost it. Just then someone spoke behind me.

"Be careful with that thing. You start with your little finger, and soon you lose your head."

"The profits go to charity," I said, "so this is humanitarian work. It would never occur to me to win money from the Red Cross."

"It's sure a year for refugees," said The Butcher, pushing aside the two panels that were there in place of a regular Norwegian door. They were supposed to give an exotic character as you arrived. We sat at a window table. It wasn't so exotic any longer. The air was dense with smoke and steam from wet clothes. Voices buzzed monotonously like a motor that never gets running properly. Now and then laughter or a loud belch broke through. Everything was as usual. Winter in Norway. Depressing and unbearable.

The Butcher raised two huge, red fingers in the air, and right away an old, tired waitress stood at our table. I ordered a beer and some cigarettes. The Butcher asked for half a bottle of vermouth and ice cubes. The waitress took our orders with a sigh and disappeared into the haze.

Without saying anything, the Butcher got up, twisted out of the huge fur that made him look like a mad bear, and walked to the restroom. The gray suit he was wearing stretched like a straight-jacket over his shoulders and back, and a lumberjack would have been inspired by his legs. His almost bald head shined nice and bright, and the few hairs still alive were combed with an optimism and diligence you wouldn't otherwise believe he had. He moved through the crowded room like a slow tank.

He came back as the waitress chugged past our table and dropped off the goods.

I took a few sips of beer, lit a cigarette and waited for him to say something. The Butcher turned the bottle around and around between his fat fingers, looked at me calmly, lifted the glass and swallowed the contents in one gulp. The ice cubes clunked against each other.

He began without a preface.

"When I plucked you out of the gutter, you didn't look much better than the hogs hanging on the hooks in my freezer. And it's been nothing but trouble with you ever since. I have to keep a sharp eye out. And every time, I've said to myself: 'Be patient.' And what's the thanks I get? New problems. More trouble. When I saw the announcement today, I thought: 'Finally! Now he's been entrusted to safer hands.' And then you call. *You call!* Do you know why I've kept you alive? For one single reason! One beautiful day when my two fine children are confirmed, I'm going to haul you out, ask them to contemplate this human refuse, and I'll say: 'Never forget this character. Never become like him!'"

He poured a new glass, evidently pleased with himself. It was a nice little story, but he hadn't told everything. I knew that. And he knew that I knew. I looked at him with my steel eyes, certain of victory.

"I need help."

The Butcher set his glass down.

"I don't bet on dead horses."

"I guess not," I said, rising. "So I'll switch to a trot and disappear. But the horses you bet on before weren't exactly spry either, were they?"

I looked at him. It's always painful to see big men embarrassed. He shrunk and got a stupid look in his face. He looked like one of Vigeland's sculptures. I don't know exactly which one, but I think it's at the bottom of the Monolith.

"Sit down," he begged. He *begged*.

I sat. The Butcher became himself again. He bent his body over the table and parked his face a few inches from mine.

"Listen carefully," he said, mild as an angel. "Listen very carefully, 'cause it'll be awhile till we talk again. Can you hear me?"

"Yes," I said. "Excellently."

"Good! I suggest you take a vacation. You look tired. I'm sure you've noticed those dark bags under your eyes."

"It's the mark of abstinence," I said.

"Could be. But you need a vacation. Tomorrow you'll go to Paris, for example. Then you can plod around the Lurve for a few months."

"The Louvre," I corrected.

"What?"

"It's pronounced *oo* not *u*. Louvre."

"Whatever." He took a deep breath. "Tomorrow you'll take a taxi to Fornebo airport, buy a ticket on the first plane to Paris, hole up in the Loorve and stay there a few months."

I looked stupidly at him.

"Obviously, I really want to go to Paris," I said, friendly. "But that might be a little difficult. I have a tiny problem with my passport, you understand. Do you understand?"

The Butcher was silent awhile. I looked at his face. It occurred to me that he had changed more than a little since I met him at the Promenade Cafe well over half a year ago. The meat had sort of loosened from his skull and slid out in all directions. His cheeks and chin were smooth as dinner plates. He eats too much behind the counter, I thought. The same way I abuse layer cakes.

"Well, then," he said slowly. "There are a lot of beautiful places here in Norway too."

I looked out the window. A red sign a little ways down the street lit up. Fredheim Hotel. Three men were waiting outside the entrance.

"I can go there," I said cheerfully and pointed. "I don't like to travel very far."

"Cute. This is no joke. You oughta take a little rest now. Don't you think so? Rest on your laurels. Norway is chock full of beautiful places. Hardanger, for example."

"I'll come up with something," I said.

"For the good of us all," he added, "I wish you'd stay away for a couple of years. But just come home when my kids get confirmed."

He got up, put on his fur and rubbed his hands together.

"That's it then. Goodbye."

Then he slipped a re-sealed envelope down on the table.

"You pay," said the Butcher.

He was about to go, took a step, but changed his mind, as if he had thought of something important. He leaned over me.

"When did you start subscribing to *Aftenposten* anyway?"

"It was just lying there," I said, "on the door mat. Maybe the paper boy made a mistake."

"Obviously," said the Butcher. "Obviously."

And then he disappeared. The door was big enough.

In the envelope were three thousand crowns. Plus sixty-five, a half bottle of vermouth and a beer. He could just as well have remembered the cigarettes too. He owed me more than that.

When I came out, the snow was hanging at an angle in the air like a dirty bed sheet. I pulled my collar up and shoved my hands in my pockets. Outside Rosenberg Theater a couple stood tight up against each other looking at pictures from Fellini's *Casanova*. I walked, stoop shouldered, past them, almost invisible. I envied them. Deep inside and a long way down tumbled some unpleasant feelings. I turned toward the couple, but they were gone. All I saw was a prostitute guiding a shaking old man into the Fredheim Hotel and slamming the door afterward. I didn't feel well. But I had three thousand crowns in an envelope in my inner pocket.

But I was dead.

Sunday came into my room like a doctor with his scalpel ready. It cut through the crack in the curtains, slashed the floor in two and mutilated my face. I groaned, sat up in bed and shook the sleep off. Somewhere in the neighborhood, church bells were ringing.

I'm a man of action. While the coffee water was boiling, I packed my things and sat the suitcase, an old cardboard one I'd bought at a rummage sale, by the door. I ate breakfast standing up. Biscuits and coffee. Somewhere in the back of my head I had a raw cold sensation like you get when there's something you think you've forgotten or missed. Then I poured another cup of coffee, made the bed and walked around the room one more time. No personal papers left behind. No photographs. No calvados. The only thing was *Aftenposten.* I opened it to the death announcements. Hans Georg Windelband. I was getting tired of seeing my name. It's a clean announcement, I said to myself. You can be proud of it. No poem or irrelevant information. Just a black cross, a name and a date. Finished. I hung the tatters over the handrail in the stairwell so someone else could have a free copy. Then I took a last survey; everything was in order. I turned off the light, grabbed the suitcase and left. The nameplate on the door posed no problem. I didn't have one. There was no name on the mailbox either. I never got letters.

The sun was shining like an operating room light. The sky was blue and disinfected. Snow had fallen during the night, once white, now smeared with the morning patients' dirt and crap. I stopped on the sidewalk and thought about it. The world is an open book, but I didn't know the title. And all journeys are a detour home. I shrugged my shoulders, whistled an out-of-tune melody and walked in the same direction as the night before. I stopped outside the Fredheim Hotel. The door was locked. I found a doorbell and set my suitcase in the new snow. It took a whole cigarette before a gray head peeked out and looked suspiciously at me.

"Do you have a vacancy?" I asked.

The head continued looking at me. I lifted my suitcase, and finally the door was opened all the way.

I followed the head, which belonged to an old, crooked man. The place didn't look too attractive. To the right was a flimsy table with a bouquet of plastic flowers shoved down in a dull loving cup. Battered chairs were placed on each side. There was nothing hanging on the walls. The wallpaper was decorated with exotic animals and must have been chosen by a colicky patient.

"A room," the man said slowly, laying his arm across the reception counter. "How long?" he added, glancing up at the board where the room keys hung. Only two were missing.

"Three weeks," I said. "Maybe longer."

"Three weeks," he repeated listlessly.

His eyes glided over me like two transparent jelly fish.

"800 crowns. In advance."

I gave him eight hundreds. He looked at them in astonishment, smoothed out one after the other and made them disappear. Then he took down a key, maneuvered out and walked toward the stairs.

"May I borrow a telephone book?" I asked.

"No phone in the room," he said curtly.

"I have a mobile phone."

I pointed at the cardboard suitcase.

Something resembling a smile colored his face red. He nodded toward the table with the plastic flowers in the loving cup. I took the book with the "F" section for Oslo, which was lying there along with some questionable magazines, and followed him up two flights and through a trashy corridor.

The room was a practical rectangle with gray wallpaper covering the walls and ceiling. The bed was wide enough for two. In a dusty closet with clothes hangers in shocking colors, I hung two shirts, a pair of gray trousers, a blue turtleneck sweater and a narrow knitted tie. Over the sink hung a picture of me. The Butcher was right. I needed a vacation. Dark semi-circles bored into the skin under my eyes. I turned on the faucet and rinsed my face in cold water. I had put the phone book on a table, near an ashtray with a Martini advertisement on it. I started for it, but changed my mind with a sigh and went over to the window. I had a view to Hedgehaugen School, Rosenborg Theater and Rosenborg Restaurant. If I leaned out far enough and looked the other way, I could get a glimpse of the urinals down by Fagerborg Church.

But I didn't lean that far out.

I sat on a hard chair with the phone book in my lap and looked up funeral homes.

There are a lot of funeral homes in Oslo. I made a list of all of them. A suspicious number of them are on Akers Street, side by side with the government office building and the big newspapers. Most are named after someone, with the help of heirs, no doubt. Olsens' Funeral Home, for example, or Gulbrandsen and Sons Mortuary. It gave a personal and earthy impression. Hans Georg Windelband was surely taken care of in the best manner.

I stayed in the room the rest of the day. I tried to sleep, but the sounds from the adjacent rooms kept me awake. The whores at work. They never closed shop. Instead, I just lay there thinking. I was in the middle of some sort of chaos I didn't understand. I had a vague feeling of being caught up with, that the past had branded me and would never set me free. I was afraid. Damned scared. I had to get away, pure and simple. The wisest thing to do was dig up the money I had hidden in the forest, in Nordmarka, take the first boat or train out of the country and come back when the party was over. But not yet. Not yet.

Outside the sun had burned up. The sky was dark violet. Snow hung motionless in the air. The night came howling over me like a melancholy Dalmatian.

4

I had been dead for five days and felt in great shape. Mondays always fill me with optimism. New week, new start, new chance. I gave the room keys to the desk clerk. He took them silently and hung them on the board.

"How about changing the flowers," I said, friendly, pointing at the plastic bouquet.

He looked at me, uninterested.

"Plastic flowers are demoralizing," I continued. "They conceal the life process."

The mute grabbed a newspaper and spread it out over the counter.

I left.

A change of weather had made Oslo into the Venice of the North. I sailed over to Sporveis Street and anchored next to Møllhausen Bakery on Bogstad Road where I ate breakfast.

At ten-thirty I was standing in a telephone booth in the Major-stua district with the list of funeral homes and a stack of coins in front of me.

A half hour later I had learned two things. Oslo's housewives have an urgent need for telephone conversations when their husbands are at work. Moreover, they don't like to wait their turn. And funeral home representatives have dark friendly voices with an undertone of businesslike mourning. They have a simple vocabulary, almost a special language where the terminology is distinctly monotonous and sentimental. And they are short of time. But no one had taken care of a corpse that answered to the name Hans Georg Windelband.

The day's other bakery visit was a fact. I found a table farthest inside Samson at Majorstua and ordered a cup of coffee and a piece of marzipan layer cake. I knew I shouldn't. I used to be thin. Now I was getting fat. It was the fare. My diet wasn't the same as before. But I didn't miss the points of syringes. And bread and water is just a myth.

But the marzipan layer cake and the strong coffee, plus a few Hobby cigarettes, made my stomach loose and restless. I closed myself in a narrow bathroom and felt everything running through me and gushing out.

Was I beginning to get delicate? I thought. Was I as fragile as the bone china cup that barely tolerated a finger's pressure? I pulled up my pants and flushed away my refuse, the slag that confirmed that I was alive.

Was someone really dead? Tomorrow I would know. But if there was a body, then I wouldn't have much time. I'm no grave robber.

I paid for the crap and took the Røa tram up to the West Crematorium.

Why are crematoriums such bleak buildings? Are the architects to blame? Is it the fault of the ministers? Or the dead? Why doesn't light get into crematoriums? Is it our fear of death that is materialized in these buildings? Is it our contempt for life erected in concrete?

I should write features.

A black-clad gathering moved in small groups through the slush toward the parking lot. Each sluggish body pressed into its own narrow car and rolled out on Sørkedals Road. A young, finicky usher with smooth hair and a high, friendly forehead came out and removed a little name card from the heavy oak door, shook himself and went in again.

I followed him, opened the lid and ducked into the darkness. Suddenly a spotlight appeared to be lit on the right side of a mural backdrop. The usher stood under the powerful lamp and looked right at me. He held a wreath as big as a tractor wheel in his hand.

I stood there and contemplated Alf Rolfsen's fresco painting in the archways on each side midships. The whole thing culminated in a gigantic mural that looked ridiculous in the stubby room. The usher, who meanwhile had disappeared into another room, came out through a little door closer to me. He was still finicky. His clothes fit perfectly, and his hair lay like a slick lid over his head. I started to think it was a toupee. The high, friendly forehead fell steeply down to an indistinct face.

I walked toward him.

"Excuse me for disturbing you like this," I began.

A remarkable spiral body movement appeared to want to tell me that it was alright, but that I ought to get to the point.

"It concerns a funeral," I continued. "A Hans Georg Windelband is supposed to be interred here tomorrow."

"One o'clock," said the usher with a dry, weary voice.

I felt my hands beginning to shake, and my heart was stumbling.

"It seems this Windelband is an old acquaintance of mine. We knew each other a short time, and we haven't seen each other since."

I suddenly realized that I was talking too much and that what I was saying was unnecessary. The usher twisted through the same spiral movement and fastened his eyes somewhere over my left shoulder.

"I wasn't aware of his death until today," I continued. I wondered if my voice wasn't carrying my words completely. "I presume that he is here now?"

"Windelband is down there," he said, pointing at the floor. "He came Saturday."

I looked down, as if he were lying between my feet.

I took off.

"Would it be possible to see him?"

The usher shrugged his small shoulders.

"He's just lying there," he said wearily.

Then he made a sign that I should follow him. We walked down a staircase to a room right under the chapel. Two coffins sat on an iron frame ready to be shoved into the cremation oven. An older man stuck a shiny red, mild face out of a door.

"A lot to do today," he puffed heavily. "Mondays are busy."

The usher nodded.

We came to a new room. It was much larger and almost reminded me of a reception hall. White coffins were stacked up in small recesses and out on the floor. Small number tags were fastened on all of them. A strange odor filled my nose and made me nauseous.

The usher went over to two men in blue smocks who were getting a coffin ready to go to the chapel.

"He would like to see number 13," he said, pointing at me.

I walked closer.

"It's not a pretty sight."

"They've done a fine job," added the other objectively. "First class. He could easily be shown."

Something turned over in my stomach. I turned toward the room we had come from and saw a coffin disappear into a huge oven.

The usher looked at me, and I thought he smiled as he said with an expressionless voice:

"Your friend certainly isn't the same any longer."

I said nothing. I was mute.

The two men went over to the other wall and into one of the recesses. They turned toward me.

"Here he is," said one of them.

The gray-white floor tiles held my feet. I had to tear myself free. I felt sick and dirty and walked toward them. The smallest of the men lifted up the lid and pulled aside the white blanket that covered the body.

I backed up and the nausea sped through my chest and filled my mouth with rot. I swallowed several times and took deep breaths. It was the most disgusting thing I'd ever seen. The face must have been cut in two. There was no nose. A thick blue stripe went from halfway up the face down to the neck. Most of the hair was shaved off. Only on one side of the head were there some thin blonde wisps.

"A little distorted," said the usher who was standing behind me, breathing down my neck.

"Couldn't have been done better," said one of the men firmly.

The deceased must have been about my age, in the middle of his twenties. It's difficult to determine the height of someone lying down, but I estimated it to be the same as mine, around five-foot-seven. The little that was left of his blonde hair showed that he probably had started going bald. I automatically stroked my hand through my own wilted hair, which stayed behind in clusters on the pillow when I got up. Near the one temple that wasn't disfigured by the blue stripe I noticed a narrow scar. There wasn't anything else. The mutilated face didn't resemble a human being anymore. It looked like it was put together from a mixture of pieces from several different jigsaw puzzles.

I looked at it a long time.

But I couldn't recognize the face.

Not even his mother could have recognized that face.

I just missed the streetcar. It was one o'clock, and some birds were chirping hysterically in a nearby tree. I sat on a wet bench, lit a cigarette and sent some strong smoke signals down to my lungs.

They had told me that Hans Georg Windelband fell, as they smilingly said, out of a window and met a fence that had divided his face in the middle. He was sent to the emergency room, dead, obviously, patched and sewn together and laid in a coffin. That was Wednesday of last week. He stayed at Krogstøtten, the emergency room's chapel, for two days. Then he was moved up here. The funeral home was so new that it still wasn't listed in the phone book. I thought it might better be listed under moving and storage companies instead. But I had the address on a piece of paper. Krans Mortuary. Trondheim Road.

No one had gone with the coffin of Hans Georg Windelband to the crematorium. Live alone, die alone.

The streetcar came clattering down from Smestad. I got up wearily, turned toward the crematorium and thought I saw gray smoke rise to the dull sky.

I got off at the National Theater and found a taxi that drove me to Krans Mortuary.

"We got here in one piece," snickered the driver as I gave him his money.

I tumbled out and stood awhile on the sidewalk to collect myself. I was exhausted. The taxi disappeared with a whine down the empty street. In the display window was a white coffin with the lid opened and a marble headstone with the name and dates written in gold lettering: Ole Olsen. 1900-1975. I went in.

It was a nice, well-lit room with green wall-to-wall carpet that absorbed my heavy steps. On the walls hung two landscape paintings with brilliant sunsets and moose, probably ordered through a magazine.

A dark-clothed, immaculate man in his thirties suddenly stood in front of me. His face laid in friendly folds, like a nice comforter. He held his hands in front, right over his belt, waited a moment, then stuck one hand out to me. I took it automatically. It was like sticking my fingers into lukewarm water.

"How may we be of service?" he whispered.

I cleared my throat.

"It concerns a . . . a client," I began, but stopped.

The man looked at me understandingly.

"It concerns a deceased you took care of," I continued, feeling my forehead become warm and damp and my clothes too small. "His name is . . . was . . . Hans Georg Windelband."

"Yes?" said the man.

"He was an old acquaintance of mine. I just learned of his death today, and I . . . would like to get in contact with his family. Perhaps you can help me?"

"I remember Windelband," the man said slowly. "He will be interred tomorrow."

I didn't say anything.

"But we do not know his family. We got the assignment from an older gentleman, a neighbor of the deceased, I believe. I can't tell you anymore."

I thanked him and left. In any case, I knew that there was a corpse. I got nauseous just thinking about it, but other than that, I was as wise as I was dumb. Who was that poor guy in the coffin? The guy no one would be able to recognize?

I wondered if I should go up or down the street. Actually, it didn't matter. I didn't know where I was.

5

I woke up the next morning not feeling well. My stomach was bloated and full of air that rushed soundlessly out of me and filled the room with a rotten stink. I tumbled out of bed, walked stiffly over to the window and opened it. The winter air hit me like the blast of a fan.

It was ten o'clock.

I went down the corridor to the toilet. I sat there in misery for fifteen minutes. Everything ran out of me. I had to to flush several times. When I finally stood up, I felt several pounds lighter. But no sooner had I gotten to my room than I had to go out again. I ran up to the third floor and slipped into the john there. I barely got myself slung down on the toilet before it burst out. I heard a man and woman laughing rudely in the corridor.

I remained sitting there, reading all the names carved into the door and walls, the grotesque offers, the jokes, the commentaries, the drawings. I felt something sink deep inside me. I emptied myself, was empty, flushed.

At eleven o'clock I went out.

The city was white again. I moved silently and carefully up Bogstad Road towards Majorstua. A school class of seven- or eight-year-olds came singing and screaming behind me, with skis on their shoulders and little bags that were surely packed with hot cocoa, sandwiches and oranges. Nordmarka. My stomach contracted. But they probably weren't going any farther than Tryvann Lodge. I pulled over to the wall and let them pass. A young teacher with a round, kind face smiled at me. I couldn't bring myself to smile in return.

It took me fifteen minutes to walk up to Majorstua. The clock over the tram station showed eleven-twenty. I still had a little time. I didn't need to be at the West Crematorium until twelve-thirty at the earliest.

I wasn't up to any bakeries today, so I walked over to Valka instead and ordered a cup of coffee. At some of the tables people were drinking beer, men in their sixties, pensioners, and a couple of young people, probably college students. Their faces were tired, but their voices were already loud and stubborn. A lone lady was chewing on a herring sandwich. It looked like blood running from the corners of her mouth, but it was just beet juice.

I drank the coffee in tiny sips and lit a smoke. I got dizzy with the first puff. My stomach was completely empty, but I couldn't even think about food.

But I did think:

Who would come to the funeral? Probably the man who had contacted the funeral home. Anyone else? Hardly. I had no circle of friends to boast of. I had no circle of friends.

I sat there like that and thought my head empty, too. Hollowed, I went out and took the tram up to the crematorium. When we went into the tunnel at Volvat, I suddenly thought that maybe I should have bought a wreath.

Fastened on the big oak door to the chapel was a little white card with my name on it. Hans Georg Windelband. Funeral at 1 P.M. It was only ten past twelve. I sat down on a green bench a ways away, between some huge trees, so I would have a view of whoever came. I waited fifteen minutes. The low sun sneaked out from behind some clouds, blinded me and glided behind a new cloud. I smoked a few cigarettes. The usher I had talked with the day before came out on the steps, looked around, and went in again. He didn't notice me.

My stomach began to growl. I regretted not eating a sandwich at Valkyrien. I leaned back and breathed deeply, as if I thought it would help. I smoked another cigarette. But nothing happened. Above me the sky became thick and tight like a stuffy nose. I noticed I was freezing. My hands were white and stiff. I stuck them in my pockets and shivered all over.

It was quarter-to-one when he came. He had a big fur hat pulled way down his forehead and a long winter coat. He walked slowly, one leg hanging back a little. When he got to the steps he stopped and took off his fur hat and gloves. His appearance was, as far as I could tell, like old people generally look. A little hair by his ears and at the neck and a face that the years had trampled on without taking off their boots. I had no idea who he was.

He disappeared into the chapel.

I sat there another five minutes. Suddenly my heart sank several fathoms deep, down between black rocks, a long way down where everything becomes dim, where the pressure squeezes you flat and you move like a lonely flounder in an unrecognizable landscape.

She came in the gate from the streetcar stop and walked right up to the chapel. I half rose and started toward her. She hadn't seen me. Something tightened up inside me, a huge knot. I took a couple of steps forward and stopped. Then my thoughts cleared. I had to stop her. I took off running. It seemed I ran a whole lifetime. She didn't notice me until I put a hand on her shoulder.

"Berit!" I said out of breath.

She looked at me with eyes that grew and grew and threatened to pop out. Oh, her small face, that petite body of hers, just as beautiful as ever, it rushed through me. Behind my leather jacket hammered a happy heart. She remembered me. She had remembered me.

"Hans Georg," she just said. Her voice faltered.

She continued staring at me, terror stricken.

"Hans Georg. . .I thought. . ."

"Relax. This is just something I arranged to get together old friends."

I tried to smile, but my mouth didn't obey.

"What's the mean..."

I interrupted her.

"I'm in trouble," I just said. "It's not me in there; it's someone else."

She looked at me, stupefied.

"I'll be able to explain it to you later. That is, I don't get it myself yet."

We remained standing there a few seconds looking at each other. My heart mushed away like a dog team. Suddenly the church bells broke the silence. I jumped, frightened.

"I have to go now. Can we meet later? Where do you live?"

The sentences jumped out of my mouth like frogs.

"People usually bring along calling cards to funerals," she stammered and searched one out from her purse.

"I'll see you later," I said quickly and went into the chapel.

As the heavy door was gliding shut, I turned. She was still standing there. Her face was white and beautiful. Then she disappeared in a short click.

The usher from the day before stuck a program in my hand. I continued in between the rows of pews. The bells were still ringing for me. On the casket lay a wreath. On the right side, almost all the way in front, sat the old man. I sat on the other side a couple of rows behind him.

But there were only the two of us.

The program I held in my hand was decorated with a cross on the front page, my name and the date. Before the eulogy we were supposed to sing "So Take My Hands and Lead Me Forward." A door opened, and the minister came out behind the pulpit. He suddenly stopped. I thought he was going to shade his eyes and enjoy the view. Then he glided down three steps and greeted the old man. They tugged at each other's arms and some soft words were spoken. Then he came over to me. He reached out a thin, passive hand from his black robe and greeted me without moving his lips. I took his fingers silently.

We sang. It sounded thin. An organ and a violin played behind us in the gallery. Afterward everything was uncomfortably silent. The old guy coughed, bent forward and pulled a huge handkerchief up from his jacket. That went on for a few seconds. He turned toward me and smiled apologetically. It was a friendly, practiced smile. The face around it was robust, with a rusty color, surely a mixture of hard work and alcohol. His eyes were curious but not intrusive.

I smiled back as friendly as I could.

The minister spoke. Fortunately it was short. I'm sure it was due to the fact that there wasn't much to say about Hans Georg Windelband. He spoke about the fate of a lonesome life, people who walk the narrow path alone, without friends, without solace, without grounding points. He spoke, thickly sentimental, about life's hard knocks in the way people talk when they've never been knocked themselves. And he talked about God's generosity, that he also forgave suicide, forgave people who made themselves masters over death. But I thought: I wonder if he has ever stood in a window, seen the city and the concrete below, dots of people, or in front of the mirror with a razor blade in his hand, and known that the only thing that gives some people strength when they're tossed unwillingly into a meaningless life is knowing it can be ended by a simple hand movement, seeing the blood roses grow in the glass, or by a single jump, hitting the sidewalk in a brutal but faithful kiss. Maybe God also thinks sometimes of heaving himself out of his empty heaven, falling through the universe in the hope of being crushed on a planet.

I should have been a preacher.

And there was earth and resurrection.

And we sang again.

At one-thirty the casket disappeared down into the floor, down to the hard-working people under us. Soon the mutilated body would be just a pile of ashes. I felt it burning beneath my feet.

The minister came down and shook hands with both of us one more time, saying something about eternal peace, the way people talk who just live in toleration. I let go of his hand as if it were a hornet. When he finally left, the old man came over to me and mumbled something. His voice was a little mushy.

"Yeah. I was the one Hans Georg lived with," I finally made out. "He rented a room from me, I mean. Nice boy. That it should end like this!"

He wiped a shaking hand across his forehead. I had planned

exactly what I was going to say, but now my vocal cords werc tied up. I swallowcd a cough. The old man stood bent forward and looked down at the floor right in front of my feet. I think he was crying.

The usher brushed past us. He greeted me almost invisibly. One corner of his mouth just widened out a little bit. I ignored him.

"My name is Malvin Paulsen," stammered the old guy. "Did you know Hans Georg well?"

I cleared my throat and began.

"I'm Hugo. Hugo Poser. I knew him a few years back, but we haven't seen each other since then."

I exhaled, lightened, and waited for the reaction. Malvin Paulsen looked at me. His eyes had become inflamed and red.

"Yeah, he didn't have many friends, Hans Georg. No family either. No one. It was nice of you to come."

I nodded and couldn't think of anything to say. Was I that alone?

There was a long pause. I looked at the mural. At the very top, near the ceiling, was a big hand, the hand of God. But it had no body, wasn't connected to an arm. A cut-off hand with fingers spread out helplessly.

Malvin Paulsen said:

"Maybe we could have a drink together and remember Hans Georg. He was a nice boy."

We went outside. The snow tumbled down from a low, loathsome sky. The usher removed the card with my name on it and fastened a new one on the oak door. From the harbor we heard the foghorns, just like cries from trolls.

We found a taxi that had just become free. Malvin barely coaxed in his bad leg.

"The war," he puffed. "Full of grenade fragments."

The driver turned and looked at us emptily.

I looked at Malvin.

"Schweigaards Street 91," he said and sank back in the seat.

The car glided into the traffic on Sørkedals Road. We sat there without saying anything. The windshield wipers swept patiently across the front window. Punk music droned from the cassette player. At Majorstua I got out and bought a bottle of Upperten at the liquor store.

We drove on. The driver drummed his fingers against the steering wheel and tensed his neck muscles in time with the music. I was absolutely not feeling well. My stomach was empty and abandoned. I wanted to suggest eating somewhere but didn't. It would have to stand the test. Malvin eyed the liquor store bag in my lap. His lips were wet. His weathered face began to get the same color as the snow outside. He became smaller and smaller in the seat.

"It'll be good to have a shot," he said heavily.

"Yes," I answered.

"I suppose we can wait till we get there," he added uncertainly.

"Yes," I said.

I gave some tens to the driver and told him to keep the change. He snapped his fingers. Malvin Paulsen struggled out of the car and hobbled onto the sidewalk.

"That damned leg!" he cursed. "It's the weather. It's a barometer. Just let it be spring soon!"

We were standing outside his place on Schweigaards Street, an ordinary apartment building built sometime in the 1890s. It was poorly kept up: big stains on the brick were between the windows, crooked door and window frames, a nauseating, worn-down yellow color.

"Here's where he fell," said Malvin, pointing at a low fence almost buried in snow. "There's a little grass here in summer."

I looked up. It was five stories. I bet that he lived on the fourth.

We walked into a trashy lobby. Flaking paint hung loosely on the walls, an empty liquor bottle stood on the row of mail boxes. Some old furniture—a sofa with torn upholstery and two brown chairs—was sitting next to the stairs.

"Are those Hans Georg's?" I asked.

Malvin shook his head.

"Oh, no. He didn't have much. It was mostly mine. It's still up there like before."

We climbed up four flights. I had to support him the whole way. His forehead was wet and blue and his face full of ugly lines. When we finally made it, he had to rest until he'd gathered the strength to unlock the door.

We came into a pitch dark hallway. I remained on the threshold and let Malvin Paulsen continue alone. Suddenly a light bulb lit up in the ceiling. I shaded my eyes and was astonished at how short the room was. Just about six feet in front of me stood Malvin leaning against the switch. He held his fur hat in his hand. The walls were overflowing with old photographs, most of them from the war. Over a little bureau hung a big, brown-stained mirror.

Malvin came over to me.

"It's not much to brag about," he sighed.

I helped him off with his heavy coat and hung it on a wooden peg.

"Hans Georg lived there," he continued, pointing at a closed door to my right. "And there's my room."

He looked over at the opposite doorway.

"And straight ahead's the kitchen. Not 'xactly a palace. And this damned leg. And the john's out by the stairs. I freeze my ass off!"

He laughed, and I followed him into the living room. I sat down on the sofa. He got out glasses, set them on the table between us, and sank down with a sigh in a red chair. I presumed he would be there awhile.

In the corner was a TV set, and by the door was a short bookcase. I noticed Salmonsen's Encyclopedia and Nordahl Grieg's collected works. On the walls were still more photographs, a map of Norway, and a drawing of a truck. On the windowsill was a sick flower, screaming for water. The view wasn't much to brag about either. I looked right out on a brick wall and a window where a fat lady was resting her breasts.

I poured two big drinks.

"To Hans Georg," he mumbled and gulped half the glass. He sat there with a stiff but satisfied expression on his face. "To Hans Georg and the whole damn mess."

I carefully drank a mouthful. My stomach was not good-natured. For a moment everything crashed around inside me. Then I picked up the pieces, stuck a cigarette between my lips, and laid the pack on the table.

I wanted to get Malvin talking.

"How long did Hans Georg live here?" I asked.

"He moved in early last fall. Right after summer."

There was a pause. I crushed the cigarette in an overfilled ashtray.

"I'd quit my job," he continued. "After twenty-five years. My leg got worse. And age! You don't 'xactly get any younger with the years."

He looked at me and smiled with his run-over face.

"I worked in moving. Good business these days. Folks gotta migrate like reindeer."

He took a formidable gulp and wiped his mouth with the back of his hand.

"Where did you know Hans Georg from?" I asked.

"It's a little strange, actually. He was just there one day. At the door. Asked if I had a spare room to rent out. I did. So he moved in. I didn't need that room anyway. And, so we split the rent."

Malvin's glass was empty. I filled it up to the rim.

"What did he do?" I asked.

Malvin Paulsen looked at me.

"Don't know. All's I know is he paid the rent. I ain't nosey."

I stopped talking. The lady in the neighboring window was still resting her big boobs on the window frame. She had pink cheeks and her hair was full of curlers. From the apartment above I heard a screaming kid. It was almost worse than Jens Book-Jenssen.

"Did *you* know Hans Georg well?" Malvin asked.

I chewed on that a little.

"Not especially. We met one summer a few years back. Since then I haven't seen or heard anything from him."

"He didn't have many friends, no," Malvin took over. "And his family's been dead a long time. He was prob'ly alone a little too much."

"Didn't anyone visit him?" I said.

Malvin hesitated and became restless. I noted that.

"Sure. At night, once in awhile. I heard 'em. Not that there was a lotta noise or anythin', that's not what I mean. They came, and then left right away."

"Who were they?" I asked innocently.

"No idea. God, you ask a lotta questions!"

We drank and smoked. I did some thinking, but my head was too unmanageable. I got nowhere. I took a chance on more questions.

"Did he have a job?"

"Not that I know of. He never went out. It's true. He was almost never outdoors. I used to buy food for him. Yeah, and he'd pay me afterward. I tried to get 'm to come down to where I worked at, but he didn't wanna."

I felt sick. The alcohol burned inside and clouded my feelings. I leaned back wearily on the sofa and lit another smoke. There was nothing else to do.

"For twenty-five years I worked in movin'," continued Malvin eagerly. "When I was younger, I lifted pianos all by myself. 'Stand back!' I just says. Them others thought my backbone was made outa steel. But then, there's my leg. And my nerves misfired a little. Hit the bottle. Not too much. Just enough to chase away the worst. Took the rest at arms length. No one'll say different!"

"Did you drive?" I asked.

"I packed and loaded. I could load a whole villa on a flat bed, boy! But in the end I just boxed stuff. It's mostly just rich folks who can afford a movin' company. People like the rest of us, we manage on our own. Who's got money to pay 600 crowns an hour just to get moved in a hurry. The military guys at Kølsas and the fat cats up on the hill! But sure, there were regular folks too. All in all, people are regular. For the most part. And then I'd work like hell so it wouldn't be too expensive for 'em!"

His eyes began to get cloudy. I poured him a fourth glass.

"Hans Georg didn't wanna work there, no. I don't really know what he did. But he had money for the rent. Otherwise, he was mostly always home. We talked a little. Not much. He didn't say much, no. I was the one who did the talkin', mostly."

We took a drink at the same time. He noticed that I was barely getting my tongue wet.

"So, what do *you* do?" he suddenly asked.

"For the time being, I'm unemployed. Looking for a job."

"What'd ya do before?"

I thought about that.

"Various. Odd jobs. The docks. In a library. Parks department."

"What kinda education you got? You look sorta educated."

Malvin laughed loudly. I wondered whether it was my snub nose or fat cheeks that looked intellectual. I said:

"High school. And I went to the university. Art History. Went to some lectures, but dropped out."

"Hans Georg was funny that way. He didn't have no job, but he had money. The rent came on time. I often wondered 'bout that. Maybe he inherited it. But I don't believe that neither."

I let Malvin talk. That's what I was there for. And I liked him.

"Maybe he stole some. Don't know. But I know one thing, I don't condemn him if he did. There's others who steal worse and go free!"

His voice was red hot. Life came to his face and movements. His hand rushed through his hair. He bent forward and poured another glass.

"Nobody can live decently in this here system, ya know. It's impossible. You gotta watch out all the time so ya don't become rotten yourself, too. My brother, ya know, he got that way. Was gonna be so damn great. His goal was to get outa the workin' class. That's the ideal the Social Democrats give the workers. Fight your way out of your class, rise above it, otherwise you're a failure, a nitwit."

He leaned over the table and smiled slyly.

"Guess what my brother is?" He beat me to it. "An antique dealer! Junk!"

Malvin Paulsen finished off the glass. The lady in the neighboring window had disappeared. She had gone from the frame and left behind a mediocre still life.

"How did it happen, really?" I asked.

"What?"

"When he jumped... fell out the window."

Malvin looked for the bottle. I poured for him. Emptied it.

"I didn't know a thing until they woke me up. It was night. I'd had a few shots and was sleepin'."

"Who woke you?"

"The police. And then I had to go along to the emergency room. They'd already taken him there in an ambulance. But he was stone dead."

Malvin held back a little while. It seemed painful for him to tell me any more. He took a huge gulp and swallowed fast.

"I had to look at him," he began. "It was terrible. I had to sorta... identify him. He didn't have anyone else. His face was almost gone. Hit the fence. It was awful to see."

"Did he have any identification on him?" I asked.

Malvin shook his head several times thoughtfully.

"No," he said. "That's what was strange. Not on himself and not here. Just his name and address in an appointment book. No passport or nothin'." He looked up suddenly, thoughtful and rash at the same time. "But they were sure that it was him!"

"Who?" I asked, a little confused.

"The doctor. One who autopsied Hans Georg. They had some file on him from before. Don't know just what, though. Dentist records or somethin'."

"Oh, I see," I said.

I was quiet and thought. Whoever it was, he had done a thorough job. I really wanted to have a chat with that doctor. But what good would it do. A little sloppy on a busy night of suicides. Besides, the police had all my data. They were probably just happy to tidy up their records a little.

I said:

"You mentioned the police. Were they up here, too?"

"Yeah. They asked questions and dug around just like you. What had he done lately, who visited him. But I don't know nothin'. No more 'n I've told you. And they went in his room. Looked high and low. But there was nothin' there. What'd they be lookin' for anyway?"

"Nothing. They probably just thought it was strange that he didn't have any papers or anything."

"Yeah, prob'ly."

"Why do you think he did it?" I asked quickly.

Malvin was sleepy. His head fell down a little, like a puppet's.

"Don't know," he said slowly. "Lonesome, he was. I'm not much company, ya know. Not for a young guy. And then, it was like he'd almost forgot how ta talk. He got quieter and quieter. Strange. But I liked him."

He waited a little while, stroked his hand over his face and coughed.

"And then he hit the fence, just like he'd stood there and aimed for it. Such a stupid little fence that don't do no good. And I was drunk! And now he's dead! Goddamnit!"

Malvin Paulsen fell asleep.

The room he had rented was sparsely furnished. There was just an old sofa bed in there, yellow-brown and worn, a scraped-up table, a chair and a writing desk. From the ceiling hung a kitchen lamp. It smelled bad.

I looked out the window. It was a long way down. And flying is difficult.

In the closet hung some pants and two jackets. A bunch of rolled up shirts, underwear, socks, and sweaters lay on the shelves. I went through all the pockets meticulously, but only found a comb full of light hair and a theater ticket from the Eldorado.

I tried to form an impression of him by studying his clothes. But they were completely ordinary clothes, surely bought at the fall sale at Dressman. I tried to picture that mutilated face placed over the gray tweed jacket, but it didn't help.

It occurred to me that everything appeared so impersonal, completely without character. There was nothing there to indicate a disposition, a fixed idea, a passion. The walls were naked, no books, nothing.

I went over to the writing table. It was clean. Not even a pencil. I assumed the drawer was locked, but it wasn't. But it couldn't tell me anything either, blank paper, a rubber band and some string. I actually thought it was remarkable that everything was so tidy. It was just as if someone had deliberately removed everything, wiped out all tracks.

I peeked in on Malvin Paulsen before I left. He sat on the bottom of a dark sea and would sleep for a hundred years.

I plodded down toward Grønland Marketplace. The air was thick with fog. Gray, stooped-over shadows glided past me like fish from a scattered school. My head was sore and swollen. On Stor Street, I took the Ullevål Hageby streetcar to Frydenlund Brewery. But I wasn't thirsty. I crossed the street and ate mother's leftover meatloaf at Peer Gynt Cafe. The jukebox played Jens Book-Jenssen. It didn't do that last time I was there, five years ago. "Do you want to be a hit with women nowadays." I paid and left. It was seven-thirty.

I zeroed in on the telephone booth at Bislett and got out her calling card. Berit Jensen. My heart beat wildly as I dialed the number. My fingers were numb. My throat was dry and rough as an old creek bed. We made a date for me to come over to her place the next evening.

A new young man sat at the reception desk at the Fredheim Hotel. He was a straight line and all too correctly dressed to fit in with the place's style.

"Room 24," I said.

He looked at me. Quite a long time.

"24," I repeated. "The key."

"It's out already."

"Out! I'm the one who lives there! I've paid for three weeks!"

The Line was still just as straight. He brushed away a speck of dust from something that resembled a shoulder.

"Then there must have been a misunderstanding," he said calmly. "I gave the room key to a big, angry man who. . ."

"That's enough," I interrupted him and ran up the stairs.

He was sitting half upright on the bed without having taken off his shoes. One of the spindle back chairs lay crushed under his fur coat. The Martini ashtray was on the floor, full of cigar butts.

"Butcher!" I said, closing the door behind me.

"Cozy place you've chosen, I must say."

He looked at me with empty eyes. I sat on the end of the bed. From the adjacent rooms came moaning and whimpering and all the disgusting sounds that make me miserable and sick.

"Is this where you're going to spend your vacation?" continued the Butcher.

"Knock it off," I said. "I have a headache."

"Uh-huh. Then we have something in common."

He pulled a bottle of vermouth out from under the covers, took a deep drink and handed it to me.

"How was the funeral?" he asked. "I reckoned there wouldn't be room for me there."

I didn't answer. It was silent for a long time. The Butcher took a few more mouthfuls of vermouth and lit a cigar.

"Well," he mumbled. "Well, well, well. So, who was that girl you talked to outside the chapel?"

I looked at him, surprised.

"You were there!"

The Butcher smiled. His mouth became a black hole under his nose. I heard a secret joy fill the room.

"Of course!"

He gave me the bottle again. Good old Butcher! Hogs' number one enemy!

"It was an old friend," I said. "We knew each other a few years ago. She thought that I was. . ."

"Superfluous!"

The Butcher waved avertingly with his paws.

"I think I was in love with her," I said. "Really. She's the only decent girl I've ever met."

"Except your mother. How long did it last?"

"Two weeks."

The Butcher howled.

"Yeah. I can imagine."

I took the bottle and drank a little. My mind got going and sailed through an autumnal forest full of colors and birds.

"It was right after I got out. The first time. I didn't have anyone. No one at all. I met her at a bus stop."

"Bus stop!"

"Yeah. Grønland. And then, I didn't have money for the bus. I was going nowhere. With the bus, I mean. But I got on anyway. She paid for me. I lived with her for those two weeks. In a little studio. She worked at a restaurant, or cafe. It was in '73. In the fall."

The Butcher leaned back in resignation.

"And then you dived back down in the dirt again," he said. "Why?"

I shrugged my shoulders.

"Don't know."

"Holy shoulder of beef!" he groaned. "I hope my children are getting confirmed soon."

"And then she pops up here," I continued. "At the chapel. I'm going to see her tomorrow. Strange, huh?"

"Congratulations! I'll send over a couple of kidneys for the wedding."

It became quiet again. The Butcher finished off the rest of the bottle and set it on the nightstand.

"And you think this is a good time to be flirting?" he asked slowly.

I kept quiet. But he didn't expect an answer and continued.

"What did you find out from this Malvin Paulsen?"

Again I looked at him surprised. He looked another way, out the window or up at the dirty ceiling.

"Nothing special," I said. "He told me a little about the guy who died. I examined the room he lived in, too. Nothing. Cleaned out!"

The Butcher stood up, got his fur coat and walked slowly to the door. He stopped there.

"So," he said, "what did you tell Malvin Paulsen your name was?"

"Hugo Poser."

The Butcher looked at me and smiled.

"Excellent name. Keep it."

Then he disappeared. The footsteps echoed down the corridor for a long time. It was like a ghost was walking.

6

I woke up late the next day. My head felt like an old sack. I opened my mouth and air squeaked out. As I got up, I saw that I was too fat. Sitting on the edge of the bed, I could count not three, but five rings around my stomach. My legs were the same as always. But my stomach. I took a firm hold of it with both hands and pulled. My side of pork hung out a little over my underwear, too. It was depressing. I stood all the way up and went over to the mirror. There I was. Behind a toothbrush glass, a comb, and a deodorant stick. Far inside a looking glass. My face was too round, too. But it had always been that way. I pinched my cheek. I was awake. There was enough to grab. My hair looked messy, withered, like dry grass on a blazing summer day. I looked myself over. When I stood upright, I looked slimmer, but I couldn't avoid seeing my stomach, which longed to be out in the room. Superfluous meat. Flesh. Winter white soft flab. I dug a wad of lint out on my bellybutton. I have always thought that navels are ugly, unappetizing, almost ridiculous. I pulled down my undershorts and took a look at my loosely hanging dick. My old faucet! I took hold of it, tugged a little back and forth, shook. A clear, transparent drop came into view, like dew on a heavy branch. Farther down were my feet.

When I imagine feet as hands, I get nauseous and think about apes. I had to clip my nails soon. I took my own sweet time on the toilet, showered a long time and got dressed. It was two o'clock before I went out. Five hours until I was going to be with her. I was impatient. I walked up and down a few streets restlessly. And while I was walking, I thought about everything that had happened and about my parents, who passed away many years of our Lord ago. Or maybe it wasn't so long ago. It just seems that way. 1970. They never got to see me go to college. But they got out of seeing so much else. Palace Park, the dreams, veins, jails. Words came to me like little birds and pecked a little on my brain. When was it I took the wrong step? I didn't know. Jail. And Berit. Two weeks in the fall of nineteen-hundred-and-seventy-three. The traveling. The stupid journey to the end of the night that only showed me that the earth was flat, just as I had suspected for a long time anyway. A new bird, a raven, coal black, behind my forehead: smuggling and jail. When was it? When did it all happen? I got out in 1977, springtime, early in the spring, an ice cold April day. The social worker noticed that I was one of those smart prisoners who borrowed a lot of books from the library, so she got me a job in the storeroom at the University Library. But I didn't want to be a lyric poet. I didn't want to roll dusty books between dark shelves the rest of my life, deep down in a cellar, under the earth. I wanted out, up. I wanted to be out in the light, be clear and visible. I had the plan ready. Do I regret it now? I don't know. I saved almost all the money. I learned that from Mother and Father. Maybe I couldn't stand being rich? I hid it in a money box half way between Kobberhaug Lodge and Bjørn Lake. I didn't spend it, just a little, didn't splurge. Maybe it was because of the teller I had to hit on the head. Bad conscience? I don't know. But I remember bicycling for my life away from Dam Square, over toward Voldsløkka. I pedaled like crazy through the entire city. And in the basket on the handlebars was a box with 200,000 crowns in it. I was rolling in dough. But I dug down and buried it. I learned how to save and went to the dogs that summer. The fall of '77. At Eger Marketplace. Chased out of Palace Park, chased across the asphalt and the hard stuff. I went to the dogs, but I found a friend in need. Actually, he found me. In need, we found each other. The Butcher. He helped me, I helped him. Good old Butcher. When and where? Birds, fly from your nests and tell all the world that to ye is born this day a savior: The Butcher, deep in the corner at the Promenade Cafe. The desperate Butcher. I loaned him 20,000. I struggled my way into Nordmarka, through mud and wind, rain and snow. There I found my secret box. I carried 20,000 home and paid the Butcher's gambling debts. Horses. Cards. He gave me a room and a television set. Thereses Street. Therese. The Holy Therese? He wanted to quit playing. I wanted to quit shooting. But he didn't play the piano, and I didn't shoot the piano player. We've managed it. Have we? The Butcher and I. Now someone's dead, and I don't know who, but I've seen others die. It doesn't hurt, say those who can. It's just a little unpleasant right beforehand. When you know it's coming and can't do a thing about it. Then you remember everything at once, your entire life in one thought! Someone with my name is dead, and I'm going to see Berit this evening.

A flock of birds took off from my head. I stopped. I had come to St. Hanshaugen Park, and my eyes fell hard and mercilessly on the corner between Ullevåls Road and Colletts Street, at Hansen's Bakery. I tried to fight the urge but walked in.

When I came out, I was carrying carefully, as if it were an infant I was holding, two big pieces of marzipan layer cake in my shaking hands. With cautious steps, I transported them home to the Fredheim Hotel.

"I'm gonna glue your goddamn cunt shut for good!" the man screamed.

His kisser was blood red, and he flailed his arms.

"A gentleman doesn't talk to a lady that way," said the receptionist, laying his slender hand on the man's shoulder.

The man shook it off and came toward me. I was just inside the door, holding tightly to my cake box.

"Lady! That ain't no damn lady! That's a hole!"

"And you call yourself a man! Takes you three weeks just to get it up, and by then you're so tired you pass out!" She laughed loudly and deeply and sent a triumphant look at all of us.

"Shut up, you lousy, deformed whore! Freak!"

Now the lady got mad. She swung her handbag as elegantly as a hammer thrower and hit the gentleman in the middle of the face. At first he was stunned with surprise, then he woke up. A fountain of unkind words and original names flowed out of him, then he threw himself forward to embrace his sweetheart. The receptionist tried to hold him back. He couldn't. The lady was pushed backward. The table with the plastic flowers tipped over. She tumbled further and sought protection with me. The man was just as furious and extended a clenched fist at her. It stopped precisely over my right eye. The layer cakes fell out of my hands. The woman disappeared somewhere behind me, and I felt a big bump making a place for itself in my head.

"A gentleman doesn't hit ladies," I said.

My foot hit him in the abdomen and left behind a muddy shoe print on his white shirt. He collapsed and deflated. I bent down and picked up my package. I shuddered at the thought of how those two pieces of cake must look. But just then the man came back from the dead. I saw the punch coming, but my body was too heavy and sluggish to get out of the way. I had barely raised my arms when his fist knocked the cakes out of my hands again and hit me right above the left ear. I remember a satisfied smile and a scream before my head exploded.

I came to sometime later. I was lying on my bed with something cold and damp over my forehead. Next to me sat a line that could speak.

"We're sorry. We're sorry. It won't happen again."

I got him to stop and wanted to know what time it was.

"Quarter past six," he said quickly.

I let him know that I wanted to be alone. He slid backwards out the door with a flurry of bows and scraping sounds. I stood up and attempted to orient myself. The cake box was gone. I cursed. The left side of my head was swollen, and my eye was dark blue. And the clock was approaching six-thirty. All the stores were closed. I had nothing to take with me. Only myself.

I cursed one more time.

But it didn't help.

I shaved, brushed my teeth, smeared myself with deodorant and put on the nicest clothes I had: gray pants, a white, wrinkled shirt, a woven, earth-tone tie that went well with my eyes, and an old tweed jacket. In the mirror I saw a run-down bouncer on a fortune hunt.

"Where's my cake box," I asked at the reception desk.

The Line curled up.

"The cake box. Was that yours!"

"Yes. Mine."

He looked down at the counter.

"We ate it."

"We?"

"The lady and I. We thought it was Herman's. I mean, the man who attacked you."

"Sure you did."

"I'll get you another cake tomorrow, of course."

"Marzipan," I said and left.

I got there a half hour late. I was supposed to have been there at seven. I heard the Daily Review fanfare from a television set before she opened the door and let me in with a cheerful "Hi." I shuffled after her, laid down my overcoat on the way and ended up in the living room, where Berit had set out coffee cups and dessert plates with little forks next to them. It was just the way I had imagined. The apartment was much bigger than the studio she had in '73, of course, but the principle was the same. She had secure surroundings, solid. Everything was tidy, no dishes that had been sitting around for a week, no clothes sprawled on the floor, no empty bottles behind the sofa. Everything was nice and shiny. The vacuum cleaner and dust cloth didn't get much rest here. The bookcase was full of book club books, and reproductions of famous and beloved paintings hung on the walls. The flowers in the vase were fresh and lush. On top of the TV set was a picture of her parents. I felt a little foreign around all this. I was afraid of tipping something over, breaking a cup, crushing the chair I was on the way down to.

"What did you do to your eye?" she asked.

"Seen too much," I said, coming into place on the seat.

She disappeared into the kitchen and came back with a coffee pot. When I saw what she was holding in her other hand, my eyes got full of water, and a divine joy rose up in my aching body.

"Marzipan layer cake," I whispered.

She sat the work of art in front of me and filled the cups.

"Mother baked it. It was my birthday yesterday."

Imagine having a birthday and a mother who makes marzipan layer cake! She put a piece on my plate.

"Congratulations," I said. "26?"

"Yes. A whole 26 years."

We ate the cake and drank coffee. Now and then I glanced over at her, and now and then she glanced at me. Then we laughed.

"You've put on a little weight," she said formally.

I had saved the marzipan top for last. I coiled it around the fork and hid it in my mouth.

"Maybe," I said. "I'm a bit sedentary. Isn't that what they say?"

But she was just like before. The lines had become maybe a little sharper, clearer, and her hair had grown longer, but otherwise she was the one I knew for two weeks a thousand years ago. She sat forward, holding the coffee cup with both hands, and formed her mouth into a little point. I could see that she had on a black bra. I saw it through her tight, white blouse. Her eyes lay peacefully beneath her forehead. I envied the look in her eyes. If I had eyes like that, everything would have been different. But all the years. Five damn long years. A big black hole between us, an abyss, a horse laugh. I couldn't manage to find the right pitch. I felt out of place and regretted that I had come here at all. What in the hell was I looking for after five years?

"What really happened to you?" Berit asked.

"Nothing. Nothing at all happened to me," I said not very convincingly.

"But the funeral? The death announcement?"

She looked confused.

I looked confused.

"I don't really know all the details," I began. "Someone or other has been using my name. Good joke, huh. But I don't know who it is."

I took yet another piece of cake and felt the blood ringing in my temples like two loud bells. My right eye was stiff and painful and wasn't comfortable with everything it saw.

"Can't the police find out?" said Berit.

I didn't answer. I concentrated intensely on the marzipan. I was full but not stuffed. Since she didn't get an answer, she tried a new question. It wasn't a simple one either.

"What have you been doing since I last saw you?"

It was just as if she were trying to find the lines of connection between us. It was probably done out of politeness. But it was difficult. The lines were so thin. So little time and so many years! But she had come to the funeral. She came when I was dead. I lit a cigarette and put the words into place.

"A little bit of everything," I said. "Had a few jobs. At the docks. And at the University Library," I added proudly.

"Why didn't you continue your studies?"

What was I supposed to say? Don't know, don't know. What really happened during those years, that time in the renaissance. The grass was green and hope was green and the voyage of discovery had begun. We were like gypsies. We danced through the city. Later, it turned into the dance of the dead. In any case, some of us died. And some suddenly became teachers and scholars and agronomists. Why didn't I study and please my blessed parents who are in heaven and who look down on me every day and cry?

"Don't know," I said. "Somehow didn't fit the plans."

"But it's not too late. Is it?"

She looked at me with green eyes that no one could imagine doing any harm.

"No. It's never too late, I guess. And then I did some traveling."

She became curious and perked up.

"Where to?"

"Various places. India. Turkey. North Africa. And France. Marseille. I was gone for a couple of years. Came back in '76, in the summer."

"You took off right after we," she hesitated a little, "we were together?"

"Yeah."

I hoped she wouldn't ask why, and she didn't.

"I've always wanted to travel," she said, almost merrily. "Do you remember how we talked about it?"

"Yes," I said. "I remember that."

It became quiet. Memories rose and fell inside me. Five years. Five years older. It felt as if I were trying to hold something back, or resurrect something that I didn't want to lose. I felt old, like a sick old man inside.

"And what have you been doing since then?" I asked, lighting another cigarette.

Her words were there immediately. She moved lightly and effortlessly through her past. She had reconciled herself once and for all to it, understood it. She quit working at the cafe and got a job with the Transit Service. She stayed with that for seven months. In 1975 she married a guy who worked for a moving company. They were separated a year later. No children. After that she moved home to her parents little farm in Hurdal for awhile. She worked as a hotel maid there for a time. Then she came back to Oslo again and took a job as a checker at Matkroken supermarket, right next to where I lived.

"So, you were married," I said and drank the rest of the lukewarm coffee.

"Yes." She sighed heavily. "It didn't work out. It was bad."

We sat quietly. I didn't want to ask her more. She twisted her fingers in her lap. I wanted to hold her, but it was impossible. The chair held me back. Five years held me back.

After awhile she got up and cleared the table. She went out to the kitchen, and I heard a faucet being turned on. I looked around the living room. It was a bright and friendly room. It was dark outside. I could barely hear the sound from steady traffic on Mosse Road.

"Would you like some banana liqueur?"

Berit stood in the doorway with a square bottle in her hand.

"We should really have had it with coffee, but I completely forgot," she apologized.

She poured something thick and yellow into two small glasses and pushed one of then over to me. We toasted. Something woolly and sweet rolled around in my mouth and knocked against my uvula. It was like swallowing a wet glove.

"Do you like it? It's my favorite!"

Berit looked at me, expectantly.

"Delicious," I stammered, thinking hard about my calvados.

It was just after nine o'clock. The conversation coagulated. My head ached. Berit set out a bowl of potato chips, and we crunched them between our teeth and sent restless looks around the room. I sweated. My shirt was stretched tight over my stomach. I loosened my tie and laughed a little. She laughed back and drew her legs up under herself on the sofa. That little, brown body of hers, full to the brim with secret juices! Her mouth, two rows of straight, white teeth, a childish tongue, grown-up lips. My hands became damp, and down in my pants the general commanded his troops. Oh, Berit! Say something, for God's sake! For my sake! Do something! Say something!

"Do you want to play Scrabble?" she asked.

I was dumfounded.

"Scrabble?"

She had already gotten up and was over by the bookcase to fetch the game. Her tight pants held firmly to her round behind, and I glimpsed the outline of tiny panties.

"We'll have to sit on the same side," she said, making room for me on the sofa.

I moved over next to her. Her body smelled strong and good. Scrabble, I thought. I hate games.

She dealt out seven letters for each of us. I was supposed to start. I placed them in different combinations. I came up with "body" and put it in the middle of the board. Berit added and wrote down the point total. I got four new letters.

Now it was her turn. I lit a cigarette and waited. She took her own sweet time. At last she lay "dance" out from the d in my body.

"Do you have some music?" I asked.

She went over to the bookcase and turned on the radio. Accordion music. I asked her to turn it down.

I had put together my letters to form "swat." I joined them elegantly with the e in dance. "Sweat." She continued immediately, adding "et" to the w in sweat. "Wet." She was clearly ahead of me.

There was a pause. I was stuck. I had a word but saw no place I could put it. She peeked impatiently over at me. I got clammy down my back and it tingled between my thighs.

"Wetness," she said.

"What!"

I looked at her anxiously.

"You can add 'ness' to 'wet.'"

I looked at the board and nodded.

"Of course," I said. "Wetness."

She gave me four new letters again.

I had smoked a cigarette by the time she laid her next word, "panty," out from the t in wet, so that it came over a triple letter square.

"You're winning," I determined.

"There's still a lot of letters left," she consoled.

She poured up two new glasses of banana liqueur. I shuddered. The accordion on the radio had turned into talking. Berit went over and turned it off. I was in a delicate situation. I only had consonants. I had to make use of the vowels on the board.

Finally I spelled "crew" with the help of the second e in wetness.

"Crew?" said Berit.

"Yes."

"Don't you have an s," she said suddenly.

I looked down at my letters.

"An s? Yeah, I do."

"You can get more points."

I added the s in front of the c. Berit figured the point total. I looked over at her, let my eyes swarm over her body, in between her breasts, around her wide hips, along her thighs that quivered ever so slightly.

But now the game started getting very slow. Consonants kept coming up. The only vowels I had were æ and ø. Berit won by 48 points. I exhaled, relieved.

Afterwards she made sandwiches. We didn't say much. It was just as if we were sitting there waiting for something. But it didn't come. At quarter past eleven, I left. As I was standing in the entry, putting on my coat, she came right up against me. I felt her soft, living body against mine, felt her breath on my face and neck. I thought that if we stood that way long enough she could breath life into me again. But we didn't. My clumsy hands ruined it. We laughed it off.

Outside everything was dark and wet. But she stood in the window and watched me go.

But it was not a leap year. March fell down like a shiny, newly-sharpened guillotine over the neck of an innocent man. And no one took action. No one shouted miscarriage of justice. The head rolled away, and everything instantly froze to ice.

At the hotel it became quiet too. The whimpering from the neighboring rooms disappeared. The footsteps in the corridor all walked out. Low in the sky hung a useless white sun.

It was Friday, and I ran zig-zag across Stor Street. I was frozen and hungry. At Gunerius I turned to the right, down Bru Street, and found the way to Kalles Restaurant at Lille Marketplace.

I ordered soup, the daily special, and a pint of beer, and sat down at a table in the middle of the place. A couple of older guys were playing pinball. Sweet music came out of a loudspeaker in the ceiling. There were some quarreling people who soon became friends again. I rubbed my hands together like a boy scout lighting a fire.

The dinner worked wonders. Blood flowed peaceful and warm in my body, and my face glowed. I ordered another beer and sat contented, listening to the pinball games' breathless symphony.

When I'd half-emptied the glass, in came Malvin Paulsen. He looked exhausted. But his friendly, red-edged eyes, which bore wit-

ness to a previous clearness and strength, caught me at once. He
sat down with me and ordered a bock beer from a good natured,
peasant-style waitress.

"Hugo. Hugo Poser," he greeted me. "That's your name, isn't it?"
I nodded. He got his beer and drank half the glass in one gulp.
With foam around his mouth, he said:

"I come here every day. The boys from the company eat here."
He looked around. "They ain't here now. Too early. I usually come
a little early. But you should'a seen it when we moved in the *Post-
giro*. Then it was hoppin' here!"

He raised his glass and we drank together.

"In a couple of months they'll be buryin' the urn with Hans Ge-
org," he said suddenly.

"A couple of months!" I said surprised.

"They gotta wait for the ground to thaw."

He hummed happily and added:

"And here I was thinkin' it's hot enough in hell!"

I ordered another beer to cool myself down. I had to hold on
to Malvin Paulsen. He could tell me a lot if I just asked right. I said:

"Malvin, when I knew Hans Georg he was a pretty good 400
meter runner. Did you know that?"

"400 meters! Hans Georg!"

He sounded genuinely astonished.

"He was on the district team. He could have gone a long way
if he'd just wanted to. The coach said so."

"Ya don't say," Malvin almost whispered, and a flash came over
his face. "I never would'a believed it."

"Why not? Wasn't he as active as before?"

He shook his head.

"He barely even moved!"

I held back awhile and thought about it.

"Did he still have that thick hair?" I asked. "He was known for
it. With the girls."

"Thick hair! Nope. Boy, he'd lost that, for sure. Just patches
around his head. Autumn already in the old wheat field!" Malvin
leaned toward me. "No. Must be someone else you're thinkin' of.
I mean, he must'a changed an awful lot."

It looked as if he had more to say. He got a deep depression over the base of his nose, and his eyes flickered.

"He was an odd one," he finally said. "It was sorta impossible to get contact with him. Like he didn't hear anythin' ya said. Or didn't understand. And the rare times he talked, it went so slow, just like them old senile folks, ya know. Strange boy. But I liked 'im!"

He leaned all the way over to me.

"He was interested in animals!"

"Animals? What kind of animals?"

"Camels. Strange, huh. He drew camels all over."

We ordered more beer, and I thought about deserts and caravans. Malvin patted the waitress on the rear and was showered with abusive words. He looked at me dismayed.

"There was a time when the girls stood in line to get a pat from Malvin Paulsen," he said, raising his glass majestically and drinking until his eyes were full of water. "There were times when . . ."

He was interrupted by a guy who sat down at our table. Malvin Paulsen forgot his defeat immediately and slapped the new arrival on the back.

"Long time, no see! Long time, no see!" he repeated.

"Lots of work lately," said the man.

"This is Arne Garve, a pal from the moving company. And this is Hugo Poser."

Malvin pointed back and forth across the table.

We said hello to each other. He seemed sympathetic, trustworthy, had a powerful, healthy face, blue eyes and a boyish forelock that made him look younger than his surely thirty years. He and Malvin talked shop awhile. Garve listened patiently to all the stories, about the time Malvin got a whole piano overhead and demanded to get payment, all the times he had been called in when the others couldn't budge a safe, about all the housewives who had fallen in love with him and seduced him into the bedroom while their husbands were in the dining room packing silverware and glasses. Malvin talked and talked. It wasn't the first time he had told all these stories. I guess they were his life now, what he remembered, or what he wanted to remember. So he embellished a little. But when he began to talk about the time he was torpedoed in '41 and almost didn't get the lifeboat loose from the ship, Arne Garve got a distant look in his eyes and impatiently moved his big body. He interrupted:

"I'm going to Bergen on Monday. It's probably best to take the lower route now."

Malvin agreed with that.

"You goin' alone?" he asked.

"I haven't gotten ahold of anybody to go along. In the summer it's full of college students and school boys who want to work. But in winter it's deserted. I don't like driving alone, if I can help it."

He finished rolling a cigarette with unbelievable precision and threw it into the corner of his mouth. Malvin looked at me.

"You found a job yet?" he asked.

"Nope."

"Couldn't you go to Bergen?"

He looked at Arne. Arne looked at me.

"It's okay with me, if you want to. Pays 28 crowns an hour. No overtime when we're driving, just for loading and unloading. But we try to work it so we drive as much as possible in the daytime and work in the evenings and at night. Then there's money for the helper, too."

I seriously considered the offer. The money from the Butcher wouldn't last forever. And a little change could do me good. I said yes.

"Pick you up at Majorstua at five o'clock. Gotta fill up the truck before we go. By the way, you a drinker?"

"No," I said.

"That's good," said Arne, and went to the john.

I made use of the chance to ask Malvin about something.

"Were you the one who cleaned up Hans Georg's room?" I said.

He looked at me over the beer glass for a long time. He looked like a water sprite.

"No," he mumbled. "He didn't usually keep it so neat. But that's the way it was when I was woke up. That night he died."

I left when Arne got back. The pinball players' screaming and the talking and breathing that filled the packed premises sounded like a huge chorus of frogmen.

I got home to the Fredheim Hotel by ten o'clock. Most of the windows were dark. The receptionist hung over the counter with a forsaken expression in his punctilious face. From one of the rooms I heard "Heartbreak Hotel."

I went up to the john, and when I came out in the corridor again, a lady was leaning up against my door.

"Hi," she said with a rough voice.

I stopped in front of her.

"What do you want?" I asked and knew at once that the question was superfluous. She laughed.

"The question is what do *you* want, my boy."

I unlocked the door.

"Sleep," I said.

But she sneaked in behind me and placed her body on my bed. I turned on the light and looked at her. It was the lady I had fought for down in the lobby. She didn't have outdoor clothes on, just a thin blouse and tight black pants with a shiny zipper that continued under the crotch all the way up to the waistband in back. Her face was thickly made-up, water-colors that were supposed to cover up the decadence. Her hair was bleached blonde. I could see the dark natural color at the part in the middle. Her age was some place between twenty and fifty. And then I noticed something else that I had not seen when we were in the lobby well over a week ago: she was hunchbacked.

"Did you get your cake?" she asked with a motherly voice.

"Yes."

"Was it your birthday?"

She laughed hysterically at something or other. Alcohol fumed from her body.

"No."

"Do you think layer cakes are that good?"

She laughed even wilder. I couldn't understand what was so funny.

"You've come to the wrong room," I said, pointing at the door. She remained sitting on the bed.

"How long have you been living here," she asked, giggling.

"A time. Why?"

"All alone. All alone in this nice, big canopy bed."

She laid back and stared up at the ceiling. This could take awhile.

I was still standing at the door looking at her. Her blouse strained over her huge breasts, and she had to lie in a strange position due to her humped back. She spread her legs and moved her hips.

"What have you been doing in this big bed all by yourself, then?"

I didn't answer. This was no Gallup survey. Suddenly she got up, in all her splendor. Her face became ugly and distorted.

"You lie there listening! I guess that's the only thing you're good for! Listening!"

She tightened her lips and looked at me contemptuously.

"Get out," I said, completely calm. But I noticed, to my great alarm, that I was getting excited. Her total immodesty excited me. I stuck my hand in my pocket and tried to hide my erection, just like a schoolboy who has to go up to the chalkboard right after he's been staring at a girl and thinking shameless thoughts.

She burst into a choppy laughter and came toward me.

"I suppose you don't go for cripples! Take off my clothes."

She looked at me as if we were two duelists. I didn't know what to do. Her eyes became cloudy again, and many smells came from her body that weren't exactly pleasant. Suddenly she laid a hand over the bulge in my pants.

"What do you use this for?" she asked.

I didn't answer this time either. I just noticed that my hard-on was growing toward the sky. She moved her hand and smiled. But suddenly I became furious. I knocked her arms away and pushed her away from me. She lost her balance and tumbled backwards. She ended up lying on the floor between the closet and the bed. A few nervous twitches went through her body. Her hands searched for something to throw at me, but she didn't find it.

"Pig!" she snarled and spit.

I was paralyzed. She lay there in front of me like an empty sack, in no position to stand up. I was going to say something but didn't get to it.

"You fat, impotent pig!"

I ignored the pleasantries and attempted to help her up. I started to regret kicking that man last week. But I was getting what I deserved. She stared at me savagely and spit one more time. It splashed on the floor. But little by little, as she saw how kind I was, she calmed down. I held her arm. The thin blouse had glided over her elbow. I looked at her, at the perforated skin above her wrists, the tiny sores that would never heal. the dry yellow crusts. She tore her arm away and pulled down her blouse.

"Wrong room!" she said contemptuously and sneered at me.

The door slammed shut behind her. I slung myself on the bed. The silence was like a splatter of blood against my forehead.

I was awakened by footsteps and voices out in the corridor. Right then two men came into view in the doorway. It was the receptionists. The older one pointed at me with a shaking finger. He said:

"Get out! We don't want people like you here!"

I got up and looked at them uncomprehendingly. Then I saw the lady. She stood with her hands at her sides and a smile full of victory.

The one who looked like a line came over to the bed.

"Get out of here now! Or we'll get the police!"

I looked at him calmly, very calmly.

"The police," I said softly, then began from the beginning again. "The police, I think, would be the last ones you'd call."

It was silent. I might as well go home to Thereses Street anyway. Why should I stay here, among unfriendlies. I said to the Line that getting out of there suited me just fine. Now.

"Good!" he answered.

I packed up my things. All three of them watched me. I took my time, folding my clothes nicely, not sloppily, and laid them carefully in my cardboard suitcase. When I was finished, I said:

"But since I've paid for three weeks, you owe me some money."

The older one leaped at me, stretching a bloated red face in the air.

"We don't owe you anything! Get out before we call the police."

But everyone in the room knew the threat didn't bite.

I picked up the suitcase anyway and went out in the hall. The others followed me. We were a whole procession. When we got down to the reception desk, I bent over the counter quickly, pulled out a drawer and took the money they owed me. I counted it twice to make sure no one was cheated. The two receptionists were around me immediately. I pushed them aside and continued out to Sporveis Street, wondering why no one liked me.

The room at Thereses Street was just as I left it. On the floor above sung Book-Jenssen. I turned on the TV, but the broadcast day was over.

The chair embraced me as I leaned back, resigned. I sat there, empty of thought. My neck and back ached. I lit a cigarette, but didn't taste it.

I rose to the surface, walked over to the window and looked out. The street was deserted. But I saw Matkroken, with huge advertisements for salami and chicken hung up in the window. I saw the row of cash registers, everyday customs stations. I tried to picture Berit sitting there punching in numbers with her small, gentle fingers.

I was awakened by the Butcher, who came thundering into the room, hammered on the door, and bellowed:

"My God, what a stink!"

He stormed over to the window, tore the curtains to the side and opened it wide. He turned around to me and said:

"Are you rotting inside? I wouldn't even want to use you for hot dogs!"

"Wait till I'm finished with my morning routine," I just said from deep down in the comforter.

"Did you hear about the guy who exploded?" the Butcher continued, falling down in a chair.

"No," I said. "I didn't."

"It was in the newspaper here one day. He was going to have an operation on his intestines. The doctors had to use a blow torch to cut through. Absolutely true story. But the devil was packed full of gas. You know what that means. It caught fire and he exploded. Bang! Right in the middle of the doctor's hands."

"Terrible."

"Yeah. So, you'd better be careful next time you smoke."

He laughed loud and long and straightened himself up in the

chair. I got up and got dressed. The Butcher lit one of his cigars and asked me to make coffee. He watched everything I did, looked at me with patronizing eyes, and now and then shook his head and blew big clouds of smoke over me.

"You know what," he said when the coffee was ready. "It's actually kind of funny."

"What's funny?" I asked. "I really want to know."

"This guy, he uses your name, then falls out a window and destroys his face. What do you think?"

"Maybe he thought I'd die of laughter."

The Butcher drank some coffee and continued.

"He must have known you. He must have known about you. Right? Try to think of who it might be."

I thought about it, over and over again. But I only knew what I knew: he was skinny with thinning hair, introverted and quiet. The description wasn't exactly precise.

"It's not so simple," the Butcher said, standing up. He went over to the window and stood with his back to me. "You haven't exactly been a good little boy. Have you? It could be that certain individuals, from certain environments here in Oslo, who knew you, your identity, used your name. Can you think of why?"

"No," I said. "My name was the last one I would have taken if I'd lost my passport."

"A rose by any other name. Isn't that how it goes?"

"Yeah. And what's in a name?"

He laughed a little, still standing there with his back to me. He closed the window with a bang and only then did I feel how cold it was in the room.

"The view isn't the most beautiful, but I don't suppose you complain."

"No," I said.

"No one's ever completely satisfied," he continued, taking the cigar out of his mouth. "If you're lucky on one side, the bomb hits the other. It's always like that. If you win the lottery, your house burns down."

The Butcher sighed and leaned on the windowsill.

"For example, I have two children. A boy and a girl. Twins. Two fine children. And I have a good business with a regular circle of customers. But yesterday for dinner, Olav and Kari refused to eat the lamb chops, which they've always liked before. They've become vegetarians."

I burst into laughter.

"Vegetarians! The Butcher's children are vegetarians!"

"It's really not so funny. But it'll pass. I hope. They've got a new teacher at school, in health and P.E., and that man lives on seeds and grass. Eating meat is barbarism, harmful to body and soul, not to mention immoral. So, now I'm a murderer in my children's eyes. But duty calls. I have to go now. There are still a few cannibals among us."

He stopped out in the hall, turned toward me and raised his hand. "Till we meet again, Hugo Poser!"

I sat at the window and looked down at Matkroken. People streamed in and out, loaded down with goods. Barking dogs were tied up outside waiting for their masters. New bargains were posted—cheap fish pudding, whole wheat bread for 1.95, a steal on pork, deep-frozen shrimp, candy treats, instant coffee, toilet paper. Hard-working women and men in white and red checkered coats ran around each other, gathering up shopping carts, opening doors, being polite, giving directions. The Ullevål Hageby streetcar was blocked by an automobile that had parked on the tracks. Impatient passengers waved their arms. The conductor rang all the bells. At last, five strong men had to lift the car onto the sidewalk.

But I didn't see Berit.

At twelve-thirty I went across the street and into Matkroken. There were lines at all the checkouts. People pushed and small children cried. I took a basket and threw myself into the forest of wares. I still hadn't seen Berit.

Actually, one doesn't need much to live. That's my personal experience. I put bread, butter, cheese, milk and eggs in the basket. I walked right past the beer. I had a headache from the day before. When I got to the check-out, the lines were even longer. I cleared my way and finally caught sight of her. She was busy checking a load of groceries that would soon belong to a lady with a hawk nose and wolf eyes. I placed myself at the end of her line.

Berit didn't see me, but I saw her. That was enough. She was absorbed in numbers and sales. She was the most beautiful cashier in Oslo.

Slowly but surely I approached her. It took some time, but I got nearer. I became nervous and tried to plan what I was going to say, but all of a sudden I was first in line.

"Berit," I just said. "Hi."

She smiled up at me and began to take the groceries out of my basket. I regretted that I hadn't loaded a whole shopping cart full. I should have bought everything, magazines and fruits and vegetables and toothpaste, beef, corn flakes, potato chips and band-aids! What I had took only a few seconds, then it was over. I gave her a fifty.

"Thanks for the other evening," she said.

She searched out the change and put it in a bowl in front of me.

"Strange that I haven't seen you in here before," she said.

"I always used to shop down the street," I said. "But I'll come here now."

I stood there counting the change closely. The line behind me began to murmur.

"I live across the street," I stammered and pointed out the window.

She nodded.

"You told me."

"I think I need a bag."

She gave me one. Twenty øre. I put my groceries in it.

"Are you doing anything this evening?" I asked quickly.

"Speed it up!" called a hot-headed woman's voice behind me.

"Maybe we could go out to eat."

"Find another place next time you want to pop the question," said a man.

The line shrieked with laughter.

"I'll pick you up at seven."

"That's fine," said Berit.

I stumbled out. I was so worn-out I almost couldn't manage to cross Thereses Street.

But it wasn't the evening I had expected or hoped. Berit had chicken and French fries and insisted on drinking cola. I had a fillet with a baked potato and a bottle of beer. We chatted politely about the menu, commented on the other customers, and smoked when we didn't have anything to say. The situation was impossible. It was impossible to pretend that nothing had happened, but we tried anyway. It fell apart. And we didn't admit that either.

I took her home in a taxi. The sky was crystal clear, but it would be superfluous to mention it. Berit said it wasn't the intention that I should pay for her and tried to intimidate me into taking her money. I refused, of course, but didn't quite know whether I should take it as a compliment or an insult.

She was too quick getting out of the car for me to do anything. Through the window we made a date that I should call her one of these days. She bent down and kissed me on the forehead. Then she disappeared into the dark entry.

It was barely ten-thirty, and I wasn't tired. I asked the driver to take me to Tørteberg, the last station on the journey to the Christmas star.

The line at the beer counter was of the undisciplined sort that favors those with pointy elbows and steel-toed boots. It was twenty minutes before I finally had a pint in my hand and wandered into the dark, smoke-filled environs. There was no place to sit down. I strolled around between the tables, looking at people, but no one looked at me. It was mostly young people, students, and a few deserters from other restaurants in the vicinity that closed earlier. At last I found a vacant chair out in the corridor by the restrooms. I sat down there, drank my beer and smoked my cigarettes. I thought: what does it matter if you lose your name when no one notices you anyway? That put me in a dejected mood. I got a little sick and sentimental and got back in line again.

It was getting so late now that people were afraid of not getting enough. A noticeably anxious atmosphere prevailed. Many people were buying two or three pints at one time, asked repeatedly what time the bar closed, asked for yet another bottle of wine. The unrest in the line became stronger and stronger with every second that passed. When I got up to the counter, I turned around. It hit me immediately that the mass of people resembled Christian Krohg's painting "The Struggle For Existence."

The chair in the corridor was still vacant, and I sat down there again. It really wasn't necessary to drink. I was angry with myself. I knew that I would have a headache the next day, that nothing at all would come of sitting here, that it cost money I could have used in a more sensible way. I had to laugh. The word "sensible" seemed a little misplaced just then. Sensible. What was sensible? I laughed. I'd prefer a shot of calvados. And someone to talk with. No, not talk. That wasn't necessary. I just missed one person.

I hadn't been to the bathroom in the course of the entire evening, and now I felt the pressure on the faucet becoming too great. I took my beer glass with me and went into the john. It was a big room with a mirror that met you as soon as you opened the door, a row of washstands in the middle of the floor, behind them, the toilets, and along the wall to the left, the urinals.

I was glad there was no one else in there. I stood with my feet solidly on the floor, held the beer glass in my right hand and coaxed my dick out with my free fingers. When the stream was merrily hitting the wall, I heard someone come in. But it wasn't so bad since I'd gotten going already.

A powerful hand suddenly grabbed hold of my arm and pulled me backwards hard. The beer glass crashed on the floor and the stream rotated around in the room, hitting the pant leg of a well-dressed man standing right in front of me.

"Goddamnit! This pig pissed on me!" he said excitedly.

I saw the fist coming clearly and distinctly, but I was so bewildered I didn't manage to get out of the way. The punch hit me over the mouth and sent me right to the concrete. I felt blood running down my chin, and my pants were sticky wet with piss. Another man bent over me, took hold of my shoulder and began to haul me toward a toilet bowl. But I didn't want to go. I managed to twist myself around, grab his legs and pull. He fell down flat with a roar. I got up in a crouch and hammered my fist with all my might over his heart. He screamed again, and then I screamed. The other guy kicked me in the back. It was as if my spinal column shot up into the back of my head, and I plunged forward. I remained lying with my face down in the piss that was overflowing from one of the bowls. A hand grabbed me by the hair and turned me over. I looked up at a smooth, expressionless face.

"We know who you are," he said softly, with clear enunciation, like you hear in school. "You ought to take it easy, then everything will take care of itself. Okay?" He lifted my head and drove it down on the rough stone floor.

I woke up in a toilet stall. I was sitting in just my shirt on the toilet bowl. On the floor lay my pants, soiled with excrement and piss. My jacket and shoes were gone. I felt my face and screamed in pain. A stripe of blood ran down my leg. There was a big abrasion on my dick.

I rose up gently, almost fell, but clawed the wall. My head was a clump of ground meat. I started crying. It burned my face. My legs shook beneath me like two burned matchsticks. I threw up.

It was two o'clock. I suddenly became afraid, panicked. I pulled on my sticky pants and staggered out. The mirror image that met me could not be me. I flailed with my hands, reeled on out to the corridor, stumbled, crawled on my knees, and got myself hoisted up on a chair. I sat there a few minutes. "It's not my body," flashed through me. "This is not my body." I stood up and tumbled further, into a dark room. I saw the beer counter and felt the cold night air from an open door.

"What in the hell!" I heard a voice say far away.

A flashlight was turned on and shined right in my face. Behind it a gaping security guard appeared dimly.

I mobilized the very last of my powers, swung the light out of his hand and ran out. I wandered and fell through the streets. I saw faces frozen in the ice. I dug my way through the snow and saw fathers who ate their sons and an old guy who kicked a frozen-solid head to bits. I ran and found a room that I could vaguely remember, where a cardboard suitcase sat on the floor, ready to travel or return home, where a cold bed drew me down and rolled me into a long and painful nightmare.

But I was not in the penitentiary listening to Johnny Cash. I was in Seljord listening to Arne Garve's cassette player. He had stopped at a roadhouse and was rolling a cigarette. He looked at my face and smiled.

"Monday's a bitch," he just said. "Let's eat."

I followed him into a dismal cafe with formica tables scattered around the floor and reindeer antlers on the walls. We ordered the daily special, which was surely the same every day, all year. I tried smoking, but my lungs couldn't handle it. I wasn't any better when the food came, but I realized that nourishment was necessary.

"You always look like this on Mondays?" asked Arne.

My face was a scab, and it was painful to talk.

"No. I got my head caught in an escalator Saturday."

I attempted to follow up with a smile, but it didn't work.

"You've just about been unconscious since Majorstua," he continued.

"I slept poorly last night," I mumbled.

I was miserable. Not only was I severely beaten, but all my money was in the leather jacket they took. All I had left was a tweed jacket. And a pair of black shoes that were too tight in the arches.

We finished eating without saying anything else. A rose painted cuckoo clock crowed eight o'clock. It was pitch dark outside.

"We'll spend the night at Grungedal," said Arne Garve. "Won't take a chance driving over the Haukeli Mountains now."

I nodded. A bed was everything my body yearned for. Fortunately, no bones were broken, but my skeleton was still scared out of its wits.

We walked out to the truck. I was freezing and climbed up into the cab. It was good and warm in there. In back of me hung pictures of naked girls. "This is Signe-Lill. She is eighteen and still hasn't found her true love. Maybe it's you. You would certainly enjoy caressing her beautiful and willing body. . ." I couldn't read any more. Arne looked at me and laughed.

"After all, you gotta have a little company out on the road alone."

He started the truck, set in motion a new Johnny Cash cassette and rolled a smoke. I struggled to stay awake. The prisoners at San Quentin howled and screamed. Arne lay over the steering wheel, stroking his hair away from his forehead and singing:

". . .don't call him Sue!"

He swayed in rhythm and started bouncing the gas to get the truck to swing along.

"You like Johnny Cash?" he asked.

"He's good," I said.

"He's the one and only," corrected Arne.

We figured to be in Grungedal by eleven. It was almost eight-thirty now. The steady drone from the engine grew inside me, filled me up completely. The snowbanks along the road walled us in. It was barren and deserted in every direction, just a few places where a window shined. I thought about Berit and about the guys who had beat me up, but it was painful to think. Now and then a car passed way below us. I would rather talk, or listen. I suddenly had a strong desire to talk with Arne. The music was over. My ears tickled. My breathing was slow, up and down, and something or other was squeezing my heart as if it were a lemon.

"How long have you been working with this here?" I asked.

"Six years. Since '72. Started with old Renaults that had been

driven since '56. They were junked three years ago. Then I usually
drove flatbeds for awhile before I got this rig."

Arne Garve pushed another cassette into the player.

"Really like the job," he continued. "It's like you're your own
boss. And you get to meet lotsa different people."

He placed his elbows on the wheel, put tobacco in the paper
and finished rolling the cigarette with one hand. His tongue glided
over the glue, and an instant later the rolled cigarette fit perfectly
in the corner of his mouth.

"But it's shitty sometimes too, when you get people who haven't
washed in a year. Overgrown with dirt. And then you have to pack
dirty panties and plates with rotten food stuck on them. Shit! You
heard about Dynamite Harry?"

"The guy from the Olsen gang?"

"No. Someone from the company. He's a little nearsighted, and
so he goes to pack up a bedroom one time and suddenly came
storming out to the other boys. 'I found a stick of dynamite under
the bed!' he screamed and showed it. Know what it was?"

I shook my head carefully.

"An old tampon. Hell, he got it good! After that he was just called
Dynamite Harry."

Johnny Cash sang his way through Telemark, past Morgedal and
Åmot, but he fell silent at the Vinje curves. We moved downward
at a snail's pace, and at each curve the headlights disappeared out
into a vast darkness without being stopped by anything but empty
space. I clenched the seat tightly and pressed my feet against the
floor.

"Where you know Malvin from?" asked Arne.

I hesitated.

"I knew the guy who rented from him."

"Oh, yeah. The one who took the short cut. What kinda guy was
he, anyway?"

"It was a long time since I'd seen him. I was at the funeral and
met Malvin there."

"That really bugged him. That the guy died."

"Looks like it," I said.

Arne concentrated on a curve. The centrifugal force pushed me
over against him. The road straightened itself out obediently in

front of us again, and the truck picked up speed.

"Malvin's a great guy! But his brother. . .you know him?"

"Uh-uh. Just heard about him. Antique dealer."

"Right. Sells old junk at blood prices. Lives in a huge villa up in the Grefsen hills. I get nauseous just thinkin' about him."

"Malvin isn't too keen on him either," I said.

"No, I can promise you that. But he gets some money from him once in awhile. And his brother's the one who owns the apartment on Schweigaards Street."

Arne Garve turned toward me quickly.

"Shit, how do people get so filthy rich selling old stuff!"

"Times of crisis," I said. "In times of crisis people start saving coins and stamps and all kinds of shit."

"I still don't get it," he said. "Getting rich from junk. Can't understand it."

I was tired and worn-out. The big truck rolled patiently through the landscape and darkness. Johnny Cash didn't let up. Arne Garve blinked his eyes a little and chewed on a brown cigarette butt. I lit a smoke to keep awake and looked over at Arne. He must have been conceived in the cab of a truck. His body seemed to be one with the steering wheel. His movements were identical to the truck's. He and the motor were perfectly synchronized. I admired his confidence, the way he talked, the way he controlled his surroundings. Sometimes he reminded me of Berit. She had the same control of her life, I thought, the same perspective, straightforwardness. And it wasn't because their lives were simple and easy, but they were clear about where they stood. They knew which strings to pull, and they knew who pulled theirs, I thought.

We were in Grungedal as figured. It was snowing heavily, and only a few lights gave witness to civilization. Johnny Cash gurgled his last stanza when Arne Garve swung the truck into a gas station and parked.

The hotel was right there, a mixture of Norwegian mountain farm and American cruise ship. A red-cheeked man with an Oslo dialect received us. In a room beyond the reception desk sat a few people around a cozy fireplace. Arne Garve looked very happy. He pointed in there.

"Never a problem here," he whispered.

I didn't quite understand what he meant, but I agreed.

He was not so happy when it turned out that there were no single rooms vacant, just a double room. We had no choice. Arne went up the stairs cursing under his breath.

"It can't be helped," he mumbled. "It can't be helped."

The room was small with a bed along each of the long walls. On the walls hung photographs from the surrounding districts, Rauland and Vinje. They were beautiful, barren landscapes.

I laid down on one of the beds and felt my body rocking and swaying after the long trip. Arne Garve took a shower. I remained lying there and thought about Berit and got the wild idea to call her. I tossed it off and decided to send a postcard instead. I went down to the reception desk and picked out one with a picture of a herd of goats crossing the road at Haukeligrend. When I got back to the room again, Arne Garve had changed and was ready to march out.

"Coming along?" he asked.

I shook my head.

"Hope you sleep well," he said with a grin.

I figured I would.

It was midnight when I finally got the address and three lines written. I took off my clothes and lay awhile pondering what was going on. Someone abused me Saturday night. I had no idea who they were. But *they* knew who I was. Had I done something wrong? Had I offended them? Maybe the folks at the Fredheim Hotel were still mad at me? Or did it have something to do with the death? Or both? Confusing, confusing! Oh, my life was like modern art, chaos, mass produced chaos. I had seen that the woman at the hotel used a needle. Maybe they didn't like that? Maybe someone didn't like it that I tried to ask about Hans Georg Windelband, the other one, myself. Sleep began to get the upper hand. I tried to collect my thoughts one last time, but couldn't. I fell asleep with a beautiful sentence on my lips: On the trail of lost time.

But I was abruptly awakened up a little while later. I had no idea what time it was when Arne and a woman came into the room and turned on the light.

"Who's that," said a slurred voice.

"Relax," hushed Arne. "That's my helper on the truck. Sleeps like a log. Turn off the light and come here."

"Same for me," said the lady.

I heard clothing falling and Arne's heavy breathing.

"Are you sure he's asleep?" said the woman suddenly.

I lay as calmly as I could. I was a mummy with my eyes closed and locked. The lady began to laugh loudly.

"He's got a hell of a boner!"

She came over to my bed and put her hand on the covers.

"Stiff as a rod," she declared.

She was right. The pain in the extended sore was unbearable.

"Let him be," said Arne Garve, pulling her over him.

And then the light was turned off. I saw nothing in the darkness, but was forced to hear all the melodies from eroticism's big songbook and sample all the smells from sex's spice catalog. When I finally fell asleep again, I was wet all over, had a stuffy nose, and the dreams that filled my head were insipid and banal, like everything else.

Arne Garve shook me awake the next morning. He was fully dressed and told me to hurry up. It was the crack of dawn, but I felt, unbelievably enough, a notch better. I bought a stamp at the reception desk and put the card in the mailbox at the gas station while Arne filled the diesel and checked the oil.

"Greetings to your sweetheart?" he called and laughed boyishly.

I thought about it.

"Yes!"

We set off. Johnny Cash started the day's concert, and Arne rolled a cigarette. He appeared to be in top form. And neither of us said anything about the night before.

"How's your girlfriend?" he asked.

"Oh, she's nice."

"Girls are nice, in general. Just don't marry 'em."

"So you've been married."

Arne Garve became serious.

"Yeah. I got married a couple of years ago. Didn't last too long. She was a damn nice girl though!"

He pulled out his wallet and found a picture.

"That's her," he said and gave it to me.

It was like getting a new round of beatings. My ears rang. My body turned numb.

"What do you think? Nice, huh!"

"Yes," I stammered.

I looked at the old photograph of Berit. She was sitting on a bench in a park with her hands folded in her lap and laughing in surprise at the photographer. She had a duffle coat on. Her thick hair was clipped short around her head, and her eyes were wide open, as if she had been surprised. She looked happy, fresh happiness. Her whole body smiled. I was the one who had taken the picture.

I gave it back.

"We were married for one year," said Arne. "But it's so damn hard with this job. Never know when I'm coming home, often gone for several days, sometimes weeks. It's almost like being at sea."

He rolled a new cigarette. This time he was not swift and steady. He sprinkled tobacco down on his legs.

"Damn it!" He brushed it away with a sharp motion. I let it rest. I felt surrounded on all sides, and I became more and more certain that the best thing to do was get away. Go to Nordmarka, boy, dig up your treasure before they build highrises at Appelsinhaugen!

Arne Garve spoke again.

"But I have to drive as much as possible to make money! She worked at a cafe, Peer Gynt on Pile Street, you know it. Didn't make much. And when I finally came home, hell, it was like I was just visiting. We didn't know what the hell we were supposed to do. Fell apart. Fell apart from the first day."

There was silence. Arne sent a brown blob out the window and rolled it back up.

"And then there was her politics," he said all of a sudden.

I looked at him surprised.

"Politics?"

"Yeah. She went to one of those study groups. Some regular at the cafe was converted."

This was news to me. I was curious.

"It's easy to get into politics," continued Arne. "But there's no point in taking it to bed with you, is there?"

"Didn't you agree?" I asked.

"That's not the point. Hell, she didn't talk about anything else, when we talked, that is. Do you think about fascism when you're fucking?"

"No," I said.

But I didn't say how long it had been since I had fucked.

"She pushed her opinions on me," he said aggressively, slashing. "It was like she wanted to hammer the whole system into me too! I got tired of it. Damn tired!"

"Was she as into it after you separated?" I asked carefully.

"I guess she was. Cooled down a little. Maybe she wasn't as certain anymore. But she kept up with it."

"Why'd you get married in the first place?" I asked quickly.

He looked at me, grinned, swallowed the grin.

"We thought she was gonna have a baby. False alarm. Just a swollen belly."

He pushed in a cassette, and Johnny Cash told us more about love.

We ate a solid breakfast at Haukeligrend. Arne started getting impatient. He wanted to be in Bergen before five. He pushed it. The white landscape outside the cab made me think about death and destruction. Everything was lifeless, static. We were the only thing in motion.

It was almost a relief to get into the four mile long Haukeli tunnel. Nature bores me. The only nature experiences I've had were in Palace Park and St. Hanshaugen Park. In Nordmarka I only think of business.

When we came out of the tunnel, we had to pay the toll. Arne grinned.

"Safe conduct plus view," he laughed. "This is the highest point on the road. Almost thirty-six hundred feet."

We lowered ourselves down toward Røldal. I concentrated hard on not thinking about what would happen if the truck skidded over the edge. It was a long way down. I was glad that Arne was conceived in the cab of a truck. He was a good driver and kept himself on the road.

Soon we started climbing laboriously up the sixteen switchbacks at Hardabrekkene toward Røldal Mountain. The motor puffed and groaned and Johnny Cash pressed on. Arne smiled, pleased when we got to the top. His forehead was wet with sweat. Then we were in a new tunnel, and I pretended I was on the Røa tram between the National Theater and Majorstua.

We passed some waterfalls, drove through Odda and followed highway 47 along Sør Fjord.

"It's nice here in the spring with the flowering fruit trees," said Arne.

I could picture it. But now it wasn't beautiful here. Everything was just black and white. The houses looked closed and abandoned, and the fruit orchards looked like neglected cemeteries.

We just made the ferry from Kinsarvik to Kvanndal. It was a little after twelve, and it blew bitter cold up on deck. We ate sandwiches and drank coffee in the cafeteria where some mute people with worn faces were sitting. I tried out the slot machine next to the restrooms, lost, and thought about the Butcher. Arne Garve laughed behind me, put in a crown and coaxed it into seven. He grabbed the money and put it in his pocket.

"Precision and will power," he grinned and took off down to the truck.

From Kvanndal to Bergen was just 80 miles. But the road was poor, and one side went precipitously down to Hardanger Fjord. I thought about the return trip with horror. Then, the fjord would be on my side. Now and then we had to go under a low overpass cut right into the mountain. Arne drove down the middle of the road to get under. It scraped along the edges of the container. He was humming.

"I know every single underpass in all of Norway," he bragged. "More than a few have unloaded their trucks on these here."

At five o'clock we were in Bergen. We ate a quick dinner at a tavern just outside of town, played a round of pinball, and drove to the apartment complex where the customer lived. It was just half a truck load, and the apartment was on the first floor, so it went quickly. I didn't drop anything, made no new enemies, just the opposite. The customer looked happy when we left. He even shook my hand. I was warm and touched. It wasn't an everyday affair.

The intention was originally to stay over in Bergen and drive back to Oslo the next day, but there was a change in plans. The bosses didn't want anyone to drive with an empty truck for long.

Arne was going to pick up a load in Førde and take it to Trond-heim. There he would change containers and take it along to Oslo. I was going to go with a truck busy loading up at Arna.

We were there by ten. Two guys about my age received us with swinging beer bottles, screaming and howling. They had come from a long trip up north and were almost finished emptying a quite stately villa. The truck they had was a brand new Daf with two containers. Arne looked a little envious and grunted something or other about the damn junker he had to drive.

"Just in the nick of time," said one of them. "There's just a piano and a mountain of a cabinet left."

He introduced himself as Kork, and he had a face I had seen many times on different people. It was pale and pear-shaped and reminded me of a caricature drawing of Louis XIV. His hair was blonde and greasy and hung down like two dirty kitchen curtains on his shoulders. He had been hibernating since the sixties.

Kork finished off the bottle in his hand and said with a light belch:

"The preacher man's pretty mellow. Been serving coffee and cookies the whole time. But he doesn't like it at all that we have a drink with it."

He laughed. His eyes resembled big cherries.

"It's a long way to run out to the truck every time, so we hid the bottles under the steps." He lit a smoke. "Been going nonstop since Mosjøen," he groaned. "Moonshine and fucking. Have to keep it up to stay awake. Rigged up a refrigerator in the tool box. You don't look in such great shape yourselves." He took a breath. "The piano, boys! The choir takes the piano!"

Kork marched inside. A frightened family stood there watching us. The driver came down from the cab and said hello to Garve.

"You're getting him for the trip back," said Arne, pointing at me.

"Okay."

He was thin and sinewy, with dark eyes. His hands seemed too big in relation to his lean body, and they swung back and forth like two sledgehammers.

"Espen Askeladd, driver, at your service," he said and banged a fist into my stomach.

"Hugo Poser," I moaned. "Helper with a diploma."

We took along four straps and went in. The minister and his wife watched us with anxious eyes, and their daughter, who was standing a little behind them, clamped her hands together. We adjusted the length of the straps and fastened the hooks. With four men there was no problem getting it into the truck.

"There's still that strange reliquary," said Espen Askeladd.

"It's an old heirloom," said the minister nervously. "You must be very careful."

"Don't worry, mister," Kork stopped him. "We moved a flatbread factory once and didn't break a crumb."

"Well, let's get it over with," said the minister with a strained smile.

We took the straps again and worked the cabinet out the door. My back ached, and my legs were starting to give way ever so slightly under me. When we got to the steps, Kork slipped on a sheet of ice and fell. The cabinet teetered over and hit the ground next to him. Then we heard something like a shriek. The minister rushed out, white in the face. He didn't quite know what he should direct his attention to, the cabinet or Kork. But when he saw Kork lying on his back in the snow, laughing, he turned to the heirloom.

"This is terrible," he groaned. "Is it broken?"

We got it upright. It had received some ugly scrapes, but even the decorative woodwork was intact. The minister's wife was almost on the verge of tears, and she ran around us in circles.

"Just spit polish it and place the ugly side in," said Kork from down on the ground.

Espen tried to pull himself together.

"You can fill out a damage claim," he said.

The minister calmed down.

"Yeah, we'll get it fixed. It's not too serious."

Kork got up and brushed off his knees. He was a little unsteady. The strap hung like an ornament around his neck, and he stared at the minister with a big smile.

"Well, boys!" he suddenly shouted. "One more time!"

We fastened the hooks again and pushed the cabinet into the container. The driver packed it well in wool blankets. The rest of us gathered up the empty packaging. When we were finished, the

minister asked us in for coffee. They still had some camping equip-
ment in the living room, and his wife passed out paper cups and
poured coffee from a thermos.

"Doesn't this coffee ever run out!" said Kork.

She laughed and shook her head hysterically.

"What are your plans now?" asked the minister.

"We drive straight to Oslo," said Espen. "Just got to get to Kvann-
dal in time for the ferry."

"Straight to Oslo now! Is that safe? How will you stay awake?"

"No problem, preacher man," Kork shot in. "We hang by the
straps and take a shot every ten minutes!"

He got up slowly and walked out to the steps. The minister
watched him and worried. None of us said anything.

"Fantastic moon tonight," sang Kork when he came back.

It became silent again. We slurped coffee and chain smoked.
The minister wanted to be friendly and started a conversation.

"Doesn't it get lonely sometimes on such long trips?" he asked.

Kork came back to life and waved his hand out.

"Lonely. Nah. We've got the address of every single mother from
Drammen to Bodø."

Once again it became completely silent. The minister looked
around restlessly, and his daughter disappeared into another room.
Espen Askeladd finished his coffee and stood up.

"The Oslo Express is ready," he said and walked out to the truck.
We followed him. Arne Garve grinned, said a hopeful: "See you
later," and drove his Bedford into Bergen. Kork sneaked the bottle
out from under the steps and stuck it in his pocket.

The minister looked at the truck.

"And this rig is solid, I hope." His voice rose and fell a little.

The driver nodded.

"It's all taken care of. Well-packed and first class crew."

Kork got between them.

"Everything's in the safest hands here," he said, patting the min-
ister on the back.

The family stood together on the steps and stared at us as we
drove off. In their eyes was something that suggested they didn't
figure it likely that they would see their furnishings again.

It was 62 miles to Kvanndal. The night was at its darkest, and the headlights lit up a slick and narrow road. We soon passed Øystese and straight down to the right was Hardanger Fjord. I couldn't see it. I just knew that it was 300 feet straight down. Espen took a beer bottle out of the box between his feet on the floor.

"Here we go!" he shouted and pressed the truck over the 70 mark.

Kork looked at me.

"Best driver since Malvin Paulsen crashed the radio truck at Grønland Market in '63."

I tried to relax.

"Do you know Malvin?" I asked.

"Malvin! He worked for the company for a generation. Didn't need a strap, just used his suspenders!" Kork took a little drink of whiskey. "He quit last fall. Now he just lifts beer glasses and cigarette butts."

Espen Askeladd started to drive a slalom across the road. I clawed the seat and felt nausea accelerate up through my chest. I didn't want to die now.

Kork put an arm around me.

"Are you nervous? Have a little mouthwash."

I drank from his bottle, but it didn't help. My body was beaten black and blue, and it was just as if my face were cracking.

"Come on, come on!" screamed Kork, hopping in the seat.

He dug out some J.J. Cale cassettes and put one of them in the player. The calm music sounded ridiculous now. Espen pressed the needle up to 75. He took out a flask of whiskey from the glove compartment and started drinking. I closed my eyes. Kork punched me.

"You're not nervous, are ya?" he said.

"No," I whispered.

"We picked up a hitchhiker at Mosjøen. He lasted a mile and a half. That's our record. He couldn't stand up when he got his feet on the ground."

Espen hooted and laughed and thundered through the low underpasses. Kork ducked every time and came up with a new bottle. By a miracle, we reached the ferry alive. I sat in the truck while the others went up to the cafeteria. My eyes were as big and white as golf balls. It had just started to become light outside. The fjord was coal black, and white mountains fell vertically down in the water. Here and there a house and barn clung to the mountainside. The ferry was as wide as a Norwegian farmer and butted patiently against the waves. It moved forward. I wasn't aware of the music until the cassette shot out of the player like a tongue. Silence. Then the motor of the boat started and the shaking attacked the membranes. I collapsed a little in the seat and was about to fall asleep when there was a knock on the window. I looked out.

It was the Butcher. I didn't believe my own eyes. I had to hear him speak and rolled down the window.

"What the hell are you doing here!" I asked.

"Are you doing alright?" he said.

"Relatively, yes. But what the hell are you doing here!"

"Business. Delivered some meat to Hotel Norge."

"Is that your refrigerated truck?" I said, pointing at a square box on the opposite side.

The Butcher shook his head.

"No. I drive a Volkswagen. Company car."

He motioned his head backwards at a rusty red bubble that looked ridiculous from where I was sitting.

"Coming the rest of the way with me?" he asked.

"I'm working."

"It's safer with me," he said with a crack in his voice.

I looked down at him from my window. It was funny to be higher than the Butcher. I stretched out a hand and patted him on the head.

"I'm working," I repeated. "I'm going to finish the job. I have pride in my work."

He cocked his head irritatedly and looked at me with eyes narrower than Khyber Pass.

"As you wish," he growled.

The Butcher snapped around and went back to his car. He barely fit behind the wheel. I rolled up the window and waved to him. He didn't budge.

When we got to Kinsarvik, Kork and Espen clamored up in the cab.

"Poser," said Kork, "there's three tremendous virgins on the port side. Coming along?"

"No," I said wearily.

He thought about the answer for a long time.

"Maybe the timing's not quite right," he added doubtfully, hiding his chin in his hand. "Probably needs a pulley to get it up, I bet."

"Love boat ferry ride," I mumbled.

"What!"

"Nothing."

The road along Sør Fjord was just as hellish. There were just a couple of bottles of beer left and a few drops of whiskey, and everyone was broke. Kork was beginning to get a little tired. He lit a pipe and passed it around. We were in the middle of the road, going over 6O miles an hour. To the right, it went precipitously down to an ice cold arm of the fjord, and to the left was a vertical mountain wall. Espen Askeladd cheered and sang.

"We have to get to the shop before the cashier's office closes, or there won't be any dough for tonight."

Kork agreed completely.

"Step on it!" he screamed. "Give it all you got!"

And Espen drove on.

Behind us a red Bug tried desperately to keep up.

We got to Oslo ten minutes before the office closed. I staggered in to the cashiers and picked up my pay and expense money.

"Do you have a tax card?" asked the lady in the window.

"No."

"Then we have to withhold 50 percent. What's your name?"

I had to think.

"Hugo," I mumbled. "Hugo Poser. No permanent address," I added meekly.

Outside, Kork and Espen waited for me.

"Want a ride into town?" they asked.

We'd come this far. May as well go a few yards more. We climbed into the cab, and Kork pulled out a fresh bottle of beer.

"This is the life, boys!" he hollered. "Time for a shower and an aspirin and then get it up!"

They drove me all the way home. I fell out of the truck and stood swaying on the sidewalk.

"Should we carry you upstairs with the straps?" shouted Kork. He slammed the door shut, and then he and Espen Askeladd snarled up Thereses Street toward Adamstuen and disappeared.

Matkroken was still open. But I couldn't see Berit. I didn't see a red Volkswagen either. I dragged myself up to my room and dived into a new sleep marathon.

And all the hedges grew sky high.

10

But it wasn't spring.

The sun ravaged for a couple of days and lured out some smiles and melted a bit of snow, but I know that trick. I had a good laugh the day the cold suddenly fell over the city again, knocking away the grins and freezing the creeks solid as death traps for optimists. It was the middle of March, and the emergency rooms complained about not enough staff, and the liquor stores needed police reinforcements.

I had already obtained a bottle of calvados and sat at home licking my wounds. My body was still stiff and my face too big, but I was coming around. The mirror became friendlier every day, and the neighbors didn't scream when they saw me anymore. For that matter, they rarely saw me.

Berit had come out of Matkroken a few minutes ago with some co-workers. They walked down to the streetcar stop outside the clockmaker's, and right away the streetcar came and took them toward downtown. She would be home soon. Then I would call her. I had a distinct feeling that I was about to do something stupid. But it wasn't the first time.

I drank my liquor carefully. I didn't want to make a mess of my head. I became nice and good and warm from it. Jens Book-Jenssen hovered above me and sang about girls in the good old days. I dreamed of a meeting between him and Johnny Cash. Johnny Cash would come riding down Bygdøy Avenue while the Book sat up in one of the trees throwing chestnuts at him.

I didn't think about Hans Georg Windelband so much. I thought more about Hugo Poser. He sat with a little calvados in the bottom of a green glass and gathered courage. Outside, darkness sank down from a flat sky and made the view turbid. Suddenly Book-Jenssen was quiet and it became amazingly still. To create a little sound, I stood up, walked across the floor, stomped, turned the TV on and off, and sat down by the telephone.

It took Berit a long time to answer, and the waiting made me shiver nervously. When I finally got connected, I didn't know what to say.

"Who's there?" she asked.

"It's Hu . . . Hans Georg," I corrected. My forehead was a radiator.

"Is that you! I've been waiting for you to call."

Had she! I became happy and shook a smoke loose from the pack in my hand.

"Where are you?" she asked.

"At home. On Thereses Street."

"So, you got back from your trip," she said. "Oh, and thanks for the card. It was really nice."

Small talk and nonsense. My hand shook a little and steered columns of smoke diagonally out into the room, as if I were afraid of blowing smoke in her face.

"Tomorrow's Friday," I said. "Would you like to go to a movie?"

She did. She wanted to see something romantic. My heart became big and soft as a teddy bear. We made a date to meet at Stor Marketplace in twenty-six hours. She was not as enthusiastic about my suggestion of dinner at my place, and said she had to go home first. But her voice was pleasant, and she said she was really looking forward to it.

But then, I was too.

Just as I hung up there was a careful knock on my door. I opened up, and Malvin Paulsen was outside. Just like always. One thing on top of another, and out of context besides.

"I got your address at the shop," he stuttered. "I have to talk to you."

I let him in. He looked bad. It occurred to me that he had changed considerably since the funeral, even though he looked tired and drunken then, too. There was, in spite of everything, something good natured and clean about him. He must have had a lot to drink lately, since his lips were swollen and his face was flushed.

He collapsed into a chair without taking off his overcoat. His eyes immediately found the bottle. It had cost me 123 crowns. Now it would get a tongue to roll on. I poured him a glass. He tossed it down and twisted his face like a washcloth.

"What's this stuff?" he spit out.

"Apple brandy. French apple brandy."

He reached out his glass for a refill.

"Why haven't ya got your name on the door?"

"Just moved in," I said.

He kept drinking. Malvin Paulsen was headed downward. I could see it. And the stairs he walked on were rotten. I poured a little for myself and lit a cigarette.

"You wanted to talk to me?" I said.

He was a little slow on the uptake and looked at me for a long time. He barely managed to keep his eyes open, and he had lost all control of his facial muscles. He looked ugly.

"Did you know," he began. "Did you know Hans Georg was a bank robber?"

I became cold as a bible. I didn't move, sat like statue with the glass halfway between the table and my mouth.

"Bank robber," I got out. "What in the world?"

"I'd never of believed it 'bout 'im," said Malvin softly. "I'da never believed it."

"How did you find out?"

My heart went like the pistons in a Harley-Davidson. My whole body shook. But Malvin didn't hear what I said.

"So now I know where he got his money from. Why he didn't have no job."

I waited before speaking. I had the feeling I was getting close to something now, that the keystone was right next to me. I asked again:

"How did you find out?"

Malvin looked at me. He took out his Petterøen tobacco, but it was just dregs. I gave him a Hobby from my pack. He attempted to say something. His tongue was like a dead fish in his mouth. But I was patient. I looked away, out the window, at the dismal facade right above, the curtains, which looked like dirty handkerchiefs, and the potted plants which were surely full of dead flies and snakes.

"I met 'em at Central Station," he finally got out. "I usually take a walk 'round the marketplace there. Read the papers."

He stopped. I gave him another smoke and filled his glass. It all disappeared inside him. He continued.

"They says Hans Georg Windelband was a bank robber. That he robbed a bank. In '77."

I held my breath. But I survived. I've been under water a lot.

"They a'ksed if I know where the rest of the money's at."

"The rest?" I just said.

"Yeah. That's what they said."

I leaned all the way over to him, looked in his eyes, but I was sure he didn't see me. Anyway, I said, absolutely as clearly as I could:

"*Who* was it you talked with, Malvin? *Who* told you all this?"

"Don't know. It was two fellas in their thirties or forties."

He stopped, became clear for a few seconds and looked suspiciously at me.

"Why you askin'? It was prob'ly the police."

"Of course," I said. "Sure, it must have been the police. Who else? I guess they looked like cops, then," I added quickly.

He didn't answer. He stood up unsteadily. I followed him, rising from my nightmare.

"They probably made a mistake. You'll see," I said. "I'm sure they're mistaken. Hans Georg wasn't like that. Not at all."

Malvin looked thankful.

"I don't think so neither. And I told 'em so. Your makin' a mistake, fellas."

He maneuvered over to the door. There, he turned around again.

"Zit possible for a diabetic to run the 400 meters?" he said.

I looked at him. I didn't get it.

"Didn'cha say he was good in the 400?"

I nodded.

"But he had diabetes," Malvin continued. "Anyway, he used them needles. I saw 'em."

"I see. Diabetes is nothing to fool around with."

It seemed like Malvin lost his chain of thought. His face rotated slowly. His eyes swam in mud.

"You wanna move in with me?" he asked all of a sudden.

I looked at him, overwhelmed.

"Move in with you! I live here. I wasn't thinking of moving anywhere."

"You can get the room cheap. I don't need more 'n one."

His voice was mushy and disappeared down inside him. I put my hand on his shoulder.

"I can't," I said. "But I'll come and visit you. Often. I promise!"

Once more he got that thankful look, and my throat constricted. He left.

I stood in the window and watched him. Malvin Paulsen was a hazy, hobbling shadow being devoured by a bigger darkness than what that evening held. I never saw him again.

11

A group from the Salvation Army entertained at Stor Market-place with music and singing. I admired the glow that filled their voices and the healthfulness and joy that flowed over their faces. But when they came a little too close and wanted to whisper a few words in my ear, I got away quickly and left the lady in the ridiculous uniform standing alone with a Bible in her hand and collection plates for eyes.

It was a cold and clear evening. I walked around to see if Berit was waiting somewhere else. I was restless and uneasy and buzzed like a fly between Kreditkassen Bank and Cathedral Church. I couldn't get Malvin Paulsen out of my head. *Who knew about the bank robbery? And how?* If it was the police, they probably would have picked me up a long time ago. It couldn't be the police. And those guys who beat up on me? Were they the ones who talked to Malvin? I thought they were. And I had a suspicion that I'd see them again. It occurred to me: was the whole thing with the obituary announcement and funeral planned to lure me out into the light? It sounded incredible. It was too messy. I almost had to laugh. You don't start a world war for the sake of a few coins. Or do you? But in any case, who was the corpse? What did I know about the crushed face, split by a low fence, mashed against the asphalt? He had diabetes, as Malvin put it. Fast friends with a syringe. I began to suspect the worst. But I didn't get any farther. Someone was breathing down my neck. I snapped around. It was Berit.

"You look sharp!" she said.

I *was* sharp. I had bought a new suit on sale at Dressman on Bogstad Road. The color was, perhaps, a little too red, but the price had closed the deal.

"Aren't you freezing!" she continued.

I was freezing like a dog. But I didn't have the heart to cover the suit with my ugly old overcoat.

We went to the Eldorado and saw a suitably crude and cozy movie. Whenever the people shot at each other and blood spilled and teeth flashed in the spotlights, Berit grabbed me tight, and I gladly let her. When they were nice and friendly to each other, lying in bed or sitting on the terrace with a view of the Mediterranean or the Alps, I tried putting a hand in her lap, and it slipped in. So it goes, it hit me, once and for all. Man and woman. Each with desire. So what if they don't desire each other.

I persuaded her to go along to Stortorget Inn afterwards. The waitress was sour and looked at the clock and said we'd have to be quick about it. They closed in fifteen minutes. Never time. Always too little time.

I wanted to tell her about the trip to Bergen, but suddenly I thought about Arne Garve. My face felt strange and I tried to hide behind the beer glass. My words stumbled and fell on each other.

"What is it?" she asked innocently.

I had to say it and said it:

"I rode with your ex-husband, Arne."

Now it was her face's turn to become strange. I was about to lay my hands reassuringly over her helpless, little hands when the waitress came between us again.

"Didn't you see the lights flash!"

I looked up. I could have blown her away.

"I thought there was something wrong with my eyes," I said.

"Thanks a lot for telling us."

Berit had already stood up. I had a sip left in my glass.

"Come on, hurry up!" the lady growled above her apron.

That was the last straw.

"Don't you see we're leaving, for Christ's sake!" I yelled up in her face.

Berit looked at me alarmed and began to walk quickly toward the exit. I was going to run after her, but a solid bouncer grabbed me from behind and held me tight.

"Are you makin' trouble!" he spit into my ear.

I didn't answer. It was an impossible question. He wrenched my arm up my back. It hurt. Some half-drunk goobers stared at us through scuba-mask eyes.

"Let go, goddamnit!" I snarled.

"Are you makin' trouble!" he repeated. It was the only sentence he could say.

I sensed the sickly smell of garlic and beer encircling my face. Berit disappeared out the door. I was seized by panic, or maybe I just became extremely impatient. The bouncer held me and Berit disappeared. It was not intentional. I butted my head as hard as I could backwards, smashing into the base of his nose. The grip loosened like a Christmas gift being opened. To be on the safe side, I jammed my elbow into his kidney. He grimaced and fell. Some guys attempted to stop me, but they were too drunk. I pushed them away and stormed out the door.

But Berit was gone. In the middle of Stor Marketplace stood Christian Kvart, pointing at something or other on the ground. But that wasn't Berit either. I ran toward Karl Johan Street and down to Central Station. She was nowhere. I hailed a taxi and went to her house. All the windows were dark, and the front door was locked. A cat scurried between my legs and disappeared into the darkness. I massaged the back of my head and cursed everything and everyone. I was freezing to death and paced up and down the sidewalk to keep warm. Lights came on in a couple of windows, and some anxious eyes looked down at me. But I was not the mad bomber. I chain smoked three cigarettes, and finally Berit showed up. We walked toward each other, and each of us rose from the grave.

"You're freezing," she said. "Your whole body's shaking."

I nodded. I was a glacier.

"Do you want some tea?"

Did I! We went up and in. It was cozy and warm in her apartment. Berit laughed at me and said my face was red as a poppy. I saw in the mirror that she was right. The color of my suit had rubbed off.

I sat down in the same chair as last time, and everything was just as neat and tidy. The carpet was vacuumed. No pictures hung crookedly. No stockings fouled the air. Soon Berit came with the tea and poured two big mugs.

"So you rode with Arne," she said.

"Yeah. He showed me a photograph of you. The one I took in Tøyen Park that time."

Her face became odd again, and she held tight to the tea cup.

"What did he say?" she asked carefully.

I hesitated.

"What did he say? Not much. That you'd been married. And been divorced."

Berit laughed silently. There was an undertone of bitterness or defiance when she spoke.

"Boy, that's original, isn't it! Getting married and getting divorced!"

I said nothing. I didn't like the situation. I didn't want to run with messages between ex-husband and wife.

"There was never really anything between us," she continued, milder now. "He was gone so much. Three and four weeks at a time. And then he had plans of driving abroad too. Daydreamed about Italy and Yugoslavia and so on."

I sat silently and listened. Berit and Arne. In good days and bad. For awhile I could feel the swaying from the tractor-trailer, and right away I could sense the rhythm in her body.

"But we're not enemies," she said. "It was just rash. That we got married, that is."

She became quiet. I wanted to ask her about that stuff with the politics, but fortunately I left it alone. I had no desire to pick at old wounds. But it was almost consoling to me that Berit was also hiding something, something she would rather not talk about. Or maybe Arne was just exaggerating. Maybe he just wanted to put the blame on something outside himself so that he walked free.

I looked out the window. To my great amazement, I caught sight of a leaf falling down through the air, in the middle of the yellow beam from the streetlight, the star of the show, the evening's clown, the year's first foliage. March, I just thought. Autumn in March.

Berit straightened up in the chair and rubbed the palms of her hands over her face as if she were brushing away a memory.

"How are things going with you?" she asked with a clear, transparent voice.

So, how was it going with me? I answered that it was going. There wasn't much to add. I'm modest in the food line and don't demand much of my fellow beings.

Berit poured more tea.

"Now I know I'll have to get up at night to pee," she said.

"Don't you have a chamber pot under the bed?"

She laughed.

"I do at home with Mother and Father. It's a long way to the bathroom there."

I drank tea and tried to picture Berit on the pot. It was a little difficult.

"Have you found out anything about the person who died?" she asked suddenly.

I was torn brutally from my amusing picture.

"No," I said.

"Why don't you go to the police?" she wanted to know again.

I thought it over. It must be good to have someone to go to. I shook my head and tried to laugh it off.

"He's still dead anyway," I said. "Poor devil. Whoever it is."

Berit looked tensely at me. The tea started getting cold.

"You've gotten yourself messed up in something again," she said, no, she declared.

"Again?" I said, looking past her, at the wall, through the wall, down to Oslo Fjord.

She curled up like a parenthesis.

"That time," she began, "when we first met each other. You had just gotten out of jail then, right?"

My eyes were on the bottom of Oslo Fjord. I flirted with a flounder on a sand bank.

"Yes," I said. "How did you know that?"

"I knew. And you talk in your sleep!"

My eyes were back on land. I laughed.

"No one's perfect!"

"What did you do?"

I hesitated, thought back, and a hazy, ungainly figure took form in my eyes, but was gone at once, disappearing in a gray mist, like a ship in the fog.

"What's done is done," I said. "Small stuff. Smoking hash. A couple of break-ins."

"How long were you in?"

"Three months. Ninety days."

My voice didn't want to say any more. But inside me I said: At what point did you take the wrong turn? When was it? Or was there someone else who ripped the map aside so that I fell in the gutter?

Berit understood that I didn't want to talk about it anymore.

"I'm going to my parents' for Easter," she said. I'm leaving tomorrow."

"Oh, yeah? It ought to be nice there now. And you'll get to use the chamber pot, too."

We laughed. I laughed myself away.

"I'll be back to work three days after Easter," she said when we stood out in the entry.

"Then I'll buy the whole store," I promised and put my hand on her arm.

She smiled. I drew her to me a short while and released her again.

"Take good care of yourself," she whispered peculiarly.

"Yes," I said.

I ran down the stairs. The moon was pasted properly up in the sky and let useless light down over the city. I stared at it, became momentarily crazy and screamed for a taxi.

When I got home, the Butcher was there. He sat in the middle of a column of smoke and had a glass in his hand.

"Can you really afford such expensive liquor?" he asked, lifting up the calvados bottle. It was almost empty.

"I drink in moderation," I said. "With civility. Besides, I've earned some money recently."

I went straight to the window and opened it. The Butcher eyed my new suit.

"I see. You've become a pimp."

I was offended. The Butcher's entire face grinned, and he handed me a glass.

"Yeah, yeah, boy. Welcome home from Bergen, anyway. And now it's Easter, and the wife and kids spending the holiday in the safe custody of Beitostølen."

I sat down.

"So you're a free man for the time being."

The Butcher shook his head sadly.

"Oh, no. No one's ever free. Do people stop eating because it's a holiday? Just the opposite. They eat themselves to death. They choke on their own intestines and drown in their own piss and get buried in their own shit!"

"It's been busy, then," I said.

He looked at me, expressionless.

"Oh, no. It's nothing."

The last streetcar clattered down Thereses Street. I closed the window. Before I drew the curtains I saw some youths stumble out of a doorway, and I heard a girl crying, quietly but heavily. I sat down on the bed again, and we didn't say anything for awhile. The Butcher looked big and sad. His swollen face had taken on a tragic dimension that didn't fit him. A half smoked cigar dangled in his mouth, and gray ashes fell down on his colossal stomach.

"Youth is gone," he said suddenly.

I looked at him surprised and couldn't help laughing.

"What do you mean?"

"Irredeemable. Hair's gone. Those swell kids of mine have started buying contraceptives. And I miss Marta. That's the worst."

I filled his glass and patted him on the shoulder.

"There, there," I consoled. "You still have many exciting years ahead of you."

The Butcher brushed me off.

"I often think about death," he said angrily. "Isn't that a sign of getting old?"

"No," I said. "The skeleton comes along no matter where we go."

"What the hell does that mean?"

"Thinking about death is just as natural as thinking about life," I chanted. "It's two sides of the same thing." I didn't say anything else. I thought the last formulation sounded ill-omened.

"*You* can say that," said the Butcher wearily. "You *are* dead. It even said so in the paper."

He laughed loudly but not cheerfully. I ignored the remark and said:

"Actually you start to die as soon as you're born. It's like a long sex act, an enormous fuck. And the orgasm is death. Phifft! Over."

The Butcher blinked his eyes and yawned. I stopped. I suddenly became extremely aware of my heart. It was hammering beneath my shirt. Time passed. Time passed. The seconds moved on the inside of my skin like blood red drops.

The Butcher rose from the chair. He walked three steps forward and two back, stopped abruptly, and pointed at me with his cigar like a threatening troll.

"Hans Georg Windelband," he said. "Or should I say Hugo Poser. Or whoever the hell you are. Which one of you robbed a bank?"

I saw that his forehead was shining with sweat. He was still aiming the cigar at me. An ash fell to the floor with a crash. I didn't answer.

"I've had a little chat with good old Malvin Paulsen," the Butcher continued. "I ran into him at Grønland. At Kalles Tavern."

I nodded and let him go on.

"I'm not exactly undisturbed by what's happened. Am I, huh? And now I'd like to know. That money you helped me out with that time, is it true that it was the last of your inheritance from your parents?"

"Does it matter where it came from?" I said.

The Butcher sank down in the chair. I hoped he would begin sucking on that cigar again, soon. It was irritating to have it directed at me all the time.

"So it was the bank robbery money you loaned me," he said surprisingly low and gentle. He finally stuck the cigar in his mouth.

"Yes."

"I never would have believed it. Never."

Now it was my turn to stand up.

"Everyone is so disappointed in me," I said. "Everyone! Would you not have taken the money, then! If you knew where it came from!"

The Butcher looked at me. Something came into his eyes or his face that I had only seen one time before, at the Promenade Cafe, October 1977.

"Yes," he said. "I would have taken it. I had to. You helped me. And I wanted to help you. We've helped each other, right?"

"Yes," I said.

"And we've managed. Haven't we? Haven't we done that?"

I sat down on the bed again, grabbed the calvados and drank right out of the bottle. I poured gasoline on the fire.

"But the point is," said the Butcher when we was himself again, "you've made me an accomplice!"

"Oh, shut up! You didn't have anything to do with it!"

I waved my arms at him, irritated. He blew cigar smoke between us.

"And the rest of the money?"

I lied. I had a right to.

"There is no more."

He was quiet for a long time. The room became more and more smoky. He stood up again suddenly. I saw his outline. He stopped by the window and opened it.

He declared:

"Someone took your name and died. Since then you've been beaten up, driven to Bergen, met an old girlfriend, and someone knows about your past!"

I just nodded. He continued right away.

"But where do *you* fit in?" he threw the cigar out the window. "What do you *know*?"

I inhaled. What did I know?

"The guys who beat me up could well have been from that damned hotel. Hell if I know. But the rest of it! I get the feeling that the whole thing is bait." I remembered that the Butcher didn't know about the rest of the bank money. "Bait for something or other."

"Bait! For you? Who in the hell wants to bait *you*?"

Neither of us answered that. The Butcher was back in the chair again. I thought he seemed unusually restless.

"Until now you just dug around in your own shit," he said. "You're digging in rotten soil. Isn't it about time to pat the shovel on the ground and let new flowers grow!"

I drank with one ear and listened with the other. The Butcher didn't know what he was saying. He struggled to express himself clearly. His lips formed words, but they never slipped out of the storehouse. I got the urge to take off again, get away, just walk out of this nightmare, take a quick trip through Nordmarka and disappear. But something was holding me back. I put it off. I knew I was an idiot, but there was nothing to do about it.

"Hugo Poser," said the Butcher finally. "Hugo Poser! Watch out!"

He didn't say anything more. He stood up slowly and left. In the chair where he had been sitting I found a thousand crown note. I ran to the window and looked for him. But the Butcher was gone.

12

It was a hell of an Easter. The radio reported snowslides and storms. People were taken by surprise by the bad weather, got lost and disappeared in slow spirals, inside a green dream, while they saw hands and feet grow until they doubled. Some were swept away by avalanches, squashed to death by tons of snow, or they fell down in glacial cracks and slowly froze stiff, maybe dreaming of popping up again in a hundred years when the glacier has moved a little and times are better.

But I was in no danger. Either I sat at home, safe in my hole, or I moved in the area around Bolteløkka and St. Hanshaugen. I never said where I was going, but the routes were well marked, and there were traffic lights at the most dangerous crossings. One day I captured a bottle of calvados and carried it proudly home to Thereses Street. Another day, when the fog lay low over the countryside, I strayed down to the city center. I walked through Palace Park. It was a long time since I had gone that route. I stopped at the steps, looked up at the pile of dirty and sticky wet snow. There wasn't a single footprint in it. Chased, I thought. Chased over on the other side, down. The black trees stood like skeletons and scarecrows. A police car rolled slowly behind me.

I walked on.

I didn't want this. But is was necessary. I had put it off. Now I had to do it. I walked down Karl Johan Street, and it hit me that I had never seen the city more gloomy. Abandoned, evacuated, gray and black, closed, yes, all of Oslo was closed. I was the last rat to abandon ship.

The ranks were thin even at Eger Marketplace. I didn't go there with desire and joy. To tell the truth, I'd rather have turned. Turned and walked away. I was walking backwards now, rotating the hands on the clock toward the sun. There were some people sitting outside Samson's Bakery, two boys and a girl. I knew the expression. They were almost one with the stone wall behind them. They believed that nature was beautiful. Maybe they thought the grass was green for them. They were fooling themselves. They were fooled. I bent down and spoke.

"Has someone disappeared from around here lately?"

They looked at me with eyes that resembled moons and black wicks. I repeated the question.

"Did someone go away, abruptly, all of a sudden?"

One of them made some motions with his head.

"No idea."

I stood up. Outside Bøndene Bank stood two guys, one in an Afghan fur, the other in pale, skin-tight denims. Both stared at me. I rolled down the escalator and looked around. The shop was closed. Some seedy passengers passed. Otherwise, no one. Nothing. I went to the john. It was dirty and smelled of booze and piss. No one there either. Easter, I thought. Everyone couldn't have gone to Norefjell and Geilo and Beitostølen.

I was right. The denims and Afghan fur stood behind me. It looked like they were blocking the exit.

"What the hell are you snoopin' 'round for," began one of them.

"I'm looking for my mother," I said.

They came closer. Both were several years younger than me, but they had been doing it longer. They had come in from the suburbs, from beer and liquor and people silos, right in to Eger Marketplace, no detour, no dreams. We came from the villas and the Westside, from cheese and red wine, ballad songs and amateur theater, dancing down to Palace Park in brightly-colored clothes. Damn, how nauseous and sick I got where I stood!

But since neither of them said anything more, I took the floor.

"I just wondered if you know of someone suddenly disappearing from around here?" I asked.

Now they came even closer.

"Fuck off, boy scout!"

I tried to explain myself.

"Listen, man," I said. "I'm looking for sc_nebody. I'm . . . I was one of you. Relax."

But they didn't relax. I could see that the guy in the denims was holding a knife in his hand, a switchblade. The other tried to get behind me. But I'm not as easy to fool as some would believe. I heard a click, and the knife blade came into the room. I kicked as hard as I could, hitting right under his knee. The knife squirted out of his hand like a slippery bar of soap. I shoved it under the door of a stall and took hold of his jacket and hammered my forehead against his head. Now he didn't want to dance anymore. He twisted out of my grip and toppled to the parquet. I turned around and looked at the Afghan fur. His reflexes were not what they had once been. He still didn't have his arms up ready to strike. I just looked at him. He backed up a little and began to flap his arms instead.

"Solidarity," I said. "Whatever happened to solidarity?"

But he didn't answer.

I went home. My forehead was sore. I thought: when the snow melts, when the snow melts I'm going to take my rucksack and trudge in to Kobberhaug Lodge, past Kobberhaug Lodge, and up Appelsinhaugen, down the other side, and there! Above the clouds the sky is always blue. And under the snow the birds always sing. I got home and turned on the TV. "Do you remember, do you remember."

Maundy Thursday came with a change of weather. It turned gray and mild. The atmosphere pressed the city flat. And my body was inert. I blamed myself for not keeping in decent shape. I was lazy. I ate too much marzipan. The sum of the damages is constant. I decided to do something about it. But I didn't do anything that day. And not the day after either. Good Friday was a bitter day.

And long. I sat in my cozy room on Thereses Street and thought. Malvin, I thought. Malvin must know *something.* Something *more.* I only had to ask him in the right way.

So, I went to Malvin Paulsen's, Good Friday, 1978. Besides, I had promised him I'd visit.

The empty liquor bottle on the mailbox and the discarded furniture weren't there this time. But it smelled of ten different dinners, and paint chips hung down like skin peeling off a sunburned back, and hymns resounded from all the apartments. I hurried up to the fourth floor. A man I had never seen before opened the door. But I knew who it was. It had to be the brother, the antiques dealer.

"I came to see Malvin," I said.

He turned his back and went inside. I followed him.

"Then you came too late," he said. "Malvin died yesterday."

I suddenly stopped. A wall fell down in front of me.

"Malvin's dead," I just said, my voice coming from somewhere else.

"That's what I said. He died yesterday, in the morning."

He spoke dryly and factually. I didn't like him. He was younger than Malvin, in his mid-fifties. He was thin and little and wearing a stylish dark blue suit that tapered at the waist. It was double-breasted, with shiny buttons. A burgundy tie sat tightly around that ugly turkey neck of his. His face was pale, almost completely white, and perforated with tiny black dots, and his eyes sat unmoving, each in its own dark chamber. He reached out a hand. It was slender, with long fingers, as well-manicured as a woman's.

"Gordon Paulsen," he said. "Malvin was my brother."

"Hugo Poser. I knew Malvin from the moving company."

We went into his room. Gordon had gathered up all the empty bottles and taken down the pictures from the walls. The bookcase was empty too, and the clothes lay in a heap on the sofa. In the window on the other side, the same lady was standing with her breasts on the window frame. She hadn't budged. She was surely at the movies.

"How did it happen?" I asked.

He looked surprised.

"How did it happen? Do you have to ask? Malvin drank himself to death. There wasn't a single blood vessel intact. Then he poured that last drink that made his heart explode. That was yesterday. He died drunk. Dead drunk."

He sat down in a chair and waved his arms.

"And what am I to do with all of this! A few moth-eaten clothes. Empty bottles and cigarette butts. If you see anything you want, just take it."

"No, thank you," I said. "I don't need anything." I sat down on the sofa and lit a smoke.

"That I can well understand."

Gordon Paulsen stood up and pointed into the room across the hall.

"And that dirt-bag who lived there. Extremely inconsiderate to throw oneself out the window like that."

"Yes, it certainly had an effect on Malvin," I said.

He turned around toward me suddenly.

"I don't know anything about that. I just know that guy didn't make God very happy. Or his mother either!"

"Is that right," I said. "How come?"

Gordon Paulsen sat down and looked desperate.

"When you have a brother like Malvin, you have to keep an eye out for him, you know. I mean, he was, you know, in no condition to watch out for himself. And when I heard he had picked up a roommate, literally, right off the streets, then I got worried and undertook an investigation. Besides, I *own* this building. It's *mine*."

"Investigation! What did you find out?"

I tried not to appear too interested.

"Well, of course, I didn't want to violate his privacy, but on the other hand, and out of consideration to my habitually drunken brother, and yes, for everyone here in the building for that matter, I saw myself compelled to conduct this kind of investigation."

Gordon Paulsen stopped and stared darkly at me.

"Any idiot could see that the boy didn't have a job! So where did he get his money from then? From his rich family? No way! Hans Georg Windelband had no family at all. They were dead and buried, every one. That is, insofar as it goes, an extenuating circumstance. To stand alone in this world is hard, very hard. But there are limits. I mean, you cannot excuse everything even though there are certain unfortunate circumstances to be considered. You can't eliminate personal responsibility. Then people would be just like plants, vegetables!"

I lit a new smoke and hoped for more rapid progress in the trial proceedings. Gordon sat straight in the chair and stroked a thin finger across his red mouth.

"Where did he get his money from?" I asked, looking out the window at the lady with the melons. She moved a little for my favor.

"Well. I investigated, as I said, a little here and there. I went into some government offices. I had a nice chat with the police and found out that this Hans Georg Windelband had a rather dark past."

I began to feel sick. Gordon fastened his unmoving eyes on me like two straight pins and continued:

"He was 26 when he jumped. In the early seventies he was a busy beaver. He was into the drug world and all that. You're that age yourself, so you remember that time well."

I nodded mechanically.

"In 1973 he was arrested for some little break-in, using hash, and petty stuff. He was held for three months. Then he traveled abroad, god knows where, and when he came home he was arrested for smuggling hash. What a swine! That was in '76. He was in for nine months. After that they lost track of him. He got work at a library, but it didn't last long. After that, the police never saw him. Until now."

"And then he moved in here?" I asked almost unconsciously.

"Yes. Last fall. I often told Malvin he ought to get himself a roommate, but he wouldn't hear of it. He sure liked the boy. Yes, well, to each his own."

I stood up and went out to the entry.

"What are you going to do with the room here, now?" I asked, pointing in to where the roommate had lived.

"On the trash heap, all of it! Take anything you need."

"I don't suppose there's anything here that can be sold as antiques," I said.

Gordon Paulsen didn't answer. He was standing on a chair, busy taking down the curtains. Maybe it was for the best this way, anyway. Burn everything, wipe out every trace. No one would ever know. That way, everything works out.

"Did you ever talk to this Windelband?" I asked.

"Just once, yes."

I waited patiently. Gordon Paulsen climbed down from the chair.

"I came here one time, and he and Malvin were sitting here. I think he was drunk. In any case, he looked very lightheaded. I asked him his name. I'm very interested in names, and Windelband rang a bell. But it was impossible to get a word out of him. An oyster. He was probably as good as dead by the time he stood on the windowsill."

"What do you mean?"

"Well, living people have a few attributes and signs of life that are easy to detect. For example, they talk, like we're doing, or they are sociable. Windelband was neither."

Gordon Paulsen put the dirty, faded curtains in a plastic bag and tossed it down. The lady on the other side was still looking across to us.

"What did Malvin say about his roommate?" I asked.

"Malvin was in no condition to evaluate anything."

He pulled out some drawers to see if there was anything he had forgotten.

"I said I was interested in names, right. Names are my hobby, in fact. I remember most names. And as I said, there was something about this Windelband name that rang a bell. Does it mean anything to you?"

I avoided the question.

"It's a long time ago now," continued Gordon Paulsen. "In 1970. A terrible accident, Car accident. A whole family was killed. It happened at Nesodden. Parents and grandparents, right out in the water. They all drowned. And what was their name? Windelband. The Windelband family. The only one who wasn't along was the good-for-nothing bum who rented the room here. I remember reading about it in the papers. A fine family, you understand. At the top for several generations. But there was something peculiar about the whole affair. The police couldn't see how the accident happened. They found no skid marks. The road was straight and visible. The speed wasn't too fast. And there wasn't anything wrong with the car. Then it turned out later that the company the family owned was bankrupt. They had tried to hold it up for a long time with the help of various tricks and forgeries, but it couldn't work in the long run, could it? So, zip, out into the fjord, like the old Japanese. There was a lot written about it at the time."

More and more, I wanted to leave. I couldn't stand hearing Gordon Paulsen talk. He knew more about me than I bargained. And I didn't like his eyes. When they looked at me, there was a false bottom to them. "We see you," they said, and a moment afterward: "We have seen you." I was about to go when he suddenly said: "Malvin talked about you."

I leaned over against the door frame and stared at him.

"He said you knew Windelband."

"A long time ago," I said, caught completely off guard. "Many years ago."

I couldn't take his eyes any longer. I had to look another way. Gordon Paulsen picked out something from a box on the floor.

"Here. Something to remember him by."

He tossed a book over to me. It was Dante's *Divine Comedy*, a paperback, in Danish.

"His initials are in there," continued Gordon Paulsen.

I flipped open to the first page. But it was not a W. It was two single V's. Double victory signs. Both hands in the air, middle finger and index finger spread boisterously in the air. It was Viktor Vekk.

I didn't say goodbye. It was like getting a harpoon in the back. I fumbled for the door, tumbled down the stairs, and all the pictures, all the suspicions that had germinated in me sprung out in full bloom. Viktor Vekk. Viktor Vekk! I came down to the street, stopped, holding tight to the precious book. I looked at where he fell. There was a dent in the fence. I looked at the sidewalk, but could see no sign of him, just a thin layer of snow and lots of footprints. I opened up Dante's *Comedy* once again, stared at the two magic letters, V.V. My hand and arm lost all their power, and the book fell to the ground. When I picked it up, a book mark stayed behind in the new snow. It was a playing card, with DFDS's trademark on the back. I turned it over. It was a joker.

I let it lie and stormed homeward.

I fell into my room, and there sat the Butcher. He followed me with his eyes. The white rims swayed faintly.

"Good Friday is a bitter day," he said.

I sank exhausted down on the mattress. Everything had happened so fast. I wasn't able to keep up with events. I was pursuing the field.

"Marta called from Beitostølen this morning," the Butcher continued with the same monotonous voice. "Olav sprained his ankle on the slalom hill, and Kari broke both her skis. And Marta came down with the stomach flu. And the weather is shitty."

He fell silent. I fetched two beers from the refrigerator. Someone had filled the top shelf with chops, T-bones, fillets and hearts. I looked at the Butcher. He looked elsewhere.

"Kind of you," I said, setting a beer in front of him on the table. He blushed.

"Shut up."

"You're too kind," I reiterated and put a hand on his shoulder. "You never think of yourself."

"Shut up!" he spit and blew me off. His eyebrows were like crests of foam and his forehead resembled a blood orange. He grabbed the bottle and drank.

It took time for the blood to leave his big head. He wiped his face with a white cloth, and finally, he straightened himself up and looked at me.

"Yeah, yeah," he said. "So now Malvin Paulsen has moved his last load."

"How did you know?" I asked, surprised.

The Butcher leaned back and looked at the ceiling.

"It needs a coat of paint," he said. "But you have to wash it good first."

I laid Dante's *Comedy* on the table between us.

"In any case, I found out who the guy was," I said. "V.V. Viktor Vekk."

The Butcher just repeated the name: "Viktor Vekk."

I supported myself with a pillow behind my back and leaned wearily backwards. When I closed my eyes, I saw his slender form and messy hair. My blood was film developer. But the pictures were yellowed now, like from an old album one shows to great-grandchildren at a golden wedding anniversary. I saw Viktor Vekk walking on board the King Olav with a green shoulder bag as his only luggage and a pair of huge sunglasses that almost hid his face. I looked through the chain link fence, and the sun warmed my back. He stopped and called with all his might:

"Now Viktor Vekk disappears!" He waved his arms. "Finally, Viktor Vekk disappears!"

He was going to where the rainbow begins to find a big treasure.

"You're dreaming!" said the Butcher, filling up my glass. "Tell me about Viktor Vekk."

I drank. My head was full of threads.

"I met him at the first free concert in Oslo. At St. Hanshaugen in 1971."

"Free concert?"

"Yeah. A warm Sunday in May. We'd both just finished with exams. Jesus, we were happy then! Above the stage was a huge banner that said: All power to imagination!"

"So it was after your family. . .disappeared?"

"Yeah. They didn't get to see me get into the University."

I tried to laugh, but my throat was tight. The Butcher looked troubled.

"Go on," he said.

"We started talking. We were on the same wavelength. He'd baked sweet rolls with hash in them. I ate four of them and cracked up in the diner afterwards."

The Butcher became impatient, and his hands fluttered up from the table like two dirty gulls.

"Don't bury yourself in details," he begged.

I tried to remember as best I could. I noticed that I was becoming melancholy. I felt shaggy inside, and my fingers were ten candles.

"It's not everyone who passes the entrance exam," said the Butcher, looking around the room but not finding a peg to hang his eyes on. I continued.

"We got ourselves rejected by the draft board that fall. He was a homo and I was a bed-wetter. So we hung around Palace Park and condemned buildings and V-dub microbuses. We kept it up for a year. We thought that everything was going to be one big journey upward. But it started going down. The whole scene became frayed. Harsher. Syringes took over. We lost contact for awhile. He wanted to do well at the University, art history. I went to some lectures myself. Then I was arrested for some little stuff. Got out late in the summer, in August. But you already know that. Then I saw him for the last time. He'd quit studying, wanted to get away from everything. He was going on a long journey, and he wanted me come along. But it didn't work out. I wanted to get back on my feet here again. I remember going with him down to the ship to Denmark. I didn't know if he'd get any farther than Copenhagen."

The Butcher was starting to get sleepy.

"What did you do after that?" he yawned.

I rested my head in my hands.

"I met Berit. Then I took off, too."

"Where to?"

"I got to India, at any rate," I smiled.

The Butcher fell back in the chair.

"India! Holy cow, what did you want there!"

I took a careful drink from the glass and lit a smoke.

"Don't really know. If I knew exactly what I wanted, it wouldn't have been necessary to travel. I think I was searching for something."

"Viktor Vekk?"

I looked at the Butcher. Now, I was searching for words.

"Yes," I said at last. "I looked for him. But I didn't find him."

"And then you came home, a skinny wreck in sandals, and stumbled into customs with your pockets full of hash!"

I didn't say anything. I just pictured all the people at St. Hanshaugen that Sunday in May, the bands that blasted from the stage, all the colors, the cop snooping around us suspiciously, the smell of incense and hash and homemade bread and rolls. It was a long time ago. And the future was very near.

"And why was there no more with this Berit?" the Butcher asked. He had leaned over the table to capture my attention.

"I wanted to be free," I sneered. "Didn't want to tie myself to anyone."

The Butcher stood up and proposed a toast.

"Congratulations," he said. "A toast for you and freedom. God damn, what an idiot you are. You know what? My two sweet kids were born in 1965. They're twins. I've said that before, right. So, in 1965 they were born and in 1980 they'll be confirmed. Until then, I'll watch out that nothing happens to you, but not one day longer. God damn. What an idiot I'm in the same room with!"

We finished our drinks. The Butcher always has been good at giving speeches at parties. But there are things that are not so easy to explain. I left Berit because I was forced to. She pulled us apart, just like pulling the wings off a fly. She didn't do it on purpose. She probably didn't even know she was doing it. But her whole manner, her down-to-earthness, punctured every damn dream I had. The visions burst like old condoms. It was 14 days with my finger in the soil, and I couldn't take it. I left her. I had to. If I was going to avoid changing myself. It would have taken too long to explain all this to the Butcher. He sat down and breathed heavily.

"But, anyway, Viktor Vekk disappeared?"

"It looked that way."

Suddenly I saw his face clearly in front of me again. I shivered. The background was a gray stone wall, and in his hand was a syringe. 1972. "Just this one time," he whispered.

He had tied a shoelace around his upper arm. The blood vessels were as big and clear as freeways along his wrist.

But it wasn't just this once.

And then came a new picture. It was the departure again. The green shoulder bag. Sunglasses. The sun behind me. We spoke through the chain link fence.

"You're a idiot!" he said. "Come along, damn it! Alone we're just one; together we're two!"

"No," I said. "I can't"

He laughed at me. His mouth almost covered his entire face.

"Maybe I'm going to the rainbow," he said. "Or hell. You'll regret it. This is our chance. *Ours!*"

I shook my head.

"The hell with you then!" he almost screamed, turning around and walking away to the gangplank. I heard him singing: "Break on Through to the Other Side."

The Butcher snapped his fingers right in front of me.

"Snap out of it!"

I came out of it, but had the same mood with me. We sat silently for a few minutes. We were trying to decipher what our hearts were saying. I thought about Viktor Vekk's face, which had been split down the middle. And now he was dust, fine, light gray, dust, like the cigarette ash I tapped into the empty bottle on the table.

The Butcher stood up and pointed at me with his whole hand.

"Coincidence," he said. "I don't like coincidences. There aren't any! And what doesn't exist, I don't like!"

He suddenly stopped and thought about it. He got a confused expression in his eyes that almost suited him. He began anew:

"Coincidences," he said. He counted on his fingers. "One, *Aftenposten* outside your door. Two, Malvin Paulsen's sudden death. Three, the book with the initials." The Butcher looked at me a long time. "And why on earth did he take your name!"

"No idea," I answered. "Maybe so that we could meet again?"

"Goodbye!" said the Butcher, packing himself into his huge fur. "Goodbye, Hugo Poser!"

He slammed the door shut and thundered like an avalanche down the stairs. Soon it was quiet around me. But not for long. It was never quiet very long. The gramophone upstairs let loose a new potpourri. I looked at the clock. It was almost twelve.

I went out and up the stairs. On the door it said Reidar Høybråten. I rang. It took some time. But I didn't give up. Finally, I heard slippers shuffling. There were four slippers, and they belonged to a couple in their late sixties. They stood close to each other and looked up at me frightened. And I'm not tall.

"Can I help you?" creaked the lady.

"Must you play that record so loud and so often," I said calmly.

The lady looked at her husband. He shook his little head uncomprehendingly.

"I live below you," I explained. "It bothers me."

The man cleared his throat and stretched his neck toward me.

"Well, you can't deny two old people the memories of their youth!"

"You can't do that!" asserted the lady.

"Wait till you're old yourself. Then you'll see how it is!"

"But isn't it possible to turn it down a little?"

"What did you say?"

"You play it too loud!" I shouted.

"Don't you like Jens Book-Jenssen!"

"No," I said.

"Ernst Rolf, then. Or Gerd and Otto?"

"And the Bjørklund Sisters!" the man added. "But Book is Book, you know."

"We were on 'Do You Remember,'" said the lady, coming almost all the way out into the hall. "Do you have a television set?"

"Yes," I said.

"Jens Book-Jenssen sang and Reidar got to sing along on a verse! He used to sing in the Business Union Choir."

She looked at her husband proudly. He smiled, embarrassed, looking down at his feet.

I gave up. I apologized for the interruption and went back home.

"Strange fellow," I heard behind me. "Does he really live here?"

I laid down, but never did fall asleep. I had too many thoughts in my head, and directly above my forehead shuffled four slippers in waltz tempo.

13

Saturday disappeared into Sunday. Time heals all wounds, and it was passing. On Monday, people began to stream back to the city. They filled up the empty places and occupied all the mirrors with sunburns and wind-blown faces that grinned broadly above white shirts and silk scarfs at us, the gray, city-bound with jaundice and stagefright.

Tuesday I woke up earlier than usual and was restless and impatient from the moment I stood on the cold floor. I made coffee, sliced some dried up pieces of bread, and sat down by the window. Everything was its old self again. The streetcars clattered up and down Thereses Street. Housewives dragged along shopping carts and screaming kids. Dogs whimpered and sniffed each other's sex organs, but never reached their goal. New bargains were pasted up in the windows. Delivery trucks backed into the loading dock. But winter still held an unfriendly hand around the capital city. Snow poured from a tuberculous sky, and the mercury sank like a syringe ampule.

I used the rest of the morning to wash and fix up the room. It's a dangerous pitfall that people who live alone can get into, letting everything fall to pieces around them, little by little, like dust and cancer. I had almost fallen into that trap. Now it smelled fresh and clean, no stinky socks under the bed, no hibernating dirty dishes. I was happy. I stood in the middle of the room and looked around. It was livable here again.

At one-thirty I went with a pounding heart over to Matkroken. I saw Berit immediately. I walked over to her. Her face was brown, and she had combed her hair behind her ears. I was overwhelmed.

"You look great!" I said, getting the urge to polish old parchment face in my pocket.

"It's good to be home with Mother and Father occasionally," she smiled.

A couple of customers came and interrupted us. Berit looked apologetically at me and began to ring up the groceries that were stacked in front of her. I took a cart and walked in between the shelves. I found beer, vitamin C, ice cream, baking chocolate, vegetables, candles, paper napkins and a toothbrush. I watched until Berit was free and pushed the cart up in front of her.

"Are you having a party today?" she asked.

"Yes," I said. "Me and one more. When do you get off work?"

Berit laughed. Berit almost always laughed.

"I'm off at five-thirty. What are you thinking of?"

"Everything will be ready by then. I live in number 26," I said, pointing out the window. "Second floor, to the right. There's no name on the door."

I paid and left. My heart was jumping. An idiot of a driver just about ran me down. But I survived that, too.

At five o'clock everything was set to go. The table was set, the T-bones the Butcher had given me were on the starting blocks, the beer was in the refrigerator, and the chocolate sauce for the ice cream was ready. I checked the calvados bottle and saw that there was enough. Now I just had to wait. I sat at the window, smoked a few cigarettes, and looked down at vanity's market.

At a quarter to six, Berit came out. She stopped on the sidewalk, thought it over, then set her course toward me. I reacted spontaneously, cranked up the record, took a last survey of the room and opened the door. Right away she came up the stairs and in to me.

If there's anything the Butcher knows, it's meat. The knives cut through it like butter and sun and flowery meadows. I pulled out a beer and lit the candles and was the consummate host, but, of course, there was something I'd forgotten.

"It doesn't matter," said Berit. "It's too much, just the meat."

"It's so seldom that I have dinner guests," I said apologetically. "I can slice some bread, if you'd like?"

Berit looked resigned.

"It really doesn't matter. *Forget* the potatoes."

We kept eating until the candles burned down. I was nervous and drank a little too much beer. I was afraid that she was going to be bored, not enjoy herself. I tried to come up with something amusing to talk about the entire time. But it wasn't necessary. Berit did the talking. She told me calmly about what she did during Easter, about when she won third prize in the jig fishing competition at Hurdal Lake, and about a moose that had gone through the ice by the mouth of the river. Exciting stories from real life. I listened to her, pictured her with the jig in her hand, up and down, up and down. All of a sudden I blushed due to the lewd association and attempted to picture the moose instead.

"What did you do during the holiday?" Berit asked.

"Not much. Stayed home, mostly."

But she didn't want to have calvados with coffee. She was feeling the beer already in her head and was afraid of getting drunk.

"There's nothing to be afraid of," I smiled slyly and poured one for myself.

"What did you do to your finger?" she suddenly asked.

"My finger?" I looked at her surprised.

"The nail on your index finger is completely blue."

I sat up straighter and swallowed several times.

"It's been that way a long time. Always," I said. "Haven't you noticed it before?"

She shook her head. Her hair fell forward into her face.

"I had a fight with a friend once," I explained. "He was leaving. I went with him to the dock, and then we started arguing about something or other. He wanted me to go with him, but I couldn't. He called me an idiot and said I was betraying him. Then we started pounding on each other. It wasn't so serious, almost more like playing. But in any case, I was lying on the ground, and he put the heel of his shoe on my finger and twisted. My index finger has been like this ever since. Strange you haven't noticed it before."

"Who was it?" Berit asked curiously.

I hesitated.

"His name was Viktor Vekk," I said eventually.

"Viktor Vekk. Strange name."

"Yeah."

"Where was he going?"

I lit a smoke and laughed.

"He said he was going to where the rainbow begins so he could find a huge treasure."

Berit was quiet awhile.

"I think that was well said," she said softly.

But I said nothing.

"Where is he now?" she continued. "Did he find the treasure?"

"Don't know. But in any case, he got to where the rainbow ends."

Berit looked at me intensely.

"He's dead."

I poured us some more coffee and treated myself to a shot of calvados. I deserved it. Berit didn't want any this time either. I locked the bottle in the cupboard so as not to make a bad impression.

"But you did some traveling too," she said.

I sat down heavily.

"I was trying to relive Dante's work," I said.

"Who's Dante?" Berit asked, both curious and irritated.

"He wandered through the realm of the dead to meet his beloved."

Berit looked skeptically at me. She must have thought I was drunk. But that didn't make the matter any better. I took out the book, the dog-eared paperback.

She flipped through it a little and looked at me.

"Beatrice. That's a pretty name."

I agreed.

The rest of the evening went more slowly. There was so much I wanted to do, but someone had glued me solidly to the chair and tied my arms and legs. At ten o'clock Berit stood up.

"I think I have to go now," she said. "I'm getting up early tomorrow."

I broke the chains, broke through the prison walls.

"You can sleep longer if you stay here," I said.

She looked at me a little surprised. Then she came over to me. I hugged her tightly.

"Yes," she said. "But then I'll sleep late."

I squeezed her even harder.

But she stayed.

Berit was right. We slept late. And the bed was narrow for two. But we twined into each other like two bunches of seaweed on the bottom of a soft and friendly sea. I watched her while she slept. It was a long time since I had seen her like this. Fireworks went through me. I touched her carefully with my fingertips, scared to death of frightening her, destroying her.

But it was Berit who woke up first. I was awakened by her laughter. It was like getting seltzer in the ear. I propped myself up, bewildered.

"You look like a blowfish when you sleep," Berit laughed and kissed me.

"A blowfish? How come?"

She laid down beside me.

"Your mouth gets little and round, and then your ears flap. And you have chubby round cheeks!"

She couldn't hold back the laughter.

"I've never seen a blowfish, so it's not intentional."

"They're so cute! They put you in a good mood just watching them."

She laughed even more.

I was a blowfish gliding along the aquarium glass.

I pushed my nose against her cheek.

"I want out, I want out!" I groaned in fish talk. "I want to get out of this aquarium and unite with my brothers and sisters in the oceans of the world!"

Berit pushed me away. I stuck my head under the comforter and swam over her stomach, between her breasts and up to her neck. She put her arms around my neck and held me tight.

"I'm a blowfish who's going to drive you crazy," I mumbled.

I closed my eyes and could feel her body become a wave, a breaker that came with messages from the coast on the other side. I drew myself tightly to her, glided into her, lost all reason and exploded right afterwards against a cliff and became spray and particles.

Berit was as pretty in the morning as the rest of the day. I wasn't. She was used to getting up early. She had a fixed rhythm, knew how to organize. She contemplated me, smiling, as I pulled the shirt over my head.

"You're a little overweight," she said.

I've said that before myself, too. I almost became sour.

"It's my body structure that's that way," I tried.

"You should start exercising," she continued unrelentingly. "I play handball once a week."

"I've thought about it," I said. "I really have thought about it."

We ate breakfast. I tried to suck in my gut. But it was useless in the long run. I couldn't sit like that all day. I let it out with a sigh and buttered another slice of bread.

"When did Viktor Vekk die?" Berit asked suddenly.

It startled me. When she said it, it was as if I were hearing it for the first time: Viktor Vekk is dead. Everything sank in me like an elevator. I had to hold on to the table.

"Why?" I said.

"I'm just curious. He sounds so unusual."

If I had gone along with him, everything would be different now. I put my elbows on the tablecloth and leaned on my hands.

"It was *his* funeral that day you came to the chapel," I said. Now I had said it.

"Was he the one who used your name!"

"Yes." My voice wasn't like before. I had a tape recorder rewinding in my throat.

"But, why did he do it? I don't understand."

I thought about the beautiful trees in Nordmarka, warm black currant toddies at Kobberhaug Lodge, a fresh orange at Bjørn Lake and waffles at Kikut. I ought to get the money box with the treasure in it, sneak off to Sweden over Svinesund, chase rainbows, return after a long time and say: "My passport has been stolen. My name is Viktor Vekk." I laughed inside. He would have liked that. He would have liked that.

Far away I discovered Berit. She came closer, riding a white horse. She was waiting for an answer. I looked at her through a thousand old curtains.

"Why did he take your name?" she repeated.

"Not everything he did was well thought out," I said. "Maybe he just wanted to play a joke on me. And then he died before the punch line."

"I think it's a rather crude joke," Berit said indignantly. "I don't believe it."

I had lost my appetite a long time ago. I lit a cigarette and drew the glow toward me. It was no joke. She had that right. In any case, I was the last one to laugh. But maybe I laughed best.

"Viktor Vekk was a follower of a distinctly vulgar brand of humor," I said, "who liked to use strong means."

"You really have to go to the police!" she said.

I said nothing.

At nine o'clock she left. I stood in the window and watched her. She waved up to me. I waved back. She was like wind and runes. Soon gone in a crowd of people, but still in my heart, like an awkward stone script hammered in by a poetic Viking.

The rats had come back to the sinking ship. I walked the same route: through Palace Park, down Karl Johan, and stopped at Eger Marketplace. The city was alive again, but breathless, feverish. Hemorrhages shook whole city blocks. Sirens went from ear to ear. Hair roots withered. Eyes popped out like from haddock pulled up on land. I stood at Eger Marketplace at the end of March, 1978, and watched the people: tourists in their berths for the night.

I caught the eyes of someone I knew. They were atop a pencil thin body leaning up against the handrail by the escalator. He stood with crossed arms, had on an old corduroy jacket, patched jeans with bells and fringe at the bottom, and leather boots. The right foot gaped like a battered jaw. He was my age. There was no generation gap here.

I walked over to him. He looked at me suspiciously, didn't recognize me, but I knew that deep inside the face that now stood in front of him he could make out another face. If he took his time, thought it over well enough, he would be able to draw the outline of another appearance in my round, butterball head.

We went up to the Promenade Cafe. He just wanted some coffee and smokes. I bought a Napoleon for myself.

"Hard times," he said. "Hard times. And it's gettin' worse. It's gonna be worse than ever, man."

His voice was completely without resonance. His eyes had seen too much to dream.

"You haven't become a social worker, have you?" he grinned.

"No," I said.

"It's a long time since you've been here. A year? Two years? Shit, I don't even remember your name. But I don't give a fuck, when I get coffee and smokes. Then, I'll talk to anybody at all. I'd gladly go to the john and beat off old men if there's something in it for me. I'll do anything. Smart, huh. Don'cha think it's smart."

He had conversation shock. I let him go on and ate the Napoleon in the meantime. It was terrible. It was a disgrace and an insult. When I pressed it together so the filling would ooze out at the sides, it just sprang back up as soon as I removed the fork from the top. It was foam rubber and steel springs. I drank the coffee and smoked instead.

"Best boots in the city," he said, pointing at his boots. "Been stomping since '69. Sold *Ph* and *Vibra* and knew all the vibrations from Tromsø to Copenhagen. Time, man! Look at those boots, man. Look at them!"

I looked at them. The tips made faces at me. I made use of the chance to get in a few words.

"Viktor Vekk," I said. "Do you know what's happened to him?"

"Viktor Vekk," he repeated. "Vekk. Viktoria. He did some traveling, didn't he? He took off. . .took off before the war began for serious. Then he came back. He traveled and came back. When was it, huh? Why are you asking?"

"I'm looking for him."

"Came back. In '75, I think. Or later. He was around, and then suddenly he was gone again. For awhile. Half a year, maybe. Yeah,

half a year, cause he popped up right after Christmas. Over a year
ago now. Almost a year and a half. 'Other things come and go,
but Oslo endures.' Then he went back and forth a little and then
was gone again. Haven't seen him since."

"Did you talk with him?"

"Rapped. We rapped. But not after he came back the second time.
After Christmas, that is. Last year. He locked himself up."

"How's that?"

"Kept quiet. Put it in low gear."

"Had something happened to him?"

"Changed. Empty. Empty headed."

The coffee cups were also empty. I shoved the pack of smokes
over to him. He saw the rolled up hundred sticking out between
the cigarettes.

"Do you have any idea what he did after he disappeared the last
time?" I asked.

He shook his head. His hair slapped across his face.

"Nope. Don't know. But. . ."

He stopped and looked at me and suddenly got in a big hurry.

"He often mentioned a lady. Took off with her, I think."

He had already stood up.

"What was her name?" I asked quickly.

"He didn't say. Had a nickname for her. She was a whore, I think.
Dromedary. Yeah, Dromedary, that was it."

He disappeared toward the exit. I remained sitting at the table
without turning after him. On the back of the check from the cash
register I wrote with the small block letters I learned in grade
school, once upon a time of innocence: Dromedary. I stuck the
note in my pocket and went my way.

The clock on the Freia Chocolates advertisement said two. It's
not true that Karl Johan Street is a hammock between the Royal
Palace and Eger Marketplace. Karl Johan is a bridge, a flimsy bridge
that goes from the upper class to the underworld. This thought
gave birth to an idea. I popped into a telephone booth down at
the corner of Lillegrensen and looked up the V's. I found Anton
Vekk. He lived on Holmenkoll Road. I had never met Viktor's par-
ent's before.

The taxi stopped outside a tall hedge, almost a wall. I was lucky today; there was a hole in it. I came in on a flagstone path that led up to a classic wooden villa with columns in front of the entrance. Around the house was a symmetrical garden, but there wasn't a single fruit tree there, not even a currant bush, just decorative trees and poplars. I walked up to the palace and rang the bell. It was forever before I finally heard steps. Do or die, I thought. Your name is Hugo Poser, and you are an art historian with the 1890s as your specialty.

The door was opened, and in front of me stood a middle aged woman. A mid-length black dress enveloped her thin body. Two necklaces hung a little crookedly around her neck, and her face showed clearly that it wasn't just joy and happiness here.

"Good morning," I said. "May I see Viktor Vekk?"

There was no reaction. I suddenly realized the grotesqueness in the situation but couldn't pull out now. Deep inside I consoled myself: I just want to help.

"My name is Hugo Poser. I'm an art historian, or professor of art, actually. I studied with Viktor a long time ago, and now I'd like to get in touch with him. It concerns some professional matters."

His mother's face lit up like a Christmas tree. She waved me in. I obeyed. The door banged shut, and I stood in an enormous hall on red wall-to-wall carpet.

"What did you say your name was?"

"Hugo Poser." I stuck out my hand. She fumbled with it.

"Else Vekk. I'm Viktor's mother."

She led me into another room. The room was over-furnished. There was barely floor space to stand on, and the walls were covered by paintings: portraits and landscapes, animals and buildings, sunsets and sunrises. A family of curators, I thought. Viktor had something to inherit.

We sat down at the same time, she on a fragile chair that shook beneath her, I in a deep, sea-blue sofa.

"So, you studied art history with my son?"

I nodded.

"He was a talented student," she said.

"Yes," I said. "He had an eye for it."

"Exactly. He could tell the beautiful from the ugly."

I became nauseous and had to look away. But nowhere was there a vacant surface where my eyes could rest in peace and gather strength.

"You wanted to ask him something?"

"Purely professional," I said. "He was working with Munch at that time. I myself also work with the 1890s. And I remember that he had some interesting viewpoints on 'The Scream,' Munch's 'Scream,' that is."

Else Vekk looked at me the entire time. Her mouth followed along and pulled all the words over to her on an invisible string.

"That was what I wanted to talk with him about. Isn't he here?"

A nervous twitch went through her, like a little earthquake.

"Tell me what his viewpoint was," she asked.

I thought it over and recharged my mouth.

"In a discussion at a seminar he stressed that 'The Scream' was the first audible painting in Norwegian art history. European, as far as that goes."

She looked at me, a little unconcentrated, and nodded gently several times.

"He was talented, wasn't he," she said with a sandblasted voice.

She had been drinking or taking drugs. I wagered on the latter. Her eyes were silk, and her nerves were like power cables on the outside of her skin. And they weren't grounded. There was a hold-up in the conversation. Viktor had never talked about his parents or his home. I looked around the room: copies of Roman busts, iron sculptures, wooden figures, vases, a life-size porcelain greyhound. I shivered. And Viktor Vekk had begun studying art history. A chip off the old block. But there's nothing to stop it from falling a long way off.

"Where is Viktor now?" I asked mercilessly.

She was startled again, the avalanche came. She stood up quickly and went over to an escritoire with many small drawers and panels and a big door at the bottom. She opened the biggest.

"Martini or Campari?" she said. "Or something else?"

I chose Campari. She had soda there, too. And ice cubes. The escritoire was a camouflaged refrigerator.

"We don't know where he is," she said abruptly and sat down heavily on the wobbling rococo chair.

"You don't?" I tried to appear surprised.

"Were you good friends?" she asked.

"We used to study together. For the time he was there."

She lit a More and did a toss of her head as she drew the first puff down into her lungs. I burned a Hobby.

"I haven't seen him in a long time. Since summer."

"Has something happened?" I tried carefully and sipped from the bitter, bubbling glass.

She sat mutely a few seconds, just as if she were frozen solid in that position, become a sculpture in her own living room: the cigarette teetering between two fingers, her head a little forward, her left hand clenched. Then she melted.

"You haven't seen him since '73?"

"No."

"Well. He went on a long trip. A study trip. . .late in the summer that year. He was gone for. . ."

She got up and took something from a bookshelf behind her.

"He sent this home," she said.

She laid a photograph on the table in front of me. My entire body became tender. Tender and loose and full of water. Viktor Vekk at a marketplace, Morocco, I bet, next to a donkey, with wide, white pants, sandals, t-shirt, huge sunglasses and shoulder bag.

"He was gone for three years," his mother continued. "He came home summer of '76." She stopped, searching for the correct expression. "He had gotten sick."

"Sick?"

"Yes. He got worse that fall. He was admitted at New Years. At a clinic."

"Did he get well?" I asked maliciously. I tried to ignore my own voice.

Else Vekk was distant and faint. There were short circuits all over her body.

"Viktor got out in March, last year. He lived here at home, but we didn't see so much of him. He lived his own life."

It wasn't easy for her to talk like this. She fought and battled. Her glass was empty; she filled it, spilling on the table.

"And since February we haven't seen him at all."

She sighed and drank. I thought about that point in time: *Febru-*

ary. But now it was my turn to say something. Never had I been so far from my voice.

"Maybe he's out traveling again?" I said, and it began to itch inside my head, in the middle of my brain. There was a fly in there.

She was up instantly and pulled out one of the small drawers in the escritoire. When she turned toward me, she was holding something in her hand. It was a little red book with a lion on it. A Norwegian passport.

"He can't be," she said fervently. "In any case, not far. All his papers are here."

I wondered why that was, and she answered without my needing to ask.

"He left them here when he was admitted. We took care of all his things then, his personal possessions."

She put the passport back in the drawer again. I followed her with my eyes, noting the place. There was no more to get from her for the time being. I stood up from the oceanic sofa and gave her my hand.

"Ask him to come home if you see him," she said sincerely. She hid my hand between both of hers.

"Yes," I said, knowing it was the most evil thing I had ever done.

She showed me out. To the right of the door to the entry hung a portrait of a man standing with his hands on his back, wide-legged, staring down with an expression that should force you on your knees instantly. The face was narrow. I didn't like his appearance. His skull thrust out under his hair like a toadstool.

"That's my husband," she said. "Viktor's father."

She let me out into the sour afternoon. I felt her eyes in my back the entire way down to the hedge, those upper class eyes that have suddenly become so vulnerable, frightened, flickering, they just barely, and almost not even that, manage to hold onto the pictures from the time when the aristocracy had soul and business was good.

I wanted to cry. I thought about Viktor's face in the coffin, so split and mutilated that no one would recognize him. But I knew that the day has many hours and the year has many days. And no one can stand next to a grave and lament for the rest of his life.

14

But I got a reason to study the West Crematorium and Alf Rolfsen's beautiful fresco paintings once again. Malvin Paulsen was interred Saturday, April first. I'm sure his brother must have chosen the date with great care.

There were quite a few of people in the chapel. In the first pew sat Gordon Paulsen and the rest of the family. Otherwise it was probably co-workers and neighbors for the most part. I spotted Kork and Espen Askeladd and sat down with them. They had dressed up nicely and were bright-eyed.

Kork leaned over toward my ear.

"Dug out my confirmation suit," he said, pointing at his chest, which was bulging out. "It's like tailor-made around the flask!"

He bent over, took a gulp and sent the bottle on to Espen.

"Malvin wouldn'ta had anything against it, I'm sure. Want some?"

I declined.

"Here's the program," Kork continued, laying it in his lap. "First there's music. Then some preacher or other talks. Then there's playing and whining again. And at last we carry out the casket with straps. He'da liked that!"

A little later Arne Garve came too. He sat down right behind us and stuck his head forward between Espen and Kork.

"Too bad about Malvin," he said. "He was one of the good guys."

Everyone could ratify that. Malvin had been good to have along on the heavy lifts. And he never cheated on the straps. Kork drank to that and said:

"I'll bet my dick he blows right into Heaven. Just grease up the elevator and push 'im in."

The organ started pumping, and we sang all four verses of an incomprehensible hymn. When the minister came out, I thought there was something familiar about him, but it wasn't the same one as last time. And I haven't met many ministers. Kork was about to blow up.

"God almighty! It's that bishop from Bergen, boys! The one with the coffee!"

Arne stuck his head forward again.

"Duck, guys, or he'll take you along at the same time."

The minister greeted Gordon Paulsen and a couple others and gave a relaxed talk. Espen fell asleep and Kork drank himself tight. There was more singing, and after twenty minutes the coffin with Malvin sank down in the floor. Kork clenched his fists and pounded them against his thighs.

"It sucks," he mumbled. "It's damn awful that Malvin's gone!"

Afterward, a wake was suggested. I would rather have gone right home. But Arne, Espen and Kork wouldn't let me.

We started at Valka with a few pints. Kork went on a side trip to the liquor store to fill up his inner pocket. He came back happy and shiny and sat down next to Espen Askeladd. Arne Garve said he wanted to take it kind of easy since he'd been working hard lately with a lot of night driving. Kork squeezed his eyes together.

"Driving at night! Who hasn't driven at night! When we're out on a send-off for old Malvin, we don't need any sissies!"

Arne laughed loudly. He was twice as big as Kork. He grabbed him with a huge fist and shook him up and down a little.

"No, we don't need sissies with us," he grinned.

Kork went to the john and was gone a long time. Espen ordered four new beers. He was thin and gaunt as a long-distance runner.

"You can't drink Kork under the table," he said to Arne.

"Probably not," he answered diplomatically. "I don't plan on trying either."

Kork came out ofthe john and sat down next to me. He wiped his mouth with a blue hand.

"Malvin couldn't stand not working," he said suddenly. "His job was his life. Lately he hadn't been alive."

"That's right," said Arne. "It was sorta just memories and old stories in the end. He was trying to live everything over again. And he started drinking more and more as he used up all the memories and stories."

It was quiet awhile. I looked at the three people sitting around the table. Arne was the oldest of us, thirty-something. He was born during the war, surely conceived behind a blackout curtain, or in a truck at full speed toward Sweden. While the rest of us were struggling at grade school back in the end of the golden '50s, he was rocking at Jordal Amphitheater, fighting the pigs, overturning cars and screaming, buying Sun records by Elvis and Johnny Cash, and making his parents desperate. But by the time we cast off the tweed jackets, gray pants and narrow ties, he was already old, didn't like the new music, thought long hair looked stupid, and had the urge to beat up people in Palace Park. Now we had all gotten old, the whole gang. The seventies would be over soon. The seventies, which were a winter coat, heavy and shaggy; we put on our coats and stumbled out into a cold and dead landscape.

Espen Askeladd hiccoughed.

"Malvin talked a lot of politics," he said "But, anyway, it was just talk."

"He was more into it earlier," said Arne. "No one could trip him up in a debate. But he never got it right," he added laughing.

"What do you mean?" I asked.

"No matter what we talked about, he always ended by saying that everyone had to become a communist before things could get worked out."

Kork raised his glass.

"Malvin had that right! Everybody must get stoned! Cheers!"

"You misunderstood," said Arne calmly.

Kork looked at him slyly.

"I understood *everything*," he said.

Espen broke in.

"Once he said that decent folks are communists, but that it's no use to live decently under this system."

Arne Garve nodded.

"He said that often. I'll drink to that. But I think he stopped counting sometime in the thirties."

"Let's be indecent, damn it!" shouted Kork, swinging his glass through the air.

I began to feel numb in the brain bark. The zipper in the back of my head was pulled down, and I took a walk to the john to freshen my face. When I came out, the others were on the way out. Kork put his arm around me.

"Now we hop on our horses and ride to the next bar," he said, jumping up on Espen Askeladd's back, and they took off in a wild trot down toward the taxi stop.

We went to Stortorget Inn and drank more beer. Kork went to the john more and more often. Arne Garve hung his head a little.

"Get it together," said Kork, punching at him. "Don't sit here and disgrace us!"

Espen laughed.

"He's still sore because his wife kicked him out."

He shouldn't have said that. Arne sent a lightning-fast fist across the table and hit Espen right between the eyes. He fell backward. The chair tipped over, and he went straight to the floor.

"Say it again!" screamed Arne, jumping up.

But Espen didn't get time to say anything before the bouncer and a few others were standing around our table. Kork helped the injured to his feet. Blood was running from his nose.

"We've had trouble with that one before," said the bouncer, pointing at me.

That was the sign. Two others grabbed me by the arms, snapped them up behind my back and threw me out. I didn't bother resisting. I was sick of getting beat up. I landed badly on all fours. The bouncer gave me a departing kick in the back that sent me in the direction of Cathedral Church. Right behind me came the others. Espen had packed his nose in a handkerchief. Kork ran back and forth between him and Arne and mediated.

"This is Malvin's day. Don't wreck Malvin's day! Shake hands and make up. Be comrades, damn it!"

Arne Garve thought it over and asked to be forgiven. Espen hesitated a little before taking his hand. Kork cheered, and soon that matter was resolved. When they caught sight of me standing outside Glasmagasinet department store with holes in the knees of my pants and injured hands, the atmosphere picked up immediately.

"There's the scoundrel," shouted Kork. "There 'e is!"

We decided to eat dinner at Kalles. It had sort of been Malvin's place. We ordered the most expensive thing they had, oriental kettle, and four pints. I was rather heavy-headed, but when the food got to the table, I shook off all the misery. Oriental or not, this was good home cooking! Arne fetched more beer at the counter, and while he was away, Kork suddenly became completely objective and bent over to Espen.

"Don't kid him about his old lady," he said. "Sore point, understand."

Espen felt his tender nose.

"I said I'm sorry, and it's all squared up now."

He was calm. Even though Arne Garve was bigger and heavier, he still would have had problems getting Espen to the ground, Espen with his long, thin arms with huge fists at the ends that could fly out in the air like ping-pong balls. But they didn't waste their energy, Arne and Espen. They didn't use it against each other.

Arne came back and sat four dewy beers on the table.

"My round," he said.

Kork cheered.

"So it is! So it is, boys! Malvin would've liked this. He's listening! He's watching!"

We finished eating in an uproar. Afterward we wanted coffee. Kork managed to sneak a little opaque liquid into all the cups.

"We have to have dessert," he said. "I want to have dessert!"

He set a course toward the counter. He walked in a strange manner, the way a person in his sixties ought to walk, with his feet way out in front of his head so that his body was like a slanted line up from the floor the whole time. The confirmation suit hung a little crooked now, and his face was a vague oval. Espen went to the restroom, and I sat there alone with Arne.

"I got a little mad awhile ago," he said and drank.

I had nothing to say to that and hoped the others would come back soon.

"How's it going with your girlfriend?" he continued.

I got nervous. I felt about like I did when I talked with Viktor's mother.

"Great."

He stroked the hair away from his forehead, but it fell right down again. Espen came out of the restroom door, and right after that Kork came back too. He set a dish of sweet rolls in the middle of the table.

"Sweet rolls with cream filling!" he sang and slung himself down on the chair.

But none of us were especially hungry for sweet rolls right then. He was disappointed and offended and began to eat up the pile himself.

"They gotta be homemade!" he tried. "Rolled in the back room between the old lady's tits!"

He took another one. Suddenly he became very enthusiastic and leaned over the table.

"I was at St. Hanshaugen once," he began.

Arne looked at him in amazement.

"Have you been that far?"

Espen laughed.

"He'll never make it up to the top till there's a chair lift."

Kork stuck a roll in his mouth and fell backwards.

"Real funny, boys," he mumbled. "Real funny, boys."

"What was that about St. Hanshaugen?" I asked.

He leaned forward again and tried anew.

"So, I was at St. Hanshaugen once. It's hundreds of years ago, in '71. I was just a baby butt with powder between the cheeks and vaseline on the hole. So, there was one of those free concerts there at St. Hanshaugen."

"I was there too!" I shot in.

"There, you see! He was there too," said Kork triumphantly, pointing at me. "It's not just somethin' I made up."

Espen patted him on the shoulder and asked him to continue.

"So, St. Hanshaugen. There was a free concert there in 1971. The first free concert. And there was this guy there. Ya know what he'd done?"

Kork grabbed a roll and showed it to us.

"He'd baked rolls with dope in them! Can you top that! He should'a won the Peace Prize. Melted the stuff in butter and presto! Divine rolls! It was the first and only time I've gotten high on rolls, boys. Remember that, Poser!"

"Yeah," I said.

Kork was happy.

"Just like I was sayin'. True story. I didn't dream it. I ate roll after roll and didn't understand a thing. Nothing. Farther and farther, up and out. And then I became a roll. I *became* a roll, boys!"

He sank back in the chair and chewed and chewed.

"So you were there too, Poser. Do you remember it! Damn, we didn't know each other then. Do you remember the dream, Poser." He leaned forward, hanging like an old banner over the table. "That dream. The rising dream. That you just got higher and higher. Never down. Straight to the heavens. That was dreaming. Damn!"

Arne Garve wanted to play pinball. Espen went with him. I tried to get contact with Kork again.

"Did you know that guy with the rolls?" I asked.

"He was one of the big ones. Earlier. I don't know anything else. Think he took off. Beyond the horizon."

"Did he come back?" I tried.

Kork looked at me bluntly.

"Everyone who travels comes back one way or another, I suppose," he said gently.

At eight o'clock Kalles was closing, and we had to find a new place. It wasn't so hard. We chose the shortest route and slid across the market to Olympus. The mood was reaching rooftop height. I wasn't sure whether I could drink any more, but I went along anyway. Kork rambled a ways in front of us. Suddenly he stood absolutely still, stared savagely at us and let out a huge fart.

"That'll shake 'em up in the Kremlin," he groaned.

Arne filled his lungs with air and sent a colossal belch out over the city.

"There. I broke the silence at the place of heavenly peace."

And the celebrating would not end. Kork scurried around us like a sheepdog. We sang and shouted and threw ourselves in amongst the gods at Olympus.

And there was more beer and wine there. The zipper in the back of my head went up and down. I had to take a trip to the john to do some breathing exercises. The urinals were full, so I closed myself in a stall and pulled down my pants. When I had been sitting there awhile, someone shook the door.

"Occupied," I sniveled.

The intruder gave up, but I could still see a pair of brown suede shoes in the opening at the floor.

A voice, distorted, as if it was being filtered through a handkerchief, said:

"Windelband. Mind your own business. Then everything will be alright for you. Don't get involved. And you will have a long life."

I pulled up my pants quickly, forgetting the most important thing, but I couldn't take such considerations now. I tore open the door, but there were no sinister characters there, just an old goober who was so startled when he saw me that he lost all pressure in his plumbing.

I stared frantically at his feet.

"You don't have suede shoes," I declared.

"No," he said, resigned, packing in his pilgrim's staff.

"Was there someone here a second ago?"

"Not that I saw. But I was standing with my back in that direction."

"You didn't hear any voices?"

"I mind my own business, damn it!"

He left. I followed. I staggered from table to table searching for a pair of suede shoes but didn't find them. There were just rubber boots and women's legs. The inside of my head was rolling like a lottery tumbler, but I never got the right number. The restaurant looked like a hangar or a barn. In any case, it resembled something other than a restaurant. I was drunk.

A few hours passed where the details are wiped out. I felt ill and heavy as lead. I drank a little once in awhile, but there wasn't much room for it. At regular intervals I got an encouraging slap on the back. A helicopter came into the hangar, or maybe it was cows. For a bright instant I got in contact with the gods and ordered a herring sandwich and two seltzers. It saved me. I got some elbow room and new spirit. I went in on a new round.

Some lights flashed, and the planes were ready to take off. The others pulled me up from the chair, and together we squeezed out the narrow door, out to Oslo, this city that no one leaves before it has left its mark.

But the air helped. It cleared my head. The wind blew through my brain and liberated my memory. I looked at the rest of the entourage. They were drunk. Drunk and crazy. We were the rear guard in the big atomic march. Kork had absolutely no desire to stop. His hip flask was empty, and he was not quite sure whether he would get to sleep now.

"Nightclub," he called. "Let's go to a nightclub!"

No one could find any serious arguments against the suggestion. And again we chose the shortest route. Right behind us flashed a red light, and a crowd of short-winded people was standing there. Pigalle. A breath of the big world, a fragrance of debauchery and gonorrhea.

The flock was let in just as we got there. Two big watchdogs placed themselves in the door opening, and it appeared as if we were not welcome. They growled. Maybe it was my pants they didn't like. Must be something.

Kork went all the way up to them and wanted in. He unfolded some money, but it didn't help. They pushed him backward, and they didn't need to push hard. Espen tried, too. The dogs snapped. And they wouldn't listen to Arne either, even though he petted them carefully.

Kork got pissed.

"Goddamnit! Let us in!" he screamed.

The watchdogs stuck their tails between their legs.

"I want to see some striptease!"

This time he landed in the gutter.

Arne and Espen tried too, but it was useless. We were fighting against a superior force.

Suddenly Kork pulled down his pants and started pissing on the sidewalk.

"Prettiest striper south of Folgefonna!" he shouted.

The guards leaped forward at him, but Arne and Espen stood

in their way. I pulled away a little, heard sirens from a police car, and said bye-bye.

It was two o'clock by the time I was throwing up behind the urinals at Fagerborg Church. Everything I had eaten and drunk showered out. I was a beautiful fountain. Each convulsion was like getting a saber in the back. Tears cascaded down my face, and below me the snow turned red and yellow and brown. But it helped. I straightened myself up and inhaled deeply. A little stomach acid burned in my mouth, but I felt better. I walked further on two feet. There was no one to be seen. Windows glowed in a few places, red and yellow and brown squares in the night. Then shadows glided behind the curtains, and the lights disappeared. Now the last people in Oslo were going to bed. Are their dreams safe and sound? I was thinking. Are they as happy as I am?

There was light in the window of my room too, yet I was sure I had turned it off when I went out. But nothing surprised me anymore. I slouched up the stairs and walked right in. I always remember to lock the door when I leave, but now it was open. That was logical. Someone had turned on the light.

The Butcher was standing at the sink, busy with something or other. He had on a white coat that was splattered with blood. I went over to him. In the sink was a pig's head.

"What the hell are you doing!" I burst out.

The Butcher looked at me sadly.

"You look terrible," he said.

"What the hell are you doing!" I repeated. "A pig's head!"

I was about to throw up again and had to turn away.

"I'm pickling pork," mumbled the Butcher. "You shouldn't drink so much. You can't handle it."

I sat down on the bed in resignation and took out my pack of cigarettes.

"Pickling pork! You're doing it now. Here!"

I started laughing. My stomach was in great pain. But I couldn't stop. I snapped forward and bellowed. Suddenly the Butcher got furious. He ripped the pig's head out of the sink and planted it in front of me on the table.

"I'll pickle pork when and where I want, and if you don't like it, I can pickle that hysterical head of yours instead!" he shouted. I fell back on the bed. The pig's head looked horrible. It stared at me with two stupid, horrid eyes, and blood and muck ran out all over the table. The Butcher puffed himself up like a balloon and looked like he was out of his mind. Then he slowly collapsed. The air went out of him. He was thinking better of it and poked around in the room with his hands.

"I'm sorry," he said. "Don't know what got into me."

He took the pig's head and put it back in the sink. He remained standing awhile with his back to me.

"Excuse me," he repeated. "It wasn't on purpose."

"It's alright," I said and got a washcloth.

The Butcher twisted off the white coat and sat down in the chair. I brewed myself a glass of cold water and laid down on the bed.

"I just wanted to make you some pickled pork," he said sadly. "Don't you like pickled pork?"

"Sure. It's delicious."

He hung his head a little. His few hairs stood in every direction, and thick blood vessels sprung out in his skull. I asked him to take out the calvados bottle, but he didn't want to. He got me another glass of water instead and squeezed a slice of lemon in it.

"Wakes are an old custom," he said, lighting a cigar.

Then some time passed before either of us opened our mouths to talk. I wondered how he was feeling. It was impossible to tell. I was glad I got away before the cops showed up. But I had a bad conscience. I had deserted.

The Butcher coughed and pushed the cigar butt in the ashtray. He seemed nervous.

"His parents," he said. "The family of Viktor Vekk. Do you know them?"

"I had a chat with his mother for the first time yesterday, or the day before, now. A wreck. Alcohol and pills. At least."

The Butcher got up the way he was in a habit of doing. He circled two times around his own ashes and looked down at me.

"Do *they* know about *you?*" he asked.

"Viktor must have mentioned my name to them. I'm sure of that. But they've never seen me before. So they don't know who I am."

This was getting complicated. I leaned wearily against the wall.

The Butcher sat down again.

"Tell me about the bank robbery?" he said. He wasn't looking at me.

"What is there to tell? I carried out the clumsiest bank robbery ever committed. That's why I wasn't caught."

"Were you armed?"

"Yeah. I had a grenade."

"A grenade! Good god! Where did you get it from?"

"Stole it from a Home Guard armory in Majorstua."

The Butcher looked out the window. It was night and dark and there wasn't a sound.

"Did you hurt anyone?"

"I hit one of the tellers in the head with a stick. He tried to stop me."

"And the grenade?"

"I chucked it."

The Butcher jumped.

"You *threw* it!"

"I got rid of it," I corrected. "In a lake. Bjørn Lake. Good trout there, by the way."

"How did you get away?"

"Bicycle. I ripped off a woman's bike with a basket on the handlebars from the student housing at Sogn. Cycled all through Oslo with a stocking over my head."

The Butcher steadied himself on the chair. He was looking right at me. His eyes burned like a mid-summer eve bonfire.

"How much did you get?"

I didn't hesitate before answering.

"A little over thirty thousand."

But that wasn't the truth. I was smarter than that.

"And you loaned me twenty thousand?"

He held it inside awhile. Then he asked.

"So, who else knows it was you?"

I didn't know. I started getting a headache. As usual. My head causes trouble. Anyway, something occurred to me that I had forgotten. Or I had put it out of my mind because the thought plagued me and I couldn't do a thing about it.

"Back then," I began slowly. "The time right before the bank rob-

bery, that is, I had a feeling that someone was following me. Just
a feeling. And when I was cycling breakneck across Dam Square,
there was someone standing behind a house corner staring at me."
"Who was it?"
"No idea. I just got a glimpse of him. Maybe it's just something
I imagined. That's it, probably. I was pretty sensitive around then."
It looked like the Butcher was thinking hard. The mountain
cracked.
"I assume," he said, "that you increased... that you increased
your consumption afterward."
"Can't deny it."
He sank down in the chair like a torpedoed tanker. He looked
at me. A long time. My face caught fire. Then he said:
"Oslo's a small city. Someone commits a bank robbery. Some-
one suddenly has a lot of money. Who's who? Who's done what?"
The Butcher was speaking in tongues. But the thought had hit
me too.
"Certain people must have gotten a suspicion," he ascertained.
And he added with an admonitory voice: "Hugo Poser, you ought
to get away. Go underground! Think of yourself!"
His head fell backwards. It creaked at the neck, an unpleasant
sound. The pig face stuck up just barely from the sink and was
staring eerily at me. I looked away.
"Olav and Kari have decided not to get confirmed," the Butcher
said suddenly.
"Well, it's up to them," I answered factually.
He looked at me, irritated.
"They've got a new teacher in life philosophy at school. Life phi-
losophy! Have you ever heard anything like it! No bourgeois con-
firmation for them, no. Do you know what they call me now? They
call me antichrist. And reactionary monk."
"Antichrist you ought to me pleased with," I said. "It's a compli-
ment. But the monk..."
"Shut up! And Marta! Do you know what she says? Marta, who
hasn't said anything funny since she said yes in the church! 'Judas,'
she says. 'Betrayer'. To me!"
He hauled up that big body of his and stood like a monolith on
the floor. He shook his head several times in resignation and be-

gan to pack up all his things, the coat, the knives, the pig head. He put everything in a plastic bag and went to the door.

"I'll bring the pickled pork when it's done," he said.

He was standing on the threshold when he suddenly turned around and looked at me with sad eyes. I had never seen him that way before. I wanted to say something encouraging.

"You know, it's not certain that he *took* the name," I said. "Viktor Vekk, that is. It could be that he was *given* it."

The Butcher didn't move. His round, shiny face was a stiff mask. He looked out through two holes. I let my eyes fall down his body. He was made of wet clay. I stopped abruptly when my journey came to his feet. I looked him in the eyes again. He was wearing brown suede shoes.

He disappeared. I went out to the stairs and watched him. Two pig ears stuck up from the plastic bag, and dark blood dripped on the steps. I heard the Butcher humming "Strangers in the Night."

15

I woke up right before Matkroken closed, threw on some clothes and walked over to talk to Berit. It was Saturday, and it was Roman chaos there. People were recklessly pushing shopping carts, elbowing each other, writing out checks, piling things into bags and boxes, and carrying themselves at a tilt. And in the background floated sweet muzak, like whipped cream foaming in the ears. I was miserable and got worse. I found Berit in the process of ringing up a load of diapers and a case of beer. She didn't see me until I poked her on the shoulder.

"I'm coming over this evening," I said, clearing my throat.

She looked me over.

"You look terrible," she said.

I was in complete agreement with that.

On the way downtown, I popped into Peer Gynt Cafe and forced down a little food and a bottle of beer. It was more comfortable there before, back when I was on speaking terms with the staff. Now, just a gang of bubble-clad girls sat there competing for who could pull the gum the farthest out of their mouths. And the waitress didn't want to hear me confess. I ordered another beer from her so I could wash down the lettuce. At the same time that my

shaking hand grabbed the cold, damp bottle, a strange man came
and sat at my table. He was old and looked sick and pallid. His
eyes were green squares, and his face was narrow and white, with
a much too big mouth full of black tooth stumps. He put his hands
on the tablecloth.

"Good afternoon," he said.

I was irritated. I didn't want to talk to him. Besides, other were
other tables vacant.

"Who are you?" I asked curtly.

"I'm just a guest here, like you. But you shouldn't drink beer
so early in the day."

His fragile body shook. Gray hair fell down in front of him.

"It's no concern of yours! Besides, you don't look so good
yourself."

I poured the rest of the beer into the glass and drank.

"Am I bothering you?" the man asked calmly.

"Yes," I said. "I'd rather see you move to another table."

"Oh, well. As you wish. But let me just sit a little. I have such
a bad foot. By the way, have you thought about selling your body
to science when you die?"

I didn't believe my own ears.

"Sell *what!*"

"Will," he corrected. "Your body. After all, you'll have no use for
it, strictly speaking. . ."

"You're crazy! Go away!"

The stranger continued looking at me just as calmly.

"It would be a service to society. Just a little gift, a cadaver!"

I got up. I had the urge to pound my fists into his ugly face. Those
green eyes stared up at me, two green blobs!

"You have many years left to live. But think about it. Think about
it."

I ran out. My entire body was wet, and there was hammering
behind my forehead. At the Forbunds Hotel I found an empty taxi.
I asked the driver to take me to Øvre Voll Street. He understood
the instructions and said nothing.

It was still early in the day, but the traffic was already heavy.
Cars with solitary, observant men drove slowly around and around
the magic square, a city block of love. Now and then one stopped,

opened the door and let in his beloved.

I stood on the corner of Øvre Voll Street and Tollbu Street. Some girls were standing alone, leaning up against parking meters or the wall of the building. Others stood in groups. It almost looked like a schoolyard. They displayed themselves when cars drove by, making faces and laughing when the same car passed for the third time.

I walked over to the nearest one. She couldn't have been more than seventeen. But she already had the characteristic lined face of a junkie. Her eyes were nowhere. They weren't even sad. She had flung some clumps of rouge on her herbarium dry skin, and between two tense, narrow lips dangled a long filter cigarette that almost made her fall forward. She inspected me without interest.

"Do you know Dromedary?" I asked.

"Who's askin'" came curtly.

"Just me."

"Don't know. Ask them."

She pointed at some veterans standing in a group farther away.

"Are you a cop?" she asked as I was leaving.

I turned and showed her my arm. She smiled.

The other whores' eyes followed me as I came toward them. A couple of cars slowly glided by, polished and shined for the big party. But it was difficult to decide. Round and round they drove, with scouting eyes and pounding hearts and lewd feelings.

I stopped a few steps away from the group and lit a smoke.

"Do any of you know Dromedary?" I asked.

Loud, sheer laughter from one of the ladies.

"If you're hot for a dromedary, you'll have to sneak in the zoo!"

Everyone thought that was amusing. The bursts of laughter boomed against the brick walls.

"Funny," I said. "You ought to contact the entertainment division at National Broadcasting."

The one who spoke came closer.

"What the hell do you want!" she snarled.

"Do you know who Dromedary is?" I repeated calmly.

"What do you want with her?"

I was getting tired.

"I have a message from her mommy and daddy that everything

is forgiven and that she can come back any day at all and her little girl's room is just as she left it."

It struck a note.

"You're not so bad yourself," said the lady. "Maybe we could get it on."

I flipped the smoke out in the gutter. A car stopped, and the driver's eyes sucked on one of the girls in the flock. It reeked of rut all the way to where I was standing.

"Dromedary?" I said patiently.

The nearest one looked wearily at me.

"Sporveis Street," she said. "The hotel there. Room 13."

Another taxi took me further on my adventurous expedition. I felt blown out. Everything was just meaningless chatter. The Fredheim Hotel again. I had the distinct impression that they didn't like me there. And Dromedary. I could imagine who that was.

I got out at the Rosenborg Theater and stood awhile looking at the pictures from Bertolucci's *1900*. Our century, I thought. Soon it will fade away. I felt heavy and hopeless. In one of the pictures a bunch of farm women were impaling a fascist with pitchforks. Another showed the farmers butchering a pig. It was hanging by the legs, and the entrails were oozing out of its belly.

I waited until a taxi stopped in front of the hotel and a couple came out of it onto the sidewalk. Then I took the chance. I ran across the street and went in with them. The gentleman looked at me a little nervously, straightened his coat and pulled his hat way down on his forehead. I winked encouragingly at him.

Then I got an opportunity to study that desperate wallpaper one more time. Nothing had changed. Nothing changes at such places. The plastic flowers were standing cheerfully in their silver loving cup, and behind the reception desk stood the Line, smiling punctiliously at us. When he saw me, he was suddenly out in the middle of the floor.

"What do you want here?" he growled.

"Dromedary," I just said. "Is she free?"

"What do you want with her?"

I brushed a speck of dust off his imitation shoulder.

"I came to tell her that she's won two hundred and fifty thousand in the lottery."

I sprang up the stairs to the second floor.

Room 13 was all the way down the corridor. I waited outside awhile to see whether anyone was coming after me. There was. But it was just the couple I came in with. The man still looked at me anxiously. I smiled at him, but he certainly didn't want to be friends with me. The lady pulled him into a room and shut the door.

I lit a smoke and knocked. It took a little time for something that resembled a human voice to say come in. I opened the door and confirmed the suspicion that Dromedary and I were old acquaintances. She was sitting on the bed in just a bra and skirt and didn't look the least surprised. I closed the door behind me and looked for a chair. But there were no chairs in the room. I sat down on the farthest end of the bed.

"What the fuck did you come here for?" she asked, friendly, pouring a milk glass full of whiskey.

I crushed out my smoke and looked around. I'd never been in a worse room. There were dirty clothes over everything. Bottles and flasks stood along the windowsill. The entire contents of a purse were dumped out on a table. In an open nightstand drawer were two syringes and a wad of cotton. And the stink was unbearable. It was like sitting in a mouth that's been on a drinking binge for a month. At the roof of the mouth shined a stark, naked light bulb. That was all. That was enough.

"Do you live here?" I asked.

"Did you come here to ask me that? Yeah. I live here. Isn't it nice?"

"If you hung up some pictures on the walls, it would be real cozy."

It occurred to me that not everyone in that building loved me.

"Viktor Vekk," I said quickly. "Where do you know him from?"

She looked at me with eyes that resembled two empty bottles. She emptied the milk glass. I turned away. Against all expectation she began speaking.

"From the clinic," she said. Her voice was amazingly clear. "Why are you asking?"

"I'm looking for him. It's pretty important. It was early in '77, wasn't it?"

"Yeah. We used to sit together sometimes. When we got permission. In the garden."

"Which clinic was it?" I asked carefully, as if she were made of glass.

She squirmed.

"Don't know."

"You don't know? How did you get there?"

"From the emergency room."

It started to dawn on me. I didn't know what, but something was dawning. The emergency room. Dromedary continued:

"Got pumped one night. A guy said he was gonna help me. He took me to this clinic. A private clinic, I think. No idea where it was. I was unconscious."

"What did it look like there?"

"A garden. With a high wall around it. He was going to help me."

"*Who* was going to help you?"

"Don't know his name. Never told me."

She talked softly and filled her glass again. She was a dry sponge that wanted to wipe off a chalkboard.

"What was wrong with Viktor?" I asked stupidly.

She laughed. She had a right to.

"I think we had the same problem, boy scout."

She threw out her arms. A wave of whiskey splashed the floor.

"And so it goes for me!"

"And for Viktor?"

She hesitated, collapsed a little, didn't have the power to straighten herself up. "Don't know. Haven't seen him since."

She became quiet. My nose was paralyzed by all the smells. The stark light cut my eyeballs into pieces.

"Did he get visits very often," I asked, "from his parents?"

"Parents? A man came once in awhile. His father, maybe. Never his mother."

I made a note of that, wrote it between my ears.

"What did you talk about?" I wanted to know.

"What did we talk about? What did we talk about. He didn't say much. In any case, not toward the end. Then he didn't say a thing. He became so different. In the beginning he talked a little. Often as not we didn't talk. Just sat in the garden."

I took the bottle and poured for her. Her entire body was shaking like a car engine.

"Did he say anything about what he was going to do when he got out?"

"I'm sure he hadn't made any plans."

New laughter tipped forward. She coughed it up, got something in her throat and vomited. I tapped her lightly on her misshapen back. She came around.

"He said something about furniture," she whispered. "Old furniture. Antiques."

"Antiques!" I repeated, overwhelmed. "Did he say *antiques?*"

"Think so. That he used to work with antiques."

I got up. Children's hour was over. I had heard enough for today. Dromedary watched me.

"He was never the same," she said softly, softly. "They did something to him."

I stood with my back to her. A cold stream went through my head.

"Was it just his father who visited him?" I said.

"Yeah. Once in awhile."

I left. When I came down to the reception desk, the Line was waiting. But he didn't need to ask me twice to leave.

"Wrong lottery ticket," I just said and stormed toward the door.

The world was a whore, and the sky was a pimp.

I spent the weekend in eternity. I was spit out of the whale's belly, drawn up from the deep and laid on a bed of eiderdown and milk. I slept my beauty sleep there, with white skin tight to me and careful hands that patted my scarred forehead. No kings or princesses disturbed us. No soldiers broke down the door and wanted to take us prisoner. The only sound we heard was our own rhythmical breathing and the trucks downshifting before the turn out to Mosse Road.

On Sunday, we took a walk up across Ekeberg. The weather was fresh and clear like the Norwegian flag, and the blue sky sat like a derby hat over Oslo. At the Seaman's School we stopped and enjoyed the view. I stood behind Berit and put my arms around her. She stiffened a little. Her body arced out from me. Then she relaxed and leaned her head back against my shoulder. But there was something. She seemed anxious.

I wanted to say something about the city, about the church steeples and tall buildings that there were constantly more of, The Postgiro Building, the SAS Hotel, the Index Building, Norsk Hydro. And way in back, the University buildings at Blindern. The Royal Palace looked like an old egg yolk, and I could barely glimpse the Towerhouse at St. Hanshaugen. And behind the city lay Holmenkoll Ridge, like a white, swollen eyelid, and the fjord cut in like a shiny, cold saber between the legs of a lying woman.

I said:

"Did you know Grønland Marketplace is the center of the universe?"

Berit didn't answer.

"Salvador Dali thinks it's the train station in Perpignan on the border between Spain and France, but he's wrong. It's Grønland Market."

"How come?" asked Berit, not particularity interested.

"In the first place, Dante stopped his journey there and opened a boutique for men. He's got one over in Majorstua, for that matter, but it doesn't count. And second, Olympus is there, the gathering place of the gods.

I became quiet and squeezed Berit's hand tighter. We stood like that a long time, silently, looking out over the city. The wind was soon blowing cold at our backs, and the fjord was full of foamy white ridges.

"Where was it you met Viktor Vekk?" she asked all of a sudden.

"At St. Hanshaugen."

I directed her so that she spotted the gold Tower.

"And that's where he left," she continued, pointing down at the dock where a white boat rocked in the steely water.

"Yes," I said and let go of her.

"Why didn't you go with him?"

She stood with her back to me. I wanted to talk about something else, but everything locked up inside me. I thought about whether it was Viktor or I who had been more afraid. Sometimes he said, in dead seriousness: "You're lucky not to have parents. You can do exactly what you want. *No one* can stop you." Maybe those sweet rolls he baked for the concert that warm May Sunday at St. Hans-haugen were the biggest thing he ever did. I imagine it was his father who financed his travels, the study trip, as his mother called it. Maybe it truly was his intention, to visit the Louvre, the Uffizi Gallery, the Vatican, the art centers along the Mediterranean coast: Picasso, Léger, the ruins in Rome, the Arch of Triumph. Viktor, I wasn't with you, or everything could have been different.

"Show me where he is now," said Berit.

I raised my arm and extended it over toward West Cemetery and the crematorium behind Frogner Park, just to the right of the Monolith. I was freezing and wanted to go home.

"You were close friends," she continued, half-questioning, half-stating.

"Yes," I said. "We were. As long as it lasted."

"Why don't you go tell the police?"

We walked downward. Berit seemed uneasy, and a storm was gathering. Soon I would be cast overboard again. I was in disfavor with the gods.

Someone had been to visit me. I noticed it as soon as I was in the doorway. I have a fine nose for such things. Something was in the air, a strange vibration, an intruder's outlines. And there was something on the table: a newspaper clipping. From June 10th, 1977. *Savings bank at Dam Square robbed. Robber armed with grenade. Escaped on bicycle with 200,000 crowns.* The amount was underlined with a thick, red felt-tipped pen. 200,000 crowns.

First, I lit a smoke. After that, I lit the clipping. The paper burned low and peacefully, curled together and became ashes. I went over to the window and blew the dust out into Thereses Street.

16

I had a nightmare. I was on a hike in Nordmarka. I was dressed in blue knickers, Selbu knee socks, sneakers, and a red ski jacket. On my back I carried an old Bergan rucksack with two oranges, a candy bar, a thermos of black currant juice, and a small shovel in it. Life was good and the sky was blue. At the chapel right before The Butcher—a hint of chaos here in the dream: I began to mix up a mountain and a person, but I got through it alright—I allowed myself a breather, ate one of the oranges and listened to an organist practicing for the sportsmen's church service. Then I carried on. In some places the trail was muddy, and I kind of regretted not taking high boots instead. But no sour faces! I got to Kobberhaug Lodge and sat down at one of the tables in front, in the middle of the sun, and drank my juice. I sat there for half an hour, then I walked on confidently. Over Appelsinhaugen, toward Bjørn Lake, and there, like in a nightmare, a bad dream directed by the devil himself, I saw steam shovels, cranes, tractors, trucks, and men in blue overalls and white hard hats. And there was an infernal noise from all the machines. In the ground they had dug a gigantic hole, it looked like a moon crater, and on a sign I read: Coming Soon, 2000 apartments built by Oslo Building and Savings.

I woke up. It was Monday morning, and I was swimming in sweat. I remained lying, motionless. Life is a dream, I whispered. And death? Do we wake up then? I looked at the ceiling. But my eyes whipped around and saw the inside of my head instead. There it said in writing: "What did they do to Viktor Vekk at that clinic?" My whole body turned numb when I thought about it. I wasn't able to think the thought to its conclusion. My introspective eyes read further on the blackboard: "Antiques. Viktor Vekk had worked with antiques." I noted that. But I couldn't quite believe it. The writing was replaced by a photograph: Viktor's mother on that fragile rococo chair. Antiques. A house full of antiques. The pieces began to look like a picture. But suddenly came a new caption: Bank robbery. I couldn't just think of others now. I had to think about myself, too. Someone knew about the robbery. Who was it? I had a clear feeling of being caught up with, and it was an unpleasant feeling. Is it impossible to run away from everything? In any case, I had to get up. I was a busy man with a full calendar.

I went down to Matkroken. I didn't see Berit at any of the registers. I was disappointed. I took a basket and shuffled between the shelves in the library of wares, but when I got to the other end of the store, I suddenly saw her. She was standing behind the meat counter. Berit stood behind the meat counter with a huge knife in her hand. It didn't suit her. She looked ugly. Her fingers were red, and her checkered work coat was full of obscene spots.

When she saw me, she exploded in a big smile and leaned over the glass case.

"Hi," she sang. "I've gotten a job in the meat department!"

"So I see," I said.

"It's a lot better than sitting at the cash register. And I earn more, too."

"You're covered with blood," I said.

"It doesn't matter," she laughed and raised the knife as if she were going to split my skull.

"Careful!" I burst out.

She put down the knife and exposed her teeth.

"The call of the wild," I whispered.

"What did you say?"

I shook my head.

"Nothing. Are you going to work here regularly?"

She put her hand over mine. I shivered and pulled my arm back.

"A while anyway," she said.

"I have to go now."

Berit looked uncertain.

"I can bring dinner up to you some day."

"Anytime at all," I mumbled and went back to the cash registers where strange girls' eyes body-searched me, and uninhibited hands caressed my basket's secrets.

I took the tram downtown and got off at the Stortinget underground station. There was a guy at Eger Marketplace that I wanted to talk with one more time. I had a few questions I wanted to get straightforward answers to. How was Viktor Vekk when he showed up for the last time? *How was he then?* And: What did he know about antiques? I came up to the market. But there was something that wasn't as it should be. At the entrance to the subway station was a huge crowd of people staring at something or other. And next to them was an ambulance with the rear door open. I'm curious and low, so I cleared my way forward to the front. A grotesque sight met me. Up the precipitously steep escalator came two white-clad orderlies, and between them they held a stretcher. Someone was lying on the stretcher, covered by a gray sheet and lashed down with two leather straps. They came up the escalator, and when they were close enough, I saw a foot sticking out from under the cover: a worn-out boot, with a tip that resembled a grotesque grin, a distorted mouth, an acidic smile. And the leather stuck its tongue out at everyone watching. The ambulance drove away without sirens. The crowd of people broke up like a slow explosion.

I didn't know what I should do. I just knew that hate is an aristocratic quality. I turned and walked up Karl Johan, over the bridge, from the underworld to the upper class. The cold had lasted too long. It wouldn't let go. It held tight like a little brat to his mother's skirt hem. April, the cruellest month! I walked over the bridge and thought: *death had undone so many. Sighs, short and infrequent, were exhaled, and each man fixed his eyes before his feet.* They came toward me like an Independence Day procession in the kingdom of death. Words rolled in my head, like a huge printing press, two sentences: *I do not find the Hanged Man. Fear death by water.* I walked and didn't know where I should go. I went to the National Gallery.

Karsten, oh Ludvig Karsten! Enlighten me! Show me the beauty in everything. Show me the beautiful in the hideous, the color in the gray, the rainbow in the cellar's depth. Show me the field in the early morning! But it didn't help. Nothing was like before. Karsten hung on the wall, self-portrait from 1912, as mute as an oyster, a hallucination, a joke that chased me on through the gallery. I came to Halfdan Egedius. Live hard, die young. No, live carefully and die young. Or even better: Live long and die young! Halfdan, who died from the pictures, who fooled everyone. And Lars Hertevig, beautiful and insane, who disappeared into strange foggy landscapes and stayed there, between sinister pine trees, behind overturned rocks, never coming out again. I walked on. I came to the national romantic period. Happy colors jumped at me, sky blue eyes shined and Synnøve Solbakken and happy boys hopped from picture to picture. I had been alone the whole time, but when I stood in front of "Bridal Procession in Hardanger" and tried to get in the mood, I heard footsteps behind me, and it hit me that they were coming nearer and nearer. But I didn't get time to ponder life's complexities. I was clamped tight in an iron grip, twisted around, and right in front of me stood a fellow who would not have been my first choice for an enemy, if it were up to me.

"Thanks for last time," he said.

The one holding me shook with laughter. Now I recognized them. They were both well-dressed. They resembled older Business School students. Their suits were double-breasted, and their ties were decorated with wine chateaus from the Loire Valley. But their clothing was too tight. Or they were too big. And they didn't have pretty teeth when they smiled.

"Perhaps we were a little heavy-handed, but you know how it is."

I didn't say anything. There was a long pause. I tried to move my arms, but that was a bad move. Suddenly the guy standing in front of me pounded his fist into my stomach. I wanted to collapse, but was held in place. I felt my spine quiver like a flagpole in a storm, and my stomach was squeezed up to my lungs. Half-digested food surged up in my mouth. Tears poured.

"What in the hell do you want from me!" I moaned.

The one doing the laying on of hands looked at me surprised. "You? I thought it was you who wanted something from us."

Another punch hit me in the stomach and pumped all the air out of me. I tried to scream, but the man holding me pressed a hand over my mouth and snapped my head backwards.

The aesthete massaged his knuckles and smiled broadly.

"You're a slow learner," he said softly. "We thought you understood last time. But, no. We can't go on meeting like this, can we?"

The man behind me was still holding a hairy hand over my mouth. But I don't think it would have been necessary to answer anyway.

"We don't really want to hurt you, you know. But maybe we need to. And we can be very unpleasant."

He suddenly stiffened up and listened. Someone was coming. Creaking shoes. It was one of the guards walking his rounds.

"From now on you'll keep away, right!"

One last punch slammed into my stomach. The guy behind me let go, and I snapped forward and pressed my arms over my abdomen. Through tears, like from the inside of an aquarium, I saw a knee come closer and closer. I pinched my eyes shut and felt the blood gush out of my mouth and nose when it hit. I hung in the air as the flowers of evil unfolded in a thousand places in my body, then I was sent to the ground with a karate chop that made my back feel like a tennis court.

When I woke up, I was curled up on the floor under "Bridal Procession in Hardanger," sniffling blood and phlegm. Crouched next to me sat two frightened ladies with guard's arm bands.

"We sent for a doctor, we sent for a doctor," repeated one of them hysterically. She wanted to wipe my face with her handkerchief.

I managed to get to my feet. The two ladies rose up with me. My central nervous system was out of whack, and I staggered around in some complicated dance steps.

"But what happened? How did it happen!" shouted the other lady.

She wrung her hands until her fingers were in a tight, unloosenable knot.

"It was too strong for me," I said. "It was absolutely too strong."

The grandmothers looked puzzled.

"The picture," I explained, pointing at the wall behind them. "'Bridal Procession in Hardanger.' I always get a nosebleed and have difficulty breathing when I see that picture."

I asked them to take me to the lobby. They each took an arm and pulled me along. I got to use the sink in the coat room, and over that sink hung the National Gallery's most atrocious picture. I wasn't able to look at it. But it was a remarkable picture: when I wasn't looking at it, it wasn't there. I didn't understand.

All the guards were standing at the exit when I left. I was their hero, the museum's most sensitive guest. It's people like me who give folks back their belief in art.

I slipped out the heavy door and stood there on the stairs to gather the last of my strength. The city packed me into a gray sack, and I began to walk slowly homeward. But this day there was no way around it. There was, in fact, no way to avoid the liquor store on Park Road, where I made a transaction of 123 crowns for a bottle of Calvados Mon Calva.

The Butcher was waiting for me at Thereses Street. He looked compassionately at my face, pinched his eyes shut and continued eating.

"The pickled pork is done," he said. "People are idiots if they think you can only eat it at Christmas."

I put the calvados bottle on the table and eased myself down in the comfy chair. I had plans to remain there for awhile.

"For the most part, people are idiots," the Butcher continued, swallowing the last bite. "Marta, for example. She almost chased me out of the house because I wanted to pickle pork. 'You're breaking with tradition,' she says. Nonsense, I say. You can eat pickled pork year round!"

He was working himself up. His voice became strong and his mouth bigger and bigger. I couldn't take it anymore. I wanted to have peace. I grabbed the bottle and took a gulp that I hoped would knock me out for a couple of days.

But it didn't help. I lit a smoke, and my lungs began to sing like the St. Olav's Boys' Choir. I gave up. I capitulated. I leaned my head backwards carefully, closed my eyes, and tableaus in national romantic motifs glided through my brain as if my head were a slide projector. I opened my eyes. The Butcher had cleared off the table and loomed in front of me. He laid his hand on my forehead, rumpled my hair a little, smiled, but said nothing. I was scared to death. Then he sat down, pulled out a huge cigar and began sending smoke signals.

The Butcher continued where he left off.

"I'm breaking tradition, says Marta. And then Olav and Kari come and shout: far from it. I'm the one holding on to traditions. And they call me a neo-nazi, a ruin of a father, a hopeless skeleton. There are no limits to their ingenuity. And then it's Marta's turn. She calls me a barge. Mountain of flesh, she says. Mount Flesh she thinks is the funniest. And cardboard head. And sex fascist. Can you imagine where she's learned all these expressions. God!"

I had to smile. But it hurt. The Butcher quenched himself from the calvados bottle, bellowed a little and continued.

"Do you know what those swell kids of mine came home with Saturday evening?"

He wanted me to guess. I thought it over.

"Their fiancees," I tried.

The Butcher waved his hands.

"With the police," I attempted.

Wrong again. I gave up. The Butcher's face became big and tragic.

"They came home with safety pins in their ears!"

I looked at him stupidly.

"It's true. Punk, they say. Punk Do you *know* what punk is?"

"It's something from England," I said. "Punk music. Started with unemployed youth in the big cities."

The Butcher groaned.

"Marta had a breakdown. It's *my* fault, she said."

I drank a little from the bottle.

"It'll pass," I said consolingly. "Haven't you noticed that everything passes sooner or later. As soon as some wise guys figure out there's money to make on this, then the revolution will be made harmless and everything will be over. Plain and simple."

The Butcher received the consolation with open arms.

"There's something in what you say. I did some cutting up when

I was young, too." He looked at me. "But I sure as hell didn't do it with safety pins in my ears and green hair!"

"Well, you have to keep them somewhere," I said. "And as far as hair is concerned. . ."

"Careful now," the Butcher interrupted. "Careful now."

I laughed loudly. But I shouldn't have done that. The stress was too much for my face. Two fine stripes of blood came out of my nostrils, like juice from a wall socket in an Oslo Building and Savings apartment, and my lips cracked like ice in the spring thaw. The Butcher moistened a cloth and washed me. After he had pushed cotton up in my nose, he said:

"It's getting harder. Nothing's like before. Don't you think so?"

It was impossible for me to answer. I just listened. My head was an old bag he could fill with words.

"It's not a joke any longer," he continued. "You're surrounded by enemies."

Yeah, I thought, but there was something else that plagued me: am I surrounded by friends too? And: who's who?

"Antiques," he said suddenly, "are nonsense! Useless shit! Marta wants us to buy one of those sets of furniture with just spindle-back chairs and wood carved table tops. No, I say. Steel tubes, glass and foam rubber is the thing!"

He stopped, looked down at me, and his long mouth slithered like an earthworm over his face.

"But you, on the other hand," he said. "You ought to take a little peek at some antiques, hmm?"

He stood there rocking back and forth. I became completely dizzy and had to close my eyes.

"And you can afford it, after all, can't you?"

Then he took his coat and went to the door.

"The pickled pork's in the refrigerator," he said. "First class!"

The Butcher left. I was sitting in the chair and stayed there. I thought about Gordon Paulsen, his ugly shape, his feminine hands. I thought about Viktor Vekk's mother, and his father, whom I had only seen in a painting. And I thought about Dromedary at the hotel. I wanted to talk to her again. I thought about Dromedary in my heart, which had gone dry, which was tired of all the hallucinations and all the mirages. Now I had to find the source.

17

Gordon Paulsen's business was called "Antiquity" and was on Frogner Road right at Niels Juels Street. I'm familiar with that area and easily found my way there. I was born and raised on that side of the city, so I knew what I was walking into.

But I didn't know everything.

I stopped on the opposite sidewalk. A streetcar came between me and the shop. Right afterwards, the view was unobstructed. Behind candlesticks, spinning wheels, rose-painted cribs, and scimitars, I glimpsed Gordon Paulsen and one other person, a tall lady's shape. I had no desire to talk with Gordon Paulsen, and there was a bakery right behind me. There is always a bakery nearby on the Westside. Bakeries are the Westside's bars. Wives sit there with white poodles in their laps and lead wanton lives. But anyway. I'm not narrow-minded. I went in and sat down at a window table with coffee and marzipan layer cake within reach.

I had a fine view and nothing escaped my vigilant, eagle eyes. I saw that it was beginning to rain just a little, like thin shreds of tin foil visible in the air. I didn't have anything against that. There was still dirty snow in the gutter, clumps of sand and dog shit covered the sidewalk. A big wash was needed.

But the rain was just a drop in the ocean, careful and coddled, like the voices around me, velvet and cream, pillows and poodles. Eyes swum like shrimp from table to table. Everyone acted subdued here. I waited for Gordon Paulsen to come out. I ate another piece of cake. It was of high quality, almost a piece of art. I waited patiently. I carved my initials in the table top with the fork: HGW. He was here. I waited patiently, and to he who waits it will be shown. But he doesn't always see what he expected. A car stopped outside "Antiquity," and three men got out. My heart hopped, skipped and jumped. I had never seen Viktor's father before, but I recognized him from the picture that hung in the living room of their home. He resembled his portrait to a T, and he was framed by two guys who weren't completely unlike himself. I had met them both on two occasions, but neither time had they properly introduced themselves. All three walked into Gordon Paulsen's place of business.

I thought it was taking an eternity, but it was just half an hour until they came out again, along with Gordon Paulsen. They crawled into the Volvo and disappeared with a sonic boom toward Solli Square and Drammen Road. I was still in a state of shock. My thoughts had derailed as the frozen tracks expanded in the heat of the sun. Marzipan quivered on the plate. A familiar melody sang in my ears. A little bluebird flew through the window. But I collected myself. I put myself together and stood up. I had the feeling of being on the homestretch. When I opened the door and felt the light rain against my head, I established with great calmness that everything was simple and unsolvable.

Two cow bells clanged when I walked in, and the lady was immediately on the spot. She was somewhere in her thirties, much taller than me, and her essence was built on a hair-fine balance between needlepoint and nightclubs. She walked a tight-rope between the vegetarians and the cannibals. I was speechless and impressed.

"May I help you," she said. The voice gave sound to my picture and it fit. Friendly and husky, business and balm. I was not quite sure how I should approach the situation.

"May I look around a little," I just said.

"Yes, go right ahead." Her hands found each other right under her breasts. I began looking at the garbage. I had already noticed the door to the back room. It was standing half-open. There was an office behind it, big and luxurious from what I could tell.

"Is there something special you're looking for?" the lady asked.

She was three steps behind me the entire time. At a distance, but within arm's length. I had no desire to hurt her.

"Well," I said, fastening my eyes on a seven-branched candelabrum. "I'm interested in Chinese woodcarvings."

I moved my eyes to her. She looked at me, friendly.

"Unfortunately we don't have any," she said in a manner which didn't give hope but didn't disappoint either. I was truly impressed.

"Perhaps you don't get things in from abroad?"

"I'm not the proprietor," she read me. "He's out at the moment."

"Will he be back soon?"

"He'll be away the rest of the day."

Now she was speaking in a manner that would have made most people feel regretful. But I was not. I repeated my question from a little while back in a revised form.

"Maybe you sell mostly Norwegian things?"

Oh, no. Our collection is, if anything, European. We have contacts all over Europe."

"I see. Interesting. But it must be inordinately expensive to transport these pieces home to Norway." I pointed at a pink chaise lounge. "That, for example."

"Mr. Paulsen has his own trucks," the lady explained obligingly.

"Oh," I said. "But to get the things inside Norway is expensive, I suppose. You get skinned at the border just bringing back a radio from Germany."

She smiled and shook her head.

"There is no tariff on goods more than one hundred years old," she crowed.

"Then it's just a matter of time," I replied boldly. "So, where is it you buy things, anyway?"

Now she changed. Her eyes became narrow and suspicious, as if she suddenly came on to something important. She couldn't maintain the balance any longer and fell over to the nightclubs and cannibals. But truth and justice have no limits. If you don't get an answer, you take it. I went into the office of Gordon Paulsen. I just hoped that she was not a karate expert. And she wasn't.

"*What* are you doing!" she shouted. "What *are* you doing!"

Now it was my turn to avoid answering. I dug through the papers that lay on his desk, but there was nothing of interest there, just some invoices and copies of estate sale notices from the newspapers. I tried to open the drawers, but they were locked, of course. I grabbed the lady, who was now standing next to me, by the arm and said quite calmly:

"Can't you unlock the drawers. It's so inconvenient otherwise."

She had lost her voice. I asked one more time. She shook her head. On a green sofa next to the door was a lady's purse. I walked toward it. But even though she was mute, she wasn't lame. She leaped after me and stood in the way. I wanted to try being nice as long as I could.

"The keys," I said, reaching out my hand.

She got her voice back.

"No," she said.

I didn't like doing it, but I had to. I hit her with the edge of my hand right under her left breast. She sank to the floor in astonishment and remained lying there, gasping. There was a huge ring of keys in her purse. She was completely silent now and refused me nothing. I tried all the keys, tore and tugged at all the drawers and finally found one that fit. I flipped through papers I didn't understand, periodicals, Norwegian and foreign catalogs, letters in English and French, notes, and loose-leaf binders with photographs of various furniture and objects. When I got to the last drawer, I heard the door move out in the shop. The cow bells rang and footsteps trod across the floor. I held my breath. It was too late to hide. Besides, there was nothing to hide behind. Then the footsteps stopped, shoes scraped the floor, and a crackling voice said hello. I went out to the customer. It was an older lady with a fox slung around her neck and an enormous hat.

"Finally!" she burst out when I came into view. "I want to talk to Gordon."

"We don't allow animals inside," I said.

She looked at me. She thought her ears were playing a trick on her.

"You'll have to tie up your fox outside," I said sternly and stuck my finger into the mouth of the garment.

"Antiquity has lost a customer." We each went our way, she out and I in. The other lady still lay coiled up on the floor, like a viper on a sunny rock. I dived into the last drawer. The clocks ticked and time passed. My heart pounded and death approached. I didn't know what I was searching for, but I found it, a green binder with lined pages where Gordon Paulsen, with elegant, almost Gothic script, had written down driving routes and times. I read and remembered: Marseille-Amsterdam-Oslo. Copenhagen-Oslo. Amsterdam-Gothenburg-Oslo. Milano-Hamburg-Copenhagen-Oslo. Zürich-Oslo. Fine cities, I thought. They are cities with culture and tradition, not to mention style. Marseille with its pleasant harbor district and all the boats that come from the Middle East and North Africa. Amsterdam, with canals and white bicycles. Copenhagen, with its shopping district and Tivoli and green Tuborg. Hamburg and Reperbahn, Zürich and gold. Once a month one of Gordon Paulsen's trucks came home from the Continent, the last Friday of every week.

I flipped further, the same routes every time, freight trade back and forth between Oslo and the Continent. But suddenly the script stood on its head. I understood the connection at once. I snapped the book shut and swung it around. Now I could start from the beginning. And I read until my eyes became big and wet and my heart little and hard. There was a list of delivery places, dates and times, not just in Oslo, but all of southern Norway. My blue index finger glided down the pages, and there were many familiar names there. The Fredheim Hotel, for example. I thought about the interior there, the carpet, the plastic flowers, the rooms. It said in the book that goods had been delivered to the hotel last Saturday. And I could not remember having seen any antiques.

But I had seen enough. I put the book back in the drawer, straightened up nicely after myself, and examined the lady on the floor. She was sleeping. I didn't want to wake her. On the way out I saw a big vase, a tall, crepe-thin porcelain vase with a beautiful blue design. The price tag said 12,000. I lifted it up and let go. I thought: It's not the vase itself that is most important, but the cavity inside.

I walked the shortest route to Dromedary, to hell's oasis. I fought through sandstorms, past stone palaces and concrete castles. There was something I wanted to ask her about. I wanted to hear it with my own ears: where did she get her stuff? I knew it now, but I wanted to hear it. And: What was the connection between Viktor Vekk and Gordon Paulsen? I got to Sporveis Street a little before one o'clock, to lust's alley, where endless rows of men walked restlessly up and down, old and young, thick and thin, happy and sad, but all driven by the same desire. The compass needles in their pants all pointed the same way, and blood knocked on the same door.

I went right in, expecting the worst. But nothing happened. The Line, standing behind the counter, just barely raised his eyes, looked disinterested, and bent over the ledgers again. I waited a little longer, but no one hit me from behind either. I shrugged my shoulders, what the hell, and ran up the stairs.

But something was wrong. There was something that didn't fit. The door to Dromedary's room was open. I walked slowly down the corridor, and gradually, as I approached, I sensed a strong smell of disinfectant and soap. I continued walking, even though it was unnecessary. Something collapsed inside me, a house of cards or a pile of rocks. I stopped and looked into room number 13: sparkling clean and empty. No curtains, no bedclothes. Just a gray mattress with a depression in it and a naked light bulb in the ceiling, otherwise nothing. Empty. Emptied.

I went down to the reception desk again. The Line was there, and now he raised his head all the way and looked right at me. An acidic smile. A nettle smile stuck out at the corners of his mouth. My fingers itched, and my arms burned. I stopped in front of him, but controlled myself. I wanted to settle accounts, but it wasn't necessary. I said:

"What happened to Dromedary?"

Even more nettles came into view.

"She moved."

"And her new address?"

I asked, but didn't expect an answer.

"That's kind of hard to say. She was picked up."

I said:

"I admire your use of antiques here."

The Line continued to look right at me. His mouth was frozen tight. I waved my arms and pointed around the room.

"I would characterize it as an example of fine classical taste. Everything is pure in style, simple, not to mention functional in relation to its intended purpose."

I snapped around. My eyes fell on the loving cup, god knows in what branch of athletics it was won. I ripped out the plastic flowers and slung them in the Line's kisser. Then I left. If I ever set my feet in that place again, it wouldn't be in my own shoes, at any rate.

I padded across Sporveis Street, past the Blind School, where the windows were full of people pointing with white canes and staring down at me with unmoving eyes. The sky was a low forehead that butted against the earth. The community was tightening up. Soon now, all ways out would be closed. A taxi driver walked bent over into the urinals down by Fagerborg Church. His car stood with the motor running and the door open. The thought rushed through me instantly, but I tossed it off just as fast. I wouldn't get any farther than Sognsvann. The barrier was lowered there. It would be better to wait until the snow melted, get hold of a bicycle and pedal in toward Bjørn Lake. But I got another idea. I set a course down Pile Street, turned toward the right at Park Road and stormed Lorry. I found a table back in the bowels of the cramped, smoke-filled joint, and ordered a pint. While I waited, I phoned Else Vekk.

I told her who it was and that I wanted to talk with her. A half-hour later she glided in the door, stopped under the clock and TV set and looked around. I stuck an arm in the air, and she came toward me. She was wrapped in the middle of a wolf-skin fur. Her hands were hidden in a muff, and her hair lay in symmetrical blonde curls down to her shoulders. She was elegant. Heads turned at every table. But it was only at a distance. When she stood in front of me, I could see the windowshades were pulled down. The hand she gave me shook, and her eyes were small from pills and alcohol. I helped her off with her fur, and immediately there was a flock of waiters around us. I ordered another pint and cigarettes. She wanted to have a glass of red wine.

"Is this where students congregate?" she said full of expectation, releasing her eyes.

"Artists, mostly," I informed her. "But they usually come after eight. When the House closes."

"The house?"

"The art academy."

The glasses were set on the table. We toasted. I had the gripes, but couldn't go to the bathroom now. I was the one who had to do the talking. After all, I had invited the lady here. I said:

"Have you heard anything from Viktor?"

She just looked down at the dirty tablecloth. I don't know why, but it caught my attention that the sleeves of her dress were too long. They almost covered the entire hand.

"I still would like to get hold of him," I continued and felt rotten.

"We're waiting for him," she said quietly with that hoarse, monotone voice of hers.

I drank and lit a smoke. My legs quivered under the table. The flame flickered in front of my face. But I didn't have the time to fool around. I was hungry.

"Viktor never took his exam," I said. "He went traveling before then. But I suppose he saw a lot that he can get pleasure and benefit from?"

"Yes. I'm sure of that."

The voice disappeared deep down inside her, like a breath.

"I remember that he was very interested in antiques," I said quickly. "A big part of the curriculum in art history concerns furniture, everyday household articles and such."

I couldn't hold up under her eyes. She raised her glass, but set it down again. It was soon empty.

"He had many interests," she said. "My husband got him a job with an antiques dealer once. I don't remember what his name was. An exclusive business. . ."

"Antiquity?"

"That was it, yes. My husband runs an import firm. He has many irons in the fire. He works with this man. So. . ."

"That must have been an excellent experience for Viktor," I said. "What did he do?"

"Viktor went along on the buying trips. He traveled all over Europe, was there at auctions, all the big cities. He was in Amsterdam, Marseille. . ."

I inhaled and crushed out the cigarette.

"That must have been before he got. . . sick?"

Her face became distant. Fog swirled out of her mouth and nose. Her fingers curled around the stem of the wine glass.

"Yes. It had to be. I don't remember exactly. . ."

I ordered more to drink. The waiter returned at once. The empty glasses were exchanged, and we drank simultaneously.

"Did he get any studying done while he was in the hospital?" I asked coldly.

"I never visited him. Just my husband. He wanted to spare me. He is so thoughtful. I have such. . . nerves."

I could see that. She was an electric chair.

"When he got out, he was so nice. He had become so kind, gentle, just like when he was little. He'd become almost like a child." She leaned over the table, toward me. Her face resembled a poor wax mask. *"He'd become a child."*

Her voice had just one inflection, and she said it without joy, without sorrow. I shuddered. An ice cold waterfall fell down my back. I pressed up against the wall.

"A child," I just said.

"Yes. He was so different. A big, kind child."

She quickly drank a gulp. I lit a cigarette for her.

"And then he went away?"

"He lived at home for awhile. With us. Then my husband got him his own apartment, or room."

"Where was that?"

"I don't know. It was to spare me. He was going to be completely well. I get sick if there are sick people around me. Do you understand?"

She breathed heavily and rubbed her hands against each other. A short smile lit up her face, died out.

"My husband takes care of everything. He arranges everything. I'm not strong enough. Viktor moved at the end of summer. And then he was gone. My husband told me about it. It was hard for him. In February. Viktor disappeared in February, at the end of February."

She finished off the glass. Her eyes sank backward into a dark, steel-plated room. I was mute.

"But he's coming back. That's what my husband says. I wait...every day."

If I take away the lie... I thought. But was Else Vekk the average person? I didn't have the time for literary musings, so instead I said:

"When Viktor was studying at the academy, there was a classmate of his who went to a few lectures and a couple of seminars, now, what was his name...Windelband! Hans Georg Windelband."

I'm a good actor. But then, I had an interesting audience. I could see Else Vekk slowly becoming someone else. Nothing could happen rapidly with her now, but it did happen, slowly and elaborately, like the development from amoeba to human.

"Windelband," she almost growled. "He's dead. I read the obituary in the paper. My husband showed me. *I'm glad he's dead!*"

I looked at her, terrified. In a flash the development had reached its zenith. She shined of hate all over. The lines had become utterly cruel. Her eyes were red and dark. Then she fell back through the centuries, a dizzying fall, and became relaxed and listless, almost indifferent.

"It was this Windelband who...yes, I can say it. I suppose you're not completely ignorant of what destroyed Viktor. It was Windelband who...who lured our son to...hell."

I gasped. But what could I say? I just nodded, and inside I said loud and clear: "This is a mother talking. History will judge you differently."

Else Vekk looked at the clock over the entrance. It was three-thirty. She rose up slowly. I followed her movements and automatically grabbed the hand that shook in front of me.

"I must go now. I really shouldn't be out. My doctor forbids it."

A thought hit me immediately. I thought about the sloppy autopsy and Dromedary.

"Doctor Stockman?" I said quickly.

She looked surprised and bewildered.

"No. Varp. My doctor. Doctor Varp."

"No one will discover," I said jokingly and hopefully, "that you've been out."

"No. I'll be home before anyone comes."

I helped her on with the fur. She stuck a hundred crown note in my pocket and left. Everyone watched her. When she was gone, everyone looked at me. I paid the tab and got into the brown phone booth for a second time. I found Dr. Varp in the book. He had an address out on Bygdøy. I stuck a coin in the slot and dialed his number. A weary male voice answered instantly.

"Is Dr. Varp there?" I asked.

"No. I'm sorry. He's out now."

"Can I reach him at the emergency room?"

"He's on duty there this evening, after seven."

"Thanks," I said. "Thank you very much!"

"Who may I say is calling?"

I hung up. I stood there awhile and collected myself. I was worn to the marrow. But I couldn't stand there the rest of my life. I repeated Varp's address and walked toward home. When I got to the Bislett Baths, I stopped. I could do with a little chlorine. On a sign it said that this was men's day. I paid six crowns in the window and was handed a towel. I felt better already. The buoyancy had started. I wandered through some catacomb-like corridors and tried to whistle, but it was just a hodge-podge of sound, like a crazy flock of off-course birds. A grim bag of bones sitting on a chair next to a door looked sternly at me.

There was just me and a couple of old guys in the pool. They floated around like tired hippos. Their skin was white and blue and hung in clusters. Their nuts looked like old pears clinging to their crotches. I swam slowly, back and forth. An element of friendliness filled my body. This was balm for body and soul. I was born again. I floated around in a big, green womb.

I laid on my back with legs and arms spread out the way you make angels in the snow. I closed my eyes and dreamed I was in the Dead Sea. I closed my eyes and thought about Viktor Vekk, who had become like a child. I was about to sink, kicked with my feet, and got my equilibrium again. He had freighted narcotics for Gordon Paulsen and his father all over Europe, along with camphor chests and Louis XVI chairs and sewing tables. Viktor Vekk, his mother's only son, the child who got house arrest in a room at Malvin's, who they gave a new name and pushed out the window. He knew too much. He had become a child, and children blab. Was that how it hung together? I made a few movements with my toes and fingers to stay afloat. I supposed I would never know. But now I knew the connections. I thought about Viktor Vekk as I last saw him and didn't recognize him. But I didn't want to remember him like that. I wanted to remember him the way he stood at St. Hanshaugen, in patched, brightly-colored, ragged clothes, screaming as loud as he could: "Sweet rolls! SWEET ROLLS!" I was a sentimental pig! Shit! I rolled over, took a few powerful strokes toward the steps, and crawled, dripping, up from the chlorine like Aphrodite, born from the foam of the sea.

I was the only one in the shower room. I massaged my leg muscles so they wouldn't stiffen up before evening. But just as I was going to turn off the water, I was not alone any longer. Two men came in. I turned toward them. They were naked, but I recognized them without clothes too. It seemed they wanted to shower with me.

I took a resigned step backward and got ready. I kicked one of them in the crotch as hard as I could. It was a disgusting sensation to feel his dick against the instep of my foot. He sagged with a contracted groan and hid his pride behind two hairy hands. But the other guy was already on top of me. I got an elbow in the chest and blew out all the candles on the cake. Then I was snapped open against the white tile wall.

The one I had kicked was back on his feet and surged at me. He extended a fist that scraped over my right cheek. His ring cut a deep gouge. I saw blood drip down on my feet.

"Fuck you!" he panted. "Fuck you!"

He hit me one more time, on the temple. In an instant everything turned black, and it was exactly as if I were standing in the middle of an eggbeater. I heard voices coming closer. They were a little unclear, but soon I heard every word.

"You've sorta been behaving yourself lately," said the smaller one.

The other took over immediately. They had been practicing this a long time.

"But you haven't always been that way, now, have you?"

He boxed my ears. My face burned. The first one suddenly became uneasy. It must have dawned on that slow brain of his that we were in a public bath.

"We know everything about you," he said quickly. "Do you understand! You've got nothing to go on."

"What?" I managed to force out of my bloodied mouth.

"A little of everything. You don't have a chance. Just leave things alone and nothing will happen. Understand!"

I got a hit over the ear. I barely managed to hold myself upright, but they helped. They shoved me up to the wall and said:

"So, from now on keep away! Far away! And you won't hear from us."

A fist was on its way to my chest when the door from the pool opened. I was about to shout for joy. It was the Butcher. It's the greatest thing I've ever seen. He stood in the middle of the floor, naked. His body tumbled out in all directions and almost filled the room.

The two best friends turned around toward him. The smaller one took a step to the side and went for the exit. The Butcher stopped him with one hand and shoved him back. I sent a foot into the body of the other. He screamed in surprise and stumbled into the Butcher's arms. The Butcher greeted him a little too enthusiastically. His forehead hit the man's head, and he howled and fell down to the floor. I turned toward the one by the wall, but he was no longer standing. There was a red mark where the back of his head had hit the white tile.

The Butcher grabbed my shoulder.

"We should go now," he said, flustered.

I looked around. I agreed. We hadn't left it very tidy.

The white-clad lifeguard with the whistle around his neck unlocked the lockers. He looked a little strangely at my face, but I didn't owe him an explanation. I threw on my clothes, waited a short while for the Butcher to get ready, and together we walked through the catacombs, past the bag of bones and the torches.

"Busy day," he said as we stood on the steps inhaling fresh air.

"Can't deny that."

"Let's go over to the bus stop."

We crossed the street. The Butcher looked down at me.

"Are you happy now?" he asked, almost anxious.

"I've figured out most of it," I said. "Coming up for a calvados?"

"No time. The hogs are waiting."

We stopped at the bus stop. The Butcher shifted from foot to foot. He looked nervously in all directions.

"Something wrong?" I asked.

"Short on time. Hope the bus comes soon."

"Someone left a newspaper clipping on my table," I said.

He looked at the sky, squinting. It had cleared.

"You think spring is far off?" he asked.

I didn't answer.

"I think you ought to lay low now awhile," he said quickly. "I mean, there's no point in slaving away anymore now. Is there?"

I looked at him. His face was wet, and our eyes didn't meet. The red bus appeared from behind Bislett.

"Play it safe," he almost shouted. "Restrain yourself! No nonsense!"

"Don't worry on my account," I calmed him.

He slapped my back.

"Hugo Poser! You are immortal. Because you never existed!"

He stuck a thick envelope in my pocket.

"You take that vacation we talked about," he said. No, he begged. "Promise me that!"

The bus stopped in front of us, and he hopped on. His back was like a barn door in the process of falling off its hinges. He was amorphous. I went my way too. My hair was wet and I didn't want to catch a cold. I walked home alone, to my calvados bottle and unending solitude. Slippers shuffled above me, and from a grating gramophone I heard: "She gets some money so she can buy a little chocolate and candy and such." I stood at the window with a green glass in my hand. An ambulance came with full sirens down Thereses Street and stopped at Bislett. On the windowsill, next to the dead cactus, lay the envelope from the Butcher. It contained 6,000 crowns, the last installment. We were even now. I thought: It's all over now. Now everything has begun.

18

The next day I woke up early. It's a bad habit I have from jail. I got right up and cooked three eggs. My face was still sore and didn't fit right, but otherwise I felt fine. While I smoked a cigarette and looked out on Thereses Street in dark, rain-heavy clouds, I thought about the Norwegian farmers who always paint a mistake in their rosemaled trunks, for only God is perfect. I'm not so superstitious. But I'm not perfect either. For example, I drink too much. I took a stiff shot of calvados and walked out into the city. My stomach growled before the explosion came. I set a course for the University Library.

The revolving door rolled me into the stone foyer, and I continued up the stairs, past the fresco brother's apocalyptic visions. I think I like the decor at the West Crematorium better. I stopped at the display cases on the second floor where some yellow handwritten manuscripts were being displayed. I didn't understand the symbols and hurried on. I rolled around poetry collections here once, in a cellar deep underground. Now most of the books have been transferred to microfilm. There's no room for any more reality, either.

I went into a reading room. It was quiet there until I came. Everyone turned toward me, a collective motion, collective eyes. I was alone. Then the eyes sank down to the thick, red books on every single table. Law students studying for the exam. I could have been sitting there too, among them, if everything had gone as Mother and Father wanted. I gathered courage and walked up the middle aisle. Straight through law to victory, I thought, and ended up at bookshelves that covered the entire end wall. "Medicine," it said on a black plate. I stroked my index finger over the backs of the books until my finger print wore off. I didn't find it. The volumes of *Norwegian Doctors* must be loaned out. I forgot myself completely, cursed and stomped the floor with my dirty shoes. All the students jumped in the air. A thousand eyes nailed me to a cross. The thieves on each side clenched their fists. I shrunk up and sneaked out. I sat down in the canteen on the first floor with a cup of student coffee and a sugared *lefse*. Was I asking for too much? Should I be satisfied now? Was I spoiled? It became noisy around me. Lunch time. The students tumbled in the narrow door right in front of me, and it hit me that they were so alike. It was the same person over and over again. I looked down at my cup. It was empty. But in the coffee grounds there were two faces: Dromedary's and Viktor's. The *lefse* turned to blood in my mouth. I sighed. I sighed loudly and heavily, like a student on the way to his exam.

There was a note pad on a table right by the entrance. I took it. I had my own pencil. When I was in the revolving door, half-way between out and in, I saw an old, red Volkswagen parked right down in front of the steps. I didn't have time to argue now. I went along for the ride, all the way around, back to where I came from, and out the rear door. A vacant taxi was waiting by the Business School, and I asked the driver to take me to the emergency room. He looked at me over his shoulder and blinked.

"Serious?"

"Rabies."

It didn't take long to get to Ankertorget. I told him to keep the change, and he just let my ten fall down on the floor. I went into the waiting room, where the unfortunate sat with crutches and wheelchairs, bandages around heads and hands, swollen tonsils and high blood pressure, destroyed bodies and lost souls. I stopped a veteran nurse marching through the room and asked:

"Where can I find Dr. Varp?"

"He's not on duty today."

She marched on. Wooden shoes clapped like castanets against the slate tile floor. This was no doctor novel. Without hesitation, I walked through a door and came into a long, gray corridor where a few frail people were slowly walking back and forth. I stood there until a new nurse popped up. She was a beauty with a name tag. I studied her left breast meticulously and read: Gunvor Mo.

"Gunvor," I said. "Do you know Dr. Varp."

"Of course. But he's not here now."

"I know." I took her arm and whispered: "I'm from the newspaper. *Our Land*. I'm writing an article about Dr. Varp."

Her eyes examined me. I smiled shamelessly, the way I had seen so often on the television news, and took out the pad and pencil.

"Do you want to talk to me?"

She laughed with her white teeth. Her name tag went up and down.

"Second-hand information is not to be scorned," I said. "Shall we sit down?"

We sat in two green chairs with plastic seats and wooden armrests. I scratched myself behind the ear with the pencil. I had the urge to ask her for an injection of something soothing, but she was gullible as a drunken confessor.

"Why are you writing about Dr. Varp?" she wanted to know.

"It's in connection with an article about narcotics," I said.

She nodded. I had fallen on fertile soil.

"How is he to work with?" I began, making notes on the pad.

She thought about it a long time, weighing the words on the scales of her brain and heart.

"His professional credibility gives assurance," she said slowly.

I wrote that down. I could be doing his eulogy. She continued right away.

"I think he looks at his work as a calling. Strictly speaking, he doesn't need to work here. He has his own private practice. He has for many years. It's a self-sacrifice for him to be here. Working at the emergency room doesn't rank high in status with Norwegian doctors."

"How long has he been employed here?" I asked.

"Since '75."

"He must have committed himself to the battle against narcotics," I said, looking at her. The pencil was ready like a syringe in my hand. Gunvor began from the beginning, and I was all ears and closed mouth.

"His specialty is manias and diseases of the nerves. And he's done research on brain functions. I think you can say that he is an authority in the field. But he probably has his opponents too."

That didn't surprise me. I asked, like the objective news gatherer I am:

"Why's that?"

"He came out in favor of lobotomics. Especially when he was connected with the university in Zürich in the late fifties."

My hand didn't want to write any more. My mouth became dry, and my head pounded all over.

"Zürich," I whispered. "So he's spent some time in Zürich."

"At the university there, yes. That was after he was affiliated with the Anatomical Institute here in Oslo."

I attempted to write again, but the writing pressed through three sheets. Viktor was there again. Viktor, who became a child. Viktor, who forgot how to talk. An extreme coldness froze me to ice. A bed rolled past us. The smell of freshly-washed body hung behind in the air.

I said, with a voice I had never heard before:

"You mentioned diseases of the nerves and manias."

"Yes. You must get that. He almost became famous in Zürich because he could get obsessive gamblers to quit."

"How did he do that?"

"With the help of hormone injections."

I dropped the pad on the floor, and wasn't able to pick it up. I looked at nurse Gunvor. She looked at me, surprised. I wanted to say: Gunvor, admit me to your hospital. Take good care of me. Wash me every morning and evening. And give me a white pill full of sleep every time I'm thinking too much and my brain is at the boiling point.

While pictures of the Butcher, the smooth, fat Butcher, grew behind my eyelids, I repeated:

"Hormone injections?"

"Aren't you going to write?"

I bent over slowly, like a pine tree, and plucked up the pad. I etched in runes: Varp. The Butcher. *Our Land.*

Gunvor continued.

"It was more or less an experiment. Dr. Varp is really a researcher. The treatment had shown side effects in some cases. It changed the subjects' appearance.

I got up and walked across the gray corridor. I heard the nurse's voice behind me, but no one could stop me now. I came out to the waiting room, where the same people were still waiting. They had become sicker since last time. The swellings had grown. The bandages had become red. The pupils of their eyes were white and dull. There was the sound of moaning and groaning, calls for help and prayers for deliverance. I ran out and nearly got run over by a taxi. The horn woke me up. I looked skyward. Only God is perfect. But this rosemaled trunk had a few too many mistakes. I thought it was enough to be satisfied with one.

But there was a time when I, too, was without marks or blemishes. I was a flower delivery boy. I was the quickest delivery boy in Oslo. In all of my career, between the ages of ten and thirteen, I only had one mishap. It was when the balloon tires on my DBS bicycle got caught in the streetcar tracks on Frogner Road, and I banged into the cobblestones with a potted plant under my arm and fifteen irises in a cardboard box on the rack. The secret behind a delivery boy's success is to remember addresses. Now, I remembered an address that the Butcher had mumbled to me once when we were sitting at the Promenade.

The taxi that almost ran over me was free now, so I asked the driver to take me to Smestad. I didn't have flowers with me this time. I had 6,000 crowns in my inner pocket. I sat in the back seat and twiddled my fingers, as if I were scattering a slippery deck of cards in my lap.

I got out at Bakke tavern and took the first road to the right. It was right. I stopped outside a yellow villa with a tall picket fence. I've played poker before. I won a sailboat once from someone in class, but I never got it.

An elegantly dressed man opened the door. His eyes fell on me and crawled up like Sisyphus' stone before they fell down again.

"Yes," he said. It was meant as a question.

I patted my breast pocket and winked.

"Tell the jack the king is here."

I was let in.

The first room was a mix of office and living space. I didn't hear a sound from anywhere. The head butler contemplated me one more time. His eyes were worn out from rolling uphill. They never reached the sky. But his fingers were long and lean. He had hands as nice as Gordon Paulsen's.

"Yes," I said. This time it was my turn to ask a question.

"The stakes are high today," he said.

I drew out the wad of bills as if it was just withered leaves I wanted to get rid of.

"Yes, indeed," he intoned, and I followed him.

We walked through several rooms, nice family rooms with pictures on the walls and books on the shelves. I loosened my fingers en route and froze my face tight. Long Fingers stopped outside a door with a burgundy velvet curtain in front of it. He pulled it aside and whispered:

"Here you are."

So, there I was. In the Butcher's paradise. It was a rather large room, obscured by cigarette smoke. In the middle of the floor stood a square table with a green felt top, and around it sat four men. They all turned toward us. My new friend went over to the one with his face to the door, bent down and said something I didn't hear. He nodded and got up, indicating with his hand that I could take his place. I sat down. I was in the game.

The others at the table stared at me, not all of me, but at my hands and eyes. They were men of the Butcher's age, in gray, slightly too large suits, which their wives had bought them once and for all in the early '6Os. Their skin was pale, their fingers yellow from nicotine. For a short while, everything in the room was quiet, not a movement, not a sound. Then the film began to roll. I bought myself into the game for 300 crowns. The guy right across from me shuffled the cards. They slipped into each other like a well-oiled zipper. I cut the deck. He looked at the others and put the stacks up on each other. I wiped my hands on my pant legs while he dealt. Five cards lay in front of me. I picked them up one at a time. I felt a hollow pain in my stomach and wanted a drink. I had two aces, clubs and spades, a ten, a jack, and a three. I looked at the others. They were statues. They could have stood in Frogner Park. I bought three new cards and had to pay 200 crowns. I got the desire for another shot. The first two cards I picked up were queens. The last was the ace of hearts. I was sitting there with three aces and two queens in my hand, a full house, a palace as far as I was concerned. My heart hammered against my wad of money, like a loving cashier.

The guy to the left folded. A sudden, soundless sigh came from him. His eyes drew into a dry skull. His shoulders shook. I started at 500. The two others followed me. I raised to 800. The dealer was in. The third passed. Two red spots came into his yellow cheeks.

"Double," I said. It was the first thing I said since coming into the room.

The dealer didn't jump. He just laid his money on the table, eight new hundreds. This was a speechless society. They lived by other rules. They were mute and lonesome.

I won. He had two lousy pair, kings and tens. There were 5,000 crowns in the pot. I twisted the bills around my fingers, stuck them in my pocket, and was going to stand up. Then I felt two gentle hands on my shoulders, and I sank back down.

"We usually play two hands," said a voice behind me.

I looked toward the door. There was a man there that I did not want to irritate. He stood with his arms crossed and was about as wide as he was tall, about six foot three. I couldn't see the door.

"Yes, of course," I said lowly.

The dealer from last time dealt again. The cards fell down in front of us and landed soundlessly on the green felt. I looked at the others, the two sitting on each side of me. They were without movement, static, but behind their worn-thin skin rumbled a tremendous angst, the angst of being alone with a deck of cards, alone with a wager. It was the same fear junkies have of having to travel alone, that others aren't going to come along on the needle express. It was not the money that was most important for these weary men, it was the game itself, the fear and joy, the thrill, the short second before the cards are placed on the table and everything disintegrates. It's a death wish that rides them, the hearts of gamblers!

I looked at the cards. This had to be an uncommonly good day. I had three of a kind again, three nice kings. I bought two new cards. I let them lie a few seconds with their backs up and asked myself whether I was cut out for this kind of child's play, but got no response. I was just excited, like when you take the first drag on a candy cigarette. I picked up the cards. The fourth king. I had four of a kind. Four kings. More than there are in all of Europe.

Everyone was in on the first round. There were 4,000 crowns in the pot already. Not a sound came from anyone. The cigarette smoke hung over us like a blue-gray curtain. The giant was standing absolutely still. I was afraid there would be an earthquake every time he blinked. The man who sat to my left raised the stakes by 800 crowns. I was in. The dealer was in. The fourth man hesitated a fraction of a second. He suffered that short moment, suffered happily. Then he followed.

We went another round. I saw a shiny drop falling from the head of the man to my right. He let it roll down to his eyebrow. Then he folded. The dealer followed me in the stakes. He looked confident. Uncomfortably confident. The third man also came along. I could see myself doing something amusing. I could see myself doubling.

I did.

No reaction. Five seconds passed. An eternity. The man to my left passed. His eyes turned white, a pearl of saliva came into view at the corner of his mouth. But then something happened. I couldn't point to it, but I knew it happened. The guy across from me exchanged a card. I couldn't see it, but I knew it. I stared at his hands, at his jacket sleeve, at his chest, at the table. I saw nothing. He met the stakes and whispered:

"Call."

There were 16,000 crowns in the pot. Six thousand of them were mine.

I placed three kings on the table. He acknowledged with three jacks. I mustered up courage again. I must have been mistaken. Triumphantly I turned the last king. He smiled weakly, opened the fourth jack. I wanted to laugh loudly, but the laughter coagulated. The game was not over. With exquisite elegance he turned the last card around. The joker. My heart fell several notches. I got a nasty taste in my mouth. I stared at his last card, at the wide-legged fool, he who is everything and nothing. They hadn't told me that there was a joker in the deck. I was going to protest, but it would have served no purpose. The winner crossed his arms. His face shouted neither triumph nor bad conscience. I bent over toward him, touched the cards with my fingertips, smiled, and stood up. I walked to the exit. The door guard took a step to the side and let me pass. The silence behind me was like a blow to the neck. Long Fingers waited outside. He showed me out. My head was numb, but my heart beat cold and calm. I still had enough money left for a pint at Bakke tavern, anyway.

It was too cold to sit outside, so I found a table by the window. I lit a smoke and drank half the glass. In spite of everything, it had gone quite nicely. What was a few thousand compared to the treasure in Nordmarka! I clutched the glass. I would have to go get it soon. When the sun comes. When spring comes! When the dawn comes to Norway! I relaxed, crushed the smoke and ordered another pilsner.

I waited for two hours. Then he finally came. I laid the money on the table and went out. He hurried across the intersection and down to the streetcar platform. I waited behind a post. He looked like all the other gray men who stood there. He resembled the classic bureaucrat, the postage stamp licker, squeezed flat between the upper class he would never be a part of and the proletariat he feared to end up in. He didn't resemble a gambler.

I followed him all the way home. He lived in a high rise at Marienlyst. He was very surprised when he opened the door. There was something he hadn't wagered on. I shoved him aside and went in.

"What do you want?" he stammered.

"A little of everything," I said, looking around. The walls were littered with pictures of a magician performing all his ridiculous tricks, pigeons and rabbits, waving handkerchiefs and ropes that stand on their own. I looked at the man.

"Is this you?"

He nodded.

"You never got very far," I said. "Remained a third-rate artist who fooled housewives at bazaars and people in old folks homes. And at night you dreamed of the big number, the world sensation, the Houdini dream, an elephant that disappears under a sheet. Huh!"

He looked stiffly at me. His eyes were full to the brim with hate.

"What do you want?" he repeated mechanically.

"You're still an amateur," I said. "What's your percentage?"

His face loosened up like *lutefisk*.

"I don't quite understand," he began.

"You cheated," I said. "I know it. You let me win one time. You gave me good cards. But you got better ones yourself. What's your percentage?"

He had no idea what to say. He sank into a chair. I stood over him.

"How do you know?" he asked, almost respectfully.

I sat down.

"I felt your cards with my fingertips," I explained. "Different temperatures. The joker was warm."

"And what do you want now? Money?"

I shook my head.

"Nope. Information."

"What kind of information?"

He was afraid now. His magic hands shook as he lit a cigarette.

"Who runs the playing club?" I asked.

He hesitated. But he couldn't manage to conjure me away.

"Who?" I repeated.

"Vekk. Anton Vekk is his name."

I wasn't surprised. I just became extremely sad. A rat was gnawing at my heart.

"Do you know the Butcher?" I asked softly.

The magician pulled another pigeon from his ragged top hat.

"He played there before. About a year ago. He lost big."

"Big? How much is that?"

"About 100,000. It wasn't just cards. He borrowed money from Vekk to play the horses too. He played everything!"

I thought, as clear as an accountant: He only borrowed 20,000 from me.

"Did he pay the debt?" I asked.

"Not all."

"And then? What happened then?"

"Don't know."

"You know," I said and rose halfway from the chair.

"I think he did some services," he said quickly.

"Like what?"

"That I don't know. Honest!"

I took a survey of the room. He didn't need to answer. I could find that out myself. I snapped around toward him. He jumped.

"Gordon Paulsen," I just said. "Do you know him."

He shook his head. "Does he play?"

"You *are* an amateur. You can't lie. I can see it in your mouth. It was your ruin as a magician. You can't lie."

"Gordon Paulsen is a friend of Anton Vekk."

I knew that.

"What kind of friend?" I wanted to know.

He looked a little surprised.

"What kind of friend?" he repeated.

"A good friend or a bad friend?"

He laughed. He thought I was joking.

"He delivers antiques," I said for him and smiled.

The magician tried to pretend that he didn't understand.

"Antiques?" he said with a big question mark.

"Now I understand why you never became more than a third-rate artist," I said. "The audience saw through you right from the start. Even the most senile goober at some old folks home out by a Vestland fjord knew where you hid the pigeons. But you don't need to answer. You have already."

I went to the door. There, I turned. I was on a roll.

"Dr. Varp?" I said. "Do you know that name?"

He nodded. His eyes locked up and stared right past me.

"He gets patients from the clientele at the playing club, doesn't he? That he can experiment a little on? Dr. Varp!"

The magician didn't answer. He just sat in the chair with eyes pasted on the door frame next to me. Suddenly he began to do some remarkable movements in the air with his fingers spread out. I went over to him, but he didn't pay any attention to me.

He continued the wild finger dance, becoming more and more energetic. At last he rose up, and then I saw foam around his lips. I slapped him. He screamed and sank to the floor. He remained there crying. He curled up like a child, sobbing. I left. I couldn't take any more. I'm not Aage Samuelsen. I found a taxi on Kirke Road and asked the driver to take me to Bygdøy, to Varp's villa.

It was a stone house, a huge, gray block, probably built sometime in the '3Os. I walked up and down the road outside the gate a little while, thinking. There had been a lot of villas recently. Vekk's museum at Holmenkollen, his playing joint at Smestad, and now this stone palace. They looked sturdy, these beautiful villas that stood like monuments to the advancement of business, science and human eradication. The Westside's symbols. The abodes of class. Who could imagine that these architectural pearls with such traditional, rich names on the doors were weapons storerooms for right wing extremists, secret clinics, gambling dens, and narcotics bases. I pointed proudly at my chest. I can imagine it, I said aloud. And then I walked through the gate and up the gravel path. There was still some snow on the ground, dirty and disgusting. The curtains were drawn in all the windows. I didn't see a single light. Darkness sank down from the sky as I rang the bell.

Someone came to the door. The steps were long and slow. I waited patiently and looked around. The yard was just a plain lawn, without trees or bushes. Dr. Varp must play croquet here with his patients in the summer, if they were in any condition for such complex and challenging pursuits. But the yard continued around the house, and on the other side was a cozy and intimate courtyard. Just as Dromedary had said.

The door opened.

I backed up three steps. It was the man I had met at Peer Gynt Cafe that time, the dead man who asked if I wanted sell my cadaver. He was horrid. I shivered. His eyes were two green blobs and I a spittoon.

"What do you want?" he asked, swallowing the look in his eyes.

I picked up my courage.

"I'm here to talk with Dr. Varp."

"Do you have an appointment?"

"In a manner of speaking."

He pretended to smile. It was a poor, bony grin. I walked across the threshold, and the door glided shut behind me.

"I have stomach trouble," I said to him. "The horrible food at Peer Gynt has taken its toll on my digestion."

"Dear me, that is sad to hear. I've only had good experiences there. I'm sure Dr. Varp can help you."

He pointed to a door. I followed his arm, and without moving the handle, the door opened. Dr. Varp stood with his back to me in the middle of the floor. He was a rather small man, with thick, curly hair at the neck. I went in to him. The door was closed without a sound. It was a big room, a living room with plush furniture, huge wing-back chairs, a corner sofa with lots of pillows, a bookcase that surely was packed full of first editions from the previous century, a table decorated with bottles and carafes and glasses of all shapes. And along the wall right in front of me was a big stone fireplace where two fat birch logs were crackling.

Dr. Varp turned around.

"What would you like?" he asked, friendly.

"Not too much. A couple of explanations."

He looked at me, intently. His eyes and face appeared sympathetic. He could have been on children's TV. But around his mouth he had a fan of tiny wrinkles, and it was due to the fact that he pursed his lips too much. His mouth was evil. It may well be that the eyes are the window to the soul. But the mouth is the soul's drainpipe. That's what it depends on.

"What's bothering you?"

I waved my hands, irritated.

"Cut it out," I said. "There's no point in us pretending. Let's talk frankly, hmm!"

He continued to look at me. He appeared completely relaxed, a little tired, like after a long laughter attack. Then he nodded to the two wing-back chairs in front of the fireplace on each side of a small, round table.

I sat down while he got glasses and a carafe of brandy. I could see myself living in a room like this. Then it could just as well be winter all year. Fire in the fireplace, bottles of brandy, boxes of cigars. I stared into the flames and felt my face becoming warm and crisp. I took off my jacket, and Varp sct two glasses between us on the table. We toasted, and he offered me a cigar. It was just about prefect. All that was left now was a little chat. I began:

"So, this is your clinic?"

"Yes, you could call it that. I prefer to say laboratory. I conduct research here."

"With people."

Varp looked at me. Something sorrowful came over his face.

"One cannot continue endlessly with mice, rats and rabbits. Now and then one must sacrifice something. That's the law of history."

"Why do you work at the emergency room when you have all this?"

"I like to help people. I help people there."

"And find patients for your private experiments. For example, Dromedary."

He looked directly into the fireplace and raised his glass of brandy.

"That's right. She was brought in one night. We pumped everything out of her stomach. It wasn't so little. A quarter of it would have killed an ox. I offered to help her."

"What did you do?"

Varp turned to me.

"Nothing, that time. She just was here, got some injections. I wanted to wait. I wanted to wait until she had taken her addiction further."

"And Gordon Paulsen fed her?"

Varp laughed and filled the glasses.

"This is moving quickly," he said.

"I'm a busy man."

We drank. I put the cigar down in the ashtray.

"What did you do to Viktor Vekk?" I asked quickly.

He thought about it, turning the glass in his furrowed hand.

"I helped him. I did my best."

"You should have stuck with rats," I said. "You're at home with them."

Varp was hurt. He set the glass down on the table just hard enough to appear demonstrative.

"Viktor's father asked me to do something for him," He said. "I have known the family for many years. Anton Vekk was in Zü rich the same time as I was. He had businesses there. He was in textiles at that time."

"I see," I interrupted. "So he's stayed with drugs?"

Varp looked at me reprimandingly. His forehead creased like a curtain.

"I was a friend of the family. A close friend. In the late '60s, in '69. So, I became their family doctor. Else Vekk, Viktor's mother, is a very nervous woman. It started getting serious in '69. Viktor's behavior at that time almost put an end to her. But I suppose I don't need to tell you about that. You met him in. . ."

" '71."

"Yes. They hoped he was going to get back on the right track again. But you destroyed that."

"I've heard that version before," I said calmly.

"Yes, indeed. You've spoken with her yourself. She was pretty once. A beautiful woman!"

"And what happened to Viktor?" I asked.

Varp leaned back in the big chair and held the glass with both hands.

"His father wanted me to cure him of his addiction. He had carried it too far. Heroin, large amounts."

"While he was driving antiques for Gordon Paulsen?" I said contemptuously.

"His dependence was created a long time before that. You ought to know. So, I was going to cure him. That was Christmas, 1976, when he came home after all that traveling. He was here for three months. I attempted chemical lobotomy. That is when one paralyzes portions of the brain that are functioning abnormally. It works only partially. I let him go home in March. He had gotten better. It was going well for awhile, then he had a relapse in June. Anton Vekk wanted me to bring him here again. At first I tried hypnosis, but that's a treatment I don't have much confidence in."

"Well, it worked on the magician, anyway," I said.

Varp smiled, leaned his head back and emptied the glass.

"In the end there was just one possibility left. His brain was sick."

He looked at me suddenly. His lips drew together.

"When there's gangrene in the leg, then one must remove it,

right! To save the rest of the body. I cut the nerves from the frontal lobes to the brain center."

Varp stroked his fingers up and down his temples and looked at me.

"I thought the result was very positive."

I finished off the glass and trembled. The voice that was speaking was without pitch. It didn't stumble on the words. It could talk through glass and stone.

"It would have been better to eliminate the entire head so he couldn't talk at all," I said softly.

Varp didn't react. He continued his report.

"As I said, I was pleased with the result. He moved home to his family in August. But it appeared that he was getting on his mother's nerves. She herself is not entirely well. She couldn't quite accept, or understand, the changes in Viktor. So he was moved to a room. We wanted to give it a little time, so that everyone could get used to the new situation. But then he ended his days there, as you know."

"With my name," I added. "In a way, that's why I'm sitting here."

"Viktor told me about you. He felt strongly attached to you. In fact, he did everything to find you when he was sent home after the first operation. And he found you, actually. But he didn't dare talk to you. It was a side effect, unfortunately. He had an abnormal fear of talking with other people. The only one who was able to get close to him at this time was Dromedary. Unbelievably enough. But he kept up with you. One could almost say he shadowed you. He saw you rob the bank at Dam Square."

Varp refilled the glasses and laughed deep inside his body.

"Quite a chance meeting, eh. But no one went to the police. You should thank us. Anton Vekk came up with a plan. He loved his son. And he loves his wife. It's true. He knew that it would kill her if Viktor died or never got better. When we saw that Viktor was, yes, going downhill somewhat after the last operation, we gave him your name, just in case."

He paused and looked at me. His evil mouth became even smaller, almost disappearing in his furrowed face.

"Else Vekk is waiting for her son. She'll be waiting until her death."

"And it was you who performed the autopsy," I said.

Varp nodded.

The logs in the fireplace crackled like snare drums. It was the only sound in the room. I wondered if I ever would get out of there alive. But at least before I died, I would get answers to my questions.

"The Butcher," I said wearily. I said no more than that.

Varp snickered.

"He was a player. A miserable and fanatic gambler. He lost the farm, as they say. He had to sell his butcher shop. His wife moved to another city with the children."

"He doesn't have his shop or his family now?" I said, surprised.

"Neither. He played them away. Almost a year ago. And was still left with a debt of over 100,000 crowns."

"To Anton Vekk?"

"He couldn't pay, of course. He performed some services instead. He encircled you. Pure and simple. He watched out for you. So you wouldn't get in any trouble in case we needed your name."

I emptied the glass in one burning gulp. I was tired, endlessly tired. I could sleep the big sleep now.

"So he has known about the whole thing all along," I said hoarsely.

"The Butcher is naive, but good. He had instructions to watch out for you. Nothing more. He didn't know any details. Anyway, he no longer plays. I'm treating him. It changes the appearance a little, but it's the head that counts, right. *The head!* Soon his voice will be in a falsetto. A eunuch's voice. But it costs to get well. In the brain."

"You haven't cured him, either," I attempted to say calmly. "He still plays. This was his biggest gamble."

The children's hour uncle lit his cigar. I froze and sweated at the same time. I thought about the Butcher, but I couldn't stand it.

"Why did you set those baboons on me incessantly?" I asked.

"You're a little too curious. We figured you would resign yourself to the state of things. But the Butcher didn't manage to stop you. Now the case is somewhat different."

He looked at me a long time. I didn't understand what he meant.

"They won't bother you anymore."

Varp got up and walked across the floor. I had a nasty feeling that they had me on a hook. But on the other hand, they couldn't do anything to me. It's not easy to get rid of a body without further ado. There aren't too many builders who like stuffing corpses into foundation holes. And if they sink me in the North Sea, I'll be found when a diver from one of the oil platforms drowns and they go searching for him. If they kill me, it will just create more problems for them. But it surprised me anyway that they were so dead sure I would keep my mouth shut about everything I knew.

"Would you like to see my laboratory?" asked Varp, pointing at the bookcase. It glided to the side, and a door came into view. He opened it.

We went into another world. A narrow, green corridor lay directly in front of us. There were doors to each side all the way down. He opened the first one and pointed in. It was a big, white room with complex machines and an operating table. He closed the door carefully, without saying anything, and went on. He stopped outside the third door on the left side. There was no door handle, just a button on the wall.

I looked at him. His mouth quivered a little, like when you pluck a tight string. He pressed the button, and the door disappeared into the wall. He almost shoved me in. It was a sterile, naked room, without windows. In the ceiling, a dim bulb was shining, and in the middle of the floor was a sort of bed.

Varp smiled.

I punched him as hard as I could in the face. My fist hit him between the eyes, and blood spurted out of his nose. I attacked him again, twisting my fingers into his horrible face. I kept pressing my thumb into his eye until he didn't scream any longer. Then I felt two hands grab me from behind. Sometimes now, when I'm walking down a street on the other side of the planet, I can feel those hands crawling up my back. Then I pop into the nearest bar for a double shot, talk senselessly, and laugh hysterically. It can go on for an hour. It was the butler with the green eyes. I would never have believed there could be so much power in one person, especially not him. He grabbed me tight, picked me up, and threw me to the floor.

Then everything became black or white.

19

I was awakened by something dripping. It was a drop falling right beside me, against stone. The sound kept growing in me until I turned over with a scream and opened my eyes. It was dark. I remained lying there, listening. The drop fell and fell. I thought I heard the surf far, far away. I suddenly remembered what had happened. I grabbed my head with both hands and tore at it, screamed, felt down my body. My eyes saw clearer now, and I recognized my clothes. It didn't mean a thing. I got up, stumbled, got up anew. I was in a cellar, or a bomb shelter. I stood still and listened. It was waves I was hearing. I started to walk toward the sound, supported myself on the stone wall, fell again, crawled on my knees. I cut myself on some glass fragments, a broken bottle, but I didn't feel pain. I stopped, listened. Now they were nearer, the waves. I was going in the right direction. There was a curve, and when I got around it, I finally saw a point of light: the way out. I ran on all fours. My heart pounded like ten oxen. I was soon there, at the opening, a small hole, and I tumbled out into the light.

I landed on a muddy lawn and laid there looking. Right in front of me was the sea. To the right, a little lighthouse stuck up from the water. I saw land on the other side. I was by a fjord. I rose up halfway, and slowly, like waking from a deep sleep, I recognized myself again. I was at Signalen on Nesodden peninsula. I stood up and began walking down to the little pool where kids usually play in the summer. I waded there once myself, hundreds of years ago, before I learned to swim. I ran the last bit and bent down to the still water. I saw my face. There was no mistake about it. I rolled up my left shirt sleeve and found the huge birthmark just under the elbow. I was me. I was whole.

I saw Bygdøy on the other side. They must have taken me over in a boat and put me in the cellar of what was once the Signalen Hotel. I had played there before, when I was a child and we lived here in the summer. It was a spooky game. I never dared go all the way in. Now I had been there.

I think I cried a little. Once, I caught two whitings on one cast here. They curled up like bacon in the pan when Mother fried them for dinner. I was freezing. It was no later than six in the morning. The fjord was gray and lifeless. I walked along the high chain link fence over toward the pier. It poked me. My legs couldn't hold me up. I sank down on the cold ground and cried again. Here came my family, roaring along in a brand new Saab. But Father didn't turn to the right at the parking lot. It was late in the evening, and there were no people waiting for the boat. Father pressed the gas pedal to the floor. It was before they put up barriers on the edge of the pier. He steered right out to the sea.

I sat there shaking until the first boat came. It was the Prinsen, the good old Prinsen, my favorite boat! I went up on the deck, even though I was freezing. Now and then, a spring-like breeze drifted on the air. A warmth was slumbering under the sky, a sleeping insect swarm that would soon explode. I spit in the water and watched the pier become smaller and smaller. The lighthouse outside Signalen blinked patiently, a short red flash. Two small boats puttered into Bunne Fjord. At Ildjernet I saw the boat to Denmark. It reminded me of traveling and breaking up. It reminded me of all that. I was shivering. When I set foot on Pier B, a sad clang came from the clock in the City Hall tower. It was eight thirty.

I still had some money in my pocket. There was still hope. I hailed a taxi at the Westside rail station and was driven to Thereses Street. Matkroken hadn't yet opened. I crawled up the stairs and stumbled over the threshold. Then I suddenly stopped. I had stood that way here before, and I knew that someone had been there. I looked at the table and wondered who had started the clipping bureau. A new newspaper article was there, a quite brief piece. I sat down on the bed and read it, and when I had finished reading, my life was changed. "The teller brutally struck down during the robbery at Dam Square in the summer of 1977 is dead from the injuries. The assailant is still at large." I sank back on the bed and could not grasp it. I turned cold as a block of ice and hid myself under the comforter. Now I was a murderer. Now I could never speak. I had to sleep. But sleep would not have me. Sleep was clean, and I was leprous. I twisted off my clothes and bent my legs up under my stomach. It couldn't be true. I didn't hit him hard. I saw his face. A scared to death older man. Why did you try to stop me! You were just as scared as I was. I didn't hit hard. But now you're dead. And I get the blame. The cry came up my throat like a fishhook. It tore my intestines. Two vultures sat behind my eyes pecking at the optical nerves. I grabbed the bottle and wanted to drink myself senseless. Now I was moving in the blink between dream and day. The things around me lost their form, the contours became fleeting lines, like sticks of charcoal rubbed on a dirty piece of paper. I was shaking. I wanted to scream, primal scream. This was the last station for abstinence. I rolled the comforter into a ball. I remembered the time we gathered chestnuts on Bygdøy Avenue, hid them until winter, put them in snowballs, and won all the street wars. Later, we put razor blades in the snow. I threw myself around in the bed, pounded my face down in the pillow and cried. I drank and cried. I emptied the bottle and myself. I was empty as a cash register at midnight.

I slept or passed out. In any case, I woke up, and time had passed. I was awakened by someone knocking on the door. I wondered who it could be. Was it Mother and Father coming to fetch their only son home to heaven? Was it Viktor and Dromedary, the two of them, headless? Or maybe Jesus, who counts gamblers and murderers among his friends, maybe he's knocking on my door. Or the Butcher? Was he standing outside with his belly slashed up and the mask of a king pulled down in front of his face? It was Berit. She came over to the bed and sat on the edge.

"Are you sick?" she asked, worried.

"Exhausted," I said hoarsely.

She got up and took a look around the room. It was not a pretty sight. I managed to hide the clipping. I crumbled it up under the comforter.

"I just wanted to see how you were doing," she said. "You haven't been in the store for a long time."

Last time I was there, she was standing behind the meat counter with her hands full of blood. Berit read my thoughts. I wasn't surprised. It's the least thing.

"I'm working in the vegetable department now," she chirped.

It takes so little. I became happy and peaceful. The world is good, if you just keep looking long enough.

"Great," I said. "No more blood!"

She emptied a bag of produce out on the kitchen counter. I saw tomatoes, radishes, carrots, peppers, apples, oranges. It was a beautiful sight. It looked like the poster that hung in the dentist's office in grade school. Finally, she pulled out a huge head of cabbage and held it in the air. I screamed. She dropped it down and looked at me alarmed.

"What is it!" she stammered.

I was hiding under the comforter.

"Nothing. I just bit my lip."

She sat down on the edge of the bed again. Her hand crept along the crumpled sheet, and she discovered that I was naked. She smiled slyly. I smiled not so slyly. The electricity was gone. She looked at me a little surprised, laughed uncertainly, and laid down next to me with her clothes on.

We lay silently on our backs on the old, sweaty bedding and each stared at our point on the ceiling. An incredible thought hit me. It was like being carried along in a flood: I can have children with her. It was too much for me. I didn't have the capacity for such a thought. I heaved for breath, felt my blood pulsating through me. It was impossible. Or was it? Total confusion. My feelings were obeying the light. There was a worm hanging in front of your mouth, fool! Could I lay all my cards on the table, serve my sentence, do my duty, and marry Berit, with handcuffs and a striped suit? It was too late. It dawned on me as slowly as the moon crosses the sky. It was too late.

"Can't we go for a walk," Berit said suddenly.

"Isn't it cold?"

"No, it's nice. Almost spring."

"Where'll we go?"

"St. Hanshaugen," she said enthusiastically.

She got up and pulled me along. A moment later we were on the way up Thereses Street. I held Berit's hand. Or she held mine. Neither of us had said anything since we left. I wanted to say something pleasant, something nice. I struggled through the world and the alphabet, but my treasure hunt was fruitless. I just pointed at the corner of Ullevåls Road and Colletts Street, at Hansen's Bakery.

"I bought two pieces of marzipan layer cake there once," I said.

"Yes?"

"It's absolutely true. Two pieces of marzipan layer cake. But I never got to eat them."

Berit looked bewildered. The light changed from red, and we walked over to St. Hanshaugen. Soon, the trees would be blocking the sky. We walked as fast as our lungs let us among the barefoot skyscrapers. And we were not the only ones. Representatives from the entire human race were out promenading on this cozy evening. I felt that anything could happen now. I wanted to go up to the heights, to the outdoor restaurant and panorama of Oslo.

"This is where you met Viktor Vekk," Berit said.

"Yeah. It was here."

I pointed up at the pavilion. At the same time we heard music from there, and right away someone started singing. And there was no mistaking the voice.

"There's music here today, too," said Berit eagerly.

"It sounds like Jens Book-Jenssen," I said, sulking.

We walked on slowly. The music became stronger and clearer. There was no doubt now. It *was* Jens Book-Jenssen singing. It was swarming with old people up the steep hill.

Berit poked me.

"Want to go up and watch?"

"No."

"Why not?"

"I don't want to," I said ardently.

"Okay, then," she dropped it. "It's nothing to get mad about!" I squeezed her hand tightly, and we walked a ways without saying anything. I had so much in my heart, but there was no language for it. I inhaled the mild air deeply.

"How was it here then?" Berit asked.

It clicked in my head. I had a film in there that I couldn't rewind completely.

"Lots of people," I said. "Lots of happy, crazy people, and loud music. And over the stage was a huge transparent banner that said ALL POWER TO IMAGINATION."

"All power to imagination, " repeated Berit quietly.

"Yeah. And on the very top, Peter Christian Asbjørnsen sat watching it all."

"Who?"

"Asbjørnsen. There's a statue of him up there. The guy who worked with Moe, you know. It could have been one of their fairy tales. And there were cops everywhere. They snooped around, but we were peaceful people."

Berit had stopped. She let go of my hand and looked at me. "What went wrong?" she asked. "What really happened to all of you?"

I met her eyes, and there was a bridge between our faces.

"It went wrong the day the ones who hated us began to love us." We continued walking. I found her fingers and laced them into mine. The music was absolutely clear now. Jenssen and Blyverket. Old people swayed in rhythm and smiled in competition.

"Isn't it sweet!" Berit burst out, pointing at two old folks who were taking a few dance steps under a weeping willow.

"Sure," I said sadly and laughed.

When we rounded the duck pond, I heard someone calling a peculiar name. Berit took no notice of it, but I reacted spontaneously. "Hugo Poser!" I turned in the direction of the call and saw none other than Kork, Espen Askeladd, and Arne Garve. They were sitting on one of the white wooden benches eyeing us. There was no way out. We started walking toward them, and when Berit noticed Arne, she stiffened up completely and let go of my hand as if it were infested. He just looked from one of us to the other, astonished. His forehead was red, and he was rolling a cigarette like mad. But Kork was the same as always, his gray, pear head swayed in the wind, and Espen stared at the sky and had a face full of dimples. It was a long march, but we came through. Arne and Berit looked past each other at first, then they met.

"Hi," she said finally and put her hand on his shoulder. She was a block of ice that had to be broken loose.

Arne just nodded and looked at her hand out of the corners of his eyes.

"Out for a walk in the nice weather," he mumbled.

Kork began whistling, loud and out of tune. Espen got up and took a few steps out on the pale grass.

"How are you doing?" Berit asked.

He threw out his arms.

"Fine. Just fine. Got a new truck. Two trailers and a sleeping compartment. A Daf." He suddenly looked up at me. "Guess you won't be coming along on any more trips."

There was something in his voice which made it sound like a fact.

"No," I said. "Guess not."

It was quiet awhile. Berit took away her hand and stuck it in her pocket. Arne lit his smoke, fumbling a little with the matches. Espen stood on the grass and just looked at us. It was Kork who finally said something.

"Listen, Poser! There's an old folks dance on our hill!"

I nodded. Berit looked at me strangely. I answered to the most peculiar name.

"Old farts sitting ringside chewing pastries from church. Do you remember those rolls, Hugo! Dream rolls!"

Kork's eyes became distant.

"You mumble too much," said Espen. "I think you oughta join the folks up there."

"Shove it!" said Kork angrily and leaned forward on his elbows.

"Where'd you go off to that night?" asked Arne Garve suddenly, looking sternly at me.

"I went home."

"You went home," he aped scornfully. "You split! You were running like hell!"

Espen got in the middle.

"It's nothing to make a fuss about now. And we started the trouble anyway."

Berit looked at me uneasily. I looked at the ground. Arne Garve didn't let up.

"Were you scared?" he asked scornfully.

"Yes," I answered, to end the whole thing.

There was a chill in the air, a narrow strip of winter that would never completely disappear. Berit shivered. She was pale, and her eyes kept moving all the time. I wanted to go home. Suddenly, Arne said in a whole new tone:

"We've been sitting here talking about what we're going to do for May Day."

Kork came back to life.

"There'll be a great big parade! First Arne, then me, and Espen in back. Arne'll carry the banner, I'll play drum and Espen'll sing."

"Cut it out, once and for all," said Arne.

He looked up at Berit, and it was just as if his eyes pressed a button with her.

"There's nothing decent any longer," she began without a lead in or introduction. "It's just strategy. Catchwords and strategy. It's all just a question of *power!*"

I didn't recognize her voice. This was a side of Berit I had never experienced. She changed. She came out in a new edition. I stared in astonishment at her mouth and eyes, and knew immediately that she also had been disappointed, that she also had seen dreams fall to ruins.

"Do you mean that," said Arne, almost meekly.

"No one *believes* anything any longer. There's no *morality* any more!"

"*Morality!*"

Arne Garve looked at the others with wide open eyes.

"Yes. Exactly. Morality."

"But what the hell can a person do about it!"

"Start over. Begin all over again. Lay a new foundation. We've come out crooked."

Berit was still pale and breathing heavily, as if it were difficult for her to speak. Begin again, I thought, and it was like falling out of a window. It blew cold around my ears. For me, there was no way back. I couldn't save the world. I could barely save myself. I had to depend on Berit.

Kork looked at us and said, in a low and unfamiliar voice:

"I wish there was just one fucking huge demonstration that blew all the bullshit to hell with a single shout!"

He fell silent and hunched up even more. But all at once, he jumped up and screamed at the top of his lungs:

"To hell with all this bullshit! To hell with scumbags and dog shit and the devil and his fucking friends! To hell with hell!"

He sank down again, exhausted, and leaned on Espen's shoulder.

"Give me a megaphone," he whispered, "and I'll change the world."

A few people had stopped and were looking at us. They stood like pillars, stiffened in the dusk. They would never get home safe and sound.

But no one shouts like that fruitlessly. A green police car rolled up behind us, and two constables got out. I took Berit's arm and pulled her along.

"Time to go," I said.

We left. I didn't turn until we got to Ullevåls Road. There was no one to be seen. No one was coming after us. But nothing was like before. Berit was far away from me. She walked in her own thoughts. She was in that world that was closed to me. When we turned down Johannes Bruns Street, she suddenly said, with a strange, withered voice:

"It's too bad that Viktor died."

"Yeah?"

"I had almost begun to like him."

I looked at her, frightened. She came to a standstill. Her face became empty and emotioness. Her hands ran through her hair. I didn't know what I should say.

"What really happened to him?" she said heavily.

It was a story that was impossible to tell.

"Perhaps he can tell you himself. If he comes back."

She thought that was in bad taste. She tossed her head and looked away. A bunch of little kids came cycling past us. They rang their bells and whistled and pointed.

"Who's Hugo Poser?" she said at last.

"You don't know him."

We walked further in silence. It was remarkably still around us, no cars, no voices, the bicycles had disappeared around the corner. But when we got to Thereses Street, and I was standing with the key in my hand, the peace was broken. The needle met the grooves and it sang: "Go into your room, as small as it is. It holds something your heart holds dear."

I unlocked and let Berit in ahead of me.

She went over to the window and stood there with her back to me. She didn't look quite well.

"When will the urn with Viktor be buried?" she asked.

I closed the door and leaned wearily against it.

"Next Saturday. Twelve o'clock."

It started raining. It hammered the windowpanes. Dirt and exhaust loosened and ran in big flakes toward the frame. But she didn't want to borrow an umbrella. I wasn't to call her a taxi either. She disappeared down Thereses Street, past the glowing windows at Matkroken, where the cash registers were visible through the rain and glass. They were lined up in a row, covered with gray cowls, tied in back. Did I hear a scream? No. It was just the streetcar that picked up Berit. Nothing happens here. The people who live here are just pensioners and murderers.

20

That's the way spring came. The sun plugged into all the sockets, blew away all the clouds, and held an effective, intensive course for six days. On the seventh day, spring was a fact. The sidewalks were dry and full of sand. People trickled out from doors and entryways and stared at each other, surprised, and looked up at the clear blue sky. Marching bands wandered through the streets and practiced for Independence Day, and the trees had gotten new green gloves.

That was the day the urn with Viktor was buried. I put on my best clothes, but wasn't able to think about breakfast. I plodded down to Majorstua, where I took the Røa tram up to the crematorium. As I gave the conductor the three crowns, it hit me that I had almost no money left, just a few crumpled tens. I got the ticket, and the tram disappeared into the tunnel at Volvat. I immediately regretted that I hadn't bought myself a pair of sunglasses.

I was half an hour early. I found the bench that I'd sat on before, between huge evergreen trees. A squirrel scurried across the grass, stopped and looked at me curiously, and was gone behind a tree trunk. Some dark-clad people approached the oak door with rounded backs and sluggish steps. A jet pulled a pipe cleaner out of the sky.

I brushed off the bench and sat down. Someone was standing behind me. I noticed but didn't turn. I fished the last smoke out of the pack and couldn't find the matches. My scalp itched. A beautiful, well-cared for hand came gliding above my shoulder and lit a lighter. I drew the flame into the cigarette and shook.

Gordon Paulsen sat down next to me. I was completely sick of this guy, and turned far away.

"I usually take a walk in the cemetery in the spring," he said, stretching his head like a rooster toward the sun.

It was almost too much for me. I shot some intense puffs down into my lungs and breathed deeply.

"I study the names on gravestones," he continued, leaning back.

His face was small and dotted black, just like it was shrunken. I didn't say anything. I could have crushed him.

"And every name has its little history that I want to learn about."

I still hadn't opened my mouth. I was silent as a mirror. His red tongue rushed in and out and moistened his lips.

"I mentioned to you before that I was interested in names, didn't I? Names are my passion, in fact. Behind every single name hides a secret. Every single Olsen and Hansen that lives here has its secret."

His tongue flapped. He was a snake that sprayed poison everywhere. I felt the hate growing. I hated so intensely that I couldn't sit still. I moved out to the edge, as far away as possible.

He suddenly looked at me. His pygmy face was tense and yellow.

"Varp failed again," he said, beginning to chuckle.

I could hear the blood vessels in my neck pounding against my shirt collar.

Gordon Paulsen stood up. I was stuck to the bench. My back ached and my breath grated my lungs. He stood in front of me and said:

"Anyway, did you read in the paper that that poor teller died. That Windelband. That Windelband."

He put his hands on his back and bent forward a little.

"But we're the only ones who know Windelband's secret, eh? And we wouldn't dirty his memory, would we?"

He came even closer.

"Let the dead rest in peace."

He smiled his snake smile. The point of his tongue came into sight, as if he had coughed up his heart. I sat paralyzed. I could have strangled him in public, if it hadn't been for Berit coming in the gate just then. I was going to stand up and wave to her, but I had no strength. Gordon Paulsen passed her. I shivered. He slithered away in slow spiral movements.

"I hadn't figured on that," I said wearily as she sat down.

"Who was that you were talking with?" said Berit.

"No idea. Some crazy pensioner."

She had dressed up in a skirt and carried a handbag, but it didn't help. What an attractive couple we were! Her face was green, and her eyes were gone every time I tried to catch them.

"Sad place," I declared.

She didn't agree.

"It's pretty too, beautiful. It's so lush here."

"What are you doing the day after tomorrow?" I asked.

"Day after tomorrow?"

"Yeah. May Day. Maybe we can do something together."

She became nervous and fumbled with her handbag a little. She didn't know what to do with herself. I regretted having asked.

"I'm going to be with Arne," she said quickly, staring down at the grass.

The church usher came out from the chapel. We got up and walked over to him. He held a tall, narrow case in his hand.

"Windelband?" I asked.

He nodded. Then we walked down the gravel path, he with the strange baggage that was heavy enough to make him tilt, and behind him, Berit and I, side by side but far from each other.

We stopped on a lawn where there were just a few graves. I had been there before. It was where my parents lay. A black stone grew up from the earth with their names on it.

The usher set the case down and breathed heavily. Drops of sweat ran down his high forehead.

"The name will be carved in later," he said. "But after that there's no room for more."

There was a deep, narrow hole in the ground, and next to it lay a shovel and a pile of earth. He opened the case, took the urn out, straightened up, and held it out, just like a waiter coming to the table with a bottle of wine. I nodded. It was right. Hans Georg Windelband. Vintage '52.

A rope was fastened to the urn, and the usher lowered it down the dark shaft. When the urn hit the bottom, seven feet beneath us, he loosened the catch with a simple swing of the rope. He pulled the rope up and coiled it together.

It was over. I read the names on the headstone. I suddenly missed Mother and Father, who'd committed hari-kari eight years ago, the proud upper class. I missed them, and my legs began to quiver. But at the same time I was aware of someone watching us. I turned around slowly and met the eyes of Viktor's father. He was standing alone on the gravel path a ways away, and, like he hung on the wall, he was staring at me with the same motionless eyes.

I went over to him. Outside the fence waited a car I had seen before, on Frogner Road. I could make out three people in it, but couldn't see their faces clearly.

"Viktor died at his own hands," said his father. His voice broke, and he drew his breath with an ugly grimace. "I did what I could. You should know that."

I just looked at him. He stood with his feet a little apart. His hands crept forward from his back down into his pockets. It looked like he was freezing.

"I did everything in my power," he continued. It astonished me that he sounded so sincere.

"Murderer," I said softly but clearly. He ignored it, or it made no impression on him.

"You've just lost your name," he said to me. "It was necessary. And you've gotten back all the money you loaned out."

There was a pause. The sun broke through a cloud and hit him in the face. He looked at the ground, at the gravel.

"You're nobody now," he said suddenly, with a smile. "You were the one who should have died, not my son. But now you're nobody."

He snapped around and walked to the car that waited for him. I sneaked back to Berit. I took it calmly. Nobody could injure me any longer.

The usher was almost finished filling in the hole. He had hung his jacket over the tombstone.

"Who was that?" she asked when we had walked a ways.

I hesitated awhile before I said:

"That was Viktor's father."

The birds were singing, and people came toward us with bouquets in their hands and smiles that reached all the way around the planet. I felt nothing. It was an empty room, a tunnel. I was a looted grave. And Berit was silent and drew far back, away from me, over on the other side where I couldn't reach.

After we got to the chapel and were headed through the hedge to the streetcar stop, I heard a yell, and there was no mistaking that yell. Fifty yards away, waving at us, was the Butcher.

"Who's *that?*" Berit asked in resignation.

"The Butcher," I said. "A former friend of mine."

He came toward us.

"I've just let off Olav and Kari at Madserud," he said. "They're playing tennis. Fine, fine sport!"

The Butcher winked at me. I saw through him. He became a little feverish, continued enthusiastically, his voice hopping:

"Finally they've started doing something sensible. Want a ride?"

He pointed at his Bug.

"Have you got a cold?" I asked calmly. "Or is your voice changing?"

His face became blood red. His eyes flickered like two trapped flies. I looked at his big body, completely formless, without fixed points.

"Let's go, then!" he said energetically, almost screaming.

We remained standing, looking at each other. Berit looked at the Butcher and me, nervous and uncertain. Then we crawled into the narrow seat and rolled down Sørkedals Road.

"Spring's taken hold now," the Butcher said. He had relaxed a little. "Now there's no way back!"

He pressed the gas pedal to the floor, but it didn't help much. I turned to Berit.

"Coming to my place?"

She looked almost frightened.

"No," she said quickly. "I can't."

"How about tonight?"

"No good."

She wanted out at Majorstua. The Butcher swerved to the curb and made a quick stop.

"I'll call you," I said meekly.

She just nodded, gathered up her skirt and tumbled out.

The car jumped forward, and we hit the green light. I turned and waved to her. But Berit stood stiffly on the sidewalk with her arms right down along her sides and watched me the way she did that fall when I left her apartment.

Berit had started over.

The Butcher drove down Bogstad Road and turned down Sporveis Street. There was already a crowd of people outside the Fredheim Hotel. He picked up speed, thundered past the urinals at Fagerborg Church, and stopped at the corner of Thereses Street.

"I suppose it's over now," he said carefully, leaning on the steering wheel.

"What?"

"Everything. This here. What will you do now?"

"Finish off the rest of my calvados."

"I don't have time," he said quickly, not that I had invited him. "Have to pick up the kids at Madserud in a bit."

He looked at me. His face was a big sore. He wiped the sweat off his forehead with his jacket sleeve. Now I knew why he had bad luck as a gambler. He didn't lay his cards on the table, but they were transparent. He held his hand tight. Our eyes met in the rearview mirror. A broken blood vessel fell like a lightning bolt over his left eyeball. We sat that way a few seconds. He was waiting for me to fold. It was the Butcher's last game, and I let him win.

"Yes," I said. "You'd better hurry so you don't get there too late."

His eyes sank from the mirror. His red neck flesh became tense. I opened the door and got out. The Volkswagen with the Butcher behind the wheel drove toward Bislett. It was the last I saw of him. He disappeared there, in the traffic circle, for all time. Goodbye, Butcher!

I began to walk up Thereses Street, on the same side as Matkroken. It was just before closing time, and people were streaming out and in. Kids screamed and tugged at the dresses of their

worn-out mothers, whose arms were full of smuggled goods. Blue
men scraped the streetcar tracks clean so that the sun's reflec-
tion could climb up to Adamstua without a mouth full of sand.
Out from a side street came the Bolteløkka Marching Band play-
ing an out-of-tune march. It echoed between the houses. But all
of a sudden everything inside me became as silent as a church,
still and hushed, like in a grave. I saw a contour behind the cur-
tains in my window. And right down from the entrance was a dark
blue BMW with two men in the front seat. The car had an antenna
on the roof. I walked a few more steps and got a better look at
them. I don't mistake plainclothes cops. They don't know that they
wear uniforms in their faces. They were waiting for me.

Berit had started cleaning out.

I blended into the line going into Matkroken. The telephone by
the window was free. I dialed Vekk's number on Holmenkoll Road.
No one answered. I got my coin back, leafed through the tens in
my pocket, and went out again. They were still waiting. But they
would have to wait long time. When the entrance is closed, use
the exit.

21

I rang the bell, but no one answered. The door was locked. I walked around the house. There was an even larger garden, full of animal sculptures and small, topiary trees. I peeked in a window. No one looked out at me. I tried the kitchen door, and to my great surprise, it glided open without my needing to exert myself.

I went in. It was completely quiet. It was so quiet that it was almost noisy. I got into an uncomfortable frame of mind and wanted to get it over with as fast as possible. I found the escritoire and pulled out the drawer I had taken note of. What I was looking for was there: Viktor's passport, his birth certificate, driver's license, and a letter of identification from the postal service. I stuck everything in my pocket and wanted to get out of there. But something held me back. I stopped and listened. The sound of emptiness in every room. I walked out in the hall and carefully began climbing the stairs up to the second floor. None of the steps creaked. I came into a long corridor, with several doors on each side. It looked like a hotel. I opened the first. It was the bath. I went further and came to a room that must be intended for guests. When I opened the third door, I almost collapsed. It was Viktor's room. I could tell immediately. And it must have been that way since we met each

other. On the walls hung pictures of Pink Floyd, the Rolling Stones,
Che Guevara, the Grateful Dead. Over the desk he had stuck up
a ragged poster: Release Concert at St. Hanshaugen, May 21, 1971.
Record covers were scattered, Woodstock, Doors, Led Zeppelin.
Clothes were thrown all over, military jackets, berets, patched jeans
with fringe at the bottom, sandals, t-shirts with "Make love not
war," an Indian tunic. And it smelled peculiar in there, of incense
and sweet tobacco and fresh-baked bread. Viktor's room. It sank
into me. I closed the door again and stood in the sterile corridor
with my face hidden in my hands.

I heard a sound. Someone moaning or crying. I continued on
and stopped outside a new door. That was where it was coming
from. I peeked in the keyhole, but it was plugged with cotton. I
pressed the door handle down carefully and pushed the door open
as quietly as I could. Right in front of me lay Viktor's mother, Else
Vekk, in a big, messy bed. But she didn't react to my arrival. I went
over to her. On the nightstand was a syringe. I looked at her wrist
and arm. She was full of tracks. I looked at the syringe. It had just
been used.

She tried to fasten her eyes, but I knew she just saw shadows
and outlines and big wheels rolling toward her. I took two steps
to the side and made a little motion to see if her eyes followed.
She jumped a little, then she sank into her nightmare again. I
wanted to go. I had to go. But suddenly she started talking through
her nose.

"Is that you, Viktor? Have you come back home?"

The floor disappeared under me. She tried to stretch out her
hands, but couldn't hold them up. I cleared my throat. There was
some trash in the drainpipe. I wasn't much good.

"Yes, Mother," I said. "It's me. I've picked up my things, my pass-
port and stuff. I'm going to travel. I'll come home again soon."

She smiled, pleased. I hugged her. My hand was fluttering like
a butterfly. She smiled, happy and relieved in her nerve-shattered
face.

I tore myself loose and stormed down the stairs. Then I thought
of something. I went into the living room, found the letter-opener
on the escritoire, and placed myself in front of the painting of Vik-
tor's father. I threw the letter-oponer at his heart and hit it dead

on. Then I cut him to pieces, in all directions, until there was just an empty frame left on the wall.

Afterward, I took the streetcar to Frognerseteren. I reassured myself that I had all the papers in my pocket. There was drizzle in the air, and the sun had stuck up a rainbow over the dark forest. I began to walk into it.